Booked on Murder

Booked on Murder

A HAUNTED LIBRARY MYSTERY

Allison Brook

NEW YORK

Copyright © 2024 by Marilyn Levinson

Published in the United States by Crooked Lane Books, an imprint of The Quick Brown Fox & Company LLC.

Crooked Lane Books and its logo are trademarks of The Quick Brown Fox & Company LLC.

Library of Congress Catalog-in-Publication data available upon request.

ISBN (hardcover): 978-1-63910-845-9
ISBN (ebook): 978-1-63910-846-6

Cover design by Claudia Griesbach-Martucci

Printed in the United States.

www.crookedlanebooks.com

Crooked Lane Books
34 West 27th St., 10th Floor
New York, NY 10001

First Edition: August 2024

10 9 8 7 6 5 4 3 2 1

For Dawn Dowdle, agent and friend, who found a home for my Haunted Library Series. I miss you.

Chapter One

"**B**ut, Sally, I'm not a writer. And besides—"

My boss glowered at me from across her desk, stopping my excuse midsentence. "Carrie, I give you plenty of leeway when it comes to running your department, but if I ask you to do something, I expect you to follow through. Especially when it has the board's approval."

My mouth fell open in amazement. "Now the library board wants me to write an article about that poor woman, after ordering us to keep it under wraps like it was a national secret?" I thought a moment. "Uncle Bosco never mentioned it."

Sally had the courtesy to look abashed. "I suppose he never got a chance since I mentioned the *Gazette*'s request to the board members only this morning via our Zoom meeting. They agreed unanimously that *you* should write the article, not one of their reporters."

I sank back into my chair to absorb this information. Three weeks ago, while helping Norman Tobin, the reference librarian, put the Historical Room's collection in order in its new location in the library's new addition, I'd come upon the diary of a woman named Verity Babcock mixed in with a pile of old ledgers and pamphlets. In 1652, she'd been hanged as a witch, one of four people victimized in this manner here in Clover Ridge, Connecticut.

I tried to approach the issue from another angle. "Verity Babcock suffered a tragic miscarriage of justice. Her death is a blot on our town's history. Don't you think someone who writes for a living would do a better job publicizing her story?"

Sally's smile was triumphant. "Actually, Chuck Ryland, the editor in chief, loves the idea that a Singleton with roots going back four generations discovered this piece of local history. And when I told him what a fine writer you are, he was all for your writing the piece."

Knowing I'd lost the battle, I caved. "When does he want it?"

"Monday afternoon, latest. It's being featured in a three-page spread in Wednesday's edition."

I stared at Sally. "That's three days from today."

Sally was too busy eyeing me critically to answer. "Pretty blouse. Simple gold earrings. But you might want to put on some eye makeup and tame your hair. I have a can of hair spray you can borrow."

Feeling self-conscious, I smoothed back my hair that tended to puff out when it needed a trim. "Why are you so concerned with my appearance?"

"The *Gazette*'s sending over a photographer. He should be arriving within the hour."

* * *

I stormed into my office and slammed the door behind me. It was a quarter after three, and Trish Templeton, my part-time assistant had left for the day. Evelyn Havers, my ghostly pal made an appearance and perched in her favorite spot, the corner of Trish's desk. Today she wore a white short-sleeved blouse over a colorful skirt and black patent sling-backed pumps with kitten heels—the perfect outfit for a stylish sixty-something ghost on a sunny day in early June. I often wondered where Evelyn kept her extensive wardrobe that was always appropriate for the current season. And how did she manage to change her hairstyle so often? There were so many things I didn't know about Evelyn's life when she wasn't visiting me here at the library, and I feared I never would.

"Someone's in a foul mood," she observed.

"Sally's insisting that I write an article about finding Verity Babcock's diary for the *Gazette*.

"And? So? As I remember, you were all excited about your discovery and a bit put out when Sally got word from the board that they wanted to keep mum about it."

I nodded. I heard a scratching at the door and went to open it. Smoky Joe, the gray library cat that was actually my cat, strutted into the office, his bushy tail flying high. He strode over to his bowl and glanced up at me. Good servant that I was, I hurried to fill it with kibble.

When Smoky Joe was busy eating, I turned back to Evelyn. "You're right. As soon as I read it, I knew people had to have access to Verity's diary so they would know firsthand how terrified she was while being subjected to the most awful accusations. And lies. One of the townspeople insisted she'd used witchcraft to poison his cow, so he could acquire her land. Even worse, Verity's neighbor claimed her husband had died because he'd ingested Verity's herbal medicine."

I exhaled loudly. "Verity could read and write, and was known as an herbalist and healer. She was also a widow who owned land. No doubt, some of her neighbors were envious of her wealth and resented the prestige her healing skills gave her.

"It struck me that Verity's was an extreme case of the #metoo movement. I still think that, but being forced to write a newspaper article isn't in my job description. Sally seems to have forgotten I'm getting married two weeks from tomorrow, and I've got tons of things to take care of."

Evelyn hopped down from her perch and started pacing toward me. I shivered as she drew near. Though she tried to be considerate, sometimes she forgot that when she came close to me she brought a chill from the other side.

"Carrie, my dear, you have everything in order: the band, the photographer, and the caterers. Your father, Bosco, and Harriet are taking care of the rehearsal dinner. Victor promised to have his house and the tent setup on the back lawn in perfect order for the big event. I know you're nervous, but what requires your immediate attention?"

I ran through the wedding list of obligations that never left my mind. "I have an appointment to try on my gown tomorrow morning, and hope they got the alterations right. Dylan and I still need to work on the seating arrangements."

"And?"

I shook my head in frustration. "Right now I can't remember what else needs taking care of. The truth is, I don't like Sally foisting assignments on me. She'll do anything to bring attention to the library."

"Maybe so." Evelyn returned to the corner of Trish's desk and crossed her legs. "Is that a bad thing?"

"I feel like I'm being used. Exploited."

"And Verity Babcock?"

"She'll be exploited as a seventeenth-century #metoo victim." I released a sigh of exasperation. "But at the same time her story must be told. Verity was no witch. Her diary makes it very clear that she was targeted because she was a widow who grew herbs, which she sometimes sold to her neighbors to help them heal."

"Until one of them took her herbs and died."

I grimaced. "Not because of Verity's herbs."

"Of course not. John Whitcomb was sick. It was only when he was dying that his wife begged Verity for medicine. When he died, his distraught widow accused Verity of witchcraft," Evelyn said, repeating what I'd told her.

"Exactly." I sat quietly for a minute, musing on the last few entries in Verity's diary. "Her terror grew as one neighbor after another bad-mouthed her, drudging up old grievances. I gathered she wasn't the easiest person to get along with, but that wasn't the issue. The number of accusations grew, and a month later Verity was in jail. Six months later she was dead."

"You'll write a wonderful article about your discovery and the contents of the diary. I know you will."

"Thanks, Evelyn." Just then the perfect opening sentence came to mind. I turned to my computer to get it down before I forgot it.

When I turned around, Evelyn had disappeared. Without a word of parting, as usual. I realized my good humor was restored. Once again her common sense had made me see in a fresh new way a situation I'd been fuming about.

The phone rang. It was Uncle Bosco.

"Hello, Carrie, I hope you're not angry with me for not giving you a heads-up about your being conscripted into writing the article for the *Gazette*. Liane went for the idea as soon as Sally mentioned it at our Zoom meeting. The others agreed, and suddenly it was a done deal."

Of course Liane Walters, the president of the library board, loved Sally's suggestion. Liane was as committed as Sally when it came to promoting the library every which way. And in the twelve years she'd held the position, she had done an excellent job. It was Liane who had instigated the library's expansion, enabling us to offer many more programs and services to our patrons.

"I must admit I was a bit put out at first," I said, "but I don't mind writing the article. It's a subject dear to my heart."

"It's just with your wedding coming up in a few weeks, I feel guilty giving you extra work. I know your aunt's going to give me what for when I get home tonight, insisting that I should have stood up for you."

I smiled, thinking about my great-aunt and -uncle and how lucky I was that they had welcomed me into their home two years ago, nurturing me when I was at my lowest point. "Tell Aunt Harriet I'm fine about it. Who knows? Maybe I'll turn into a writer," I joked.

There was a knock at the door. "I have to go, Uncle Bosco. The photographer from the newspaper is here to take a few shots of me."

I put down the receiver and called out, "Come in."

A tall, string bean of a young man with a mop of dark, curly hair and a scraggly beard entered the office. Two cameras hung from straps around his neck.

"Carrie, right?"

"I am."

"Hi. Nick Fanning from the *Gazette*." He pushed aside the cameras and offered me his hand.

Smoky Joe strode over and sniffed Nick's trouser legs. Satisfied, he left through the open door.

"I imagine you want to take photos of Verity Babcock's diary," I said.

"Of course."

"Then let's head down to the new Historical Room. We'll stop by for Norman Tobin, the reference librarian. The Historical Room is really his baby. I was only helping him go through our collection and put it in some kind of order."

"That's when you discovered Verity's diary?" Nick said.

"Yes."

We left my office and walked in the direction of the new wing. Norman was waiting for us at the reference desk. I was fond of our new reference librarian. He was good-natured and very knowledge-able. He bore me no ill will, unlike his predecessor Dorothy, Evelyn's niece, who would have been furious that I was the one who had come upon the diary and not her. I made the introductions, and the three of us set out for the Historical Room.

The new Historical Room was twice the size of the old one and still required many more hours of sorting through the entire collection. But we'd already made good use of the available wall space by mounting several photos and maps around the room.

"Excuse the mess," Norman said, gesturing at the pile of papers and brochures that threatened to slide off the large table. Boxes containing old children's toys, utensils, and clothing were stacked in one corner. "Ever since Carrie discovered the diary, we've been besieged with donations, all of which require careful sorting so they can be authenticated."

I stepped behind the display case that had arrived only a week earlier. Inside was Verity Babcock's diary along with a few pamphlets from the 1600s. The three of us peered down at the diary.

It was encased in a clear acid-free sleeve. The cover was a faded brown, its corners bent, the edges worn and discolored. "Do you think we could remove it for the photos?" Nick asked.

I looked at Norman. He laughed. "I don't see why not since it was stashed haphazardly among papers and pamphlets for so many years. A forensic expert is coming to verify the diary's age and authenticity, but we have no reason to doubt that it was Verity Babcock's diary."

"You won't be able to photograph any of the diary's pages," I told Nick. "The paper Verity used is stronger than the kind we use now, but the diary is almost five hundred years old. Norman and I are the only ones who handle the diary. The forensic expert will advise us how best to keep it in good condition."

I unlocked the rear sliding door, wishing the security system we'd set up for the library's art gallery and entrances had already been extended to protect this room, and placed the diary on top of the case.

As soon as I removed the sleeve, Nick was all business. He had me pose holding the diary in various positions. Then he took a few shots of Norman and me in the midst of what appeared to be a serious discussion about the diary. Click, click, click went one camera. Then the other. Ten minutes later it was over.

"I'll send you copies of the photos so you can tell me which ones you definitely don't want me to use. And which you like but need to have touched up." He grinned. "I can perform miracles."

"Good to know," I said. "Thanks."

Nick sped off, and Norman and I returned to our duties at a slower pace.

* * *

At five o'clock, I went in search of Smoky Joe and found him behind the circulation desk, where my best friend, Angela Prisco, worked. When Angela saw me approach, she moved to block my view of Smoky Joe, who was munching away.

"So, this is how you follow my instructions regarding not giving him treats," I said.

"The poor cat was hungry. Was I supposed to let him starve?"

I tsk-tsked. "He wouldn't come here begging for food if he didn't know you kept treats for him."

Angela threw out her hands in mock despair. "What can I say? Guilty as charged."

I let Smoky Joe polish off his snack, then gathered him up in my arms.

"Are we still meeting at the bridal shop tomorrow morning at eleven?" Angela asked.

"Uh-huh. The alterations are done, and our dresses are ready for us to try on. In fact, Julia will be picking up her dress too. I asked her to join us because I want to treat my two matrons of honor to brunch."

Angela grinned. "A nice perk for being in your wedding party."

I smiled as I made a mental check list of our wedding party. Julia, my other matron of honor, was my cousin Randy's wife; their five-year-old daughter, Tacey, was my flower girl; her older brother, Mark, was our ring bearer; and Mac, Dylan's business partner who had once been his mentor and employer, was his best man. My cousin Randy and Gary Winton, who worked for Dylan, were Dylan's two groomsmen. And of course my father was walking me down the aisle.

Five minutes later, I had Smoky Joe in his carrier and was heading for my car in the parking lot behind the library. The trees were sporting green leaves, the sun was shining brightly, and all was right with the world.

Dylan and I were getting married! A sense of excitement coursed through me every time I thought about our upcoming wedding at Victor Zalinka's elegant home above the Long Island Sound. Dear friend and lovely man that he was, Victor had given us carte blanche to make whatever arrangements we liked. A very kind and generous offer, since his home was filled with modern art and pre-Columbian figures worth several million dollars.

After much discussion and weather checking of the third Saturday night in June, Dylan and I had decided to hold the marriage ceremony in the living room, the cocktail hour out on the deck that ran along the back of the house, and the dancing and dinner beneath a tent on the lawn. We'd asked Mayor Alvin Tripp, a good friend with whom I served on the town council, to officiate.

Dylan and I had already taken care of the major arrangements. Besides those tasks Evelyn had mentioned, we'd chosen our menu; ordered the tent, rental tables, and chairs, and I'd reserved several rooms at a nearby motel for our out-of-town guests. Still, every day something new cropped up that required our attention.

My cell phone's jingle sounded when I was close to home.

"Hey, Babe, just calling to say I should be home by six thirty. Are we eating in or out?"

"In. I have an article to write for the newspaper, and I'd like to start on it this evening."

"Fine with me. Maybe we can finish the seating plan too."

"Sure. Why not?"

"See you in a few."

I smiled as I disconnected. In two weeks and one day I was going to be Mrs. Dylan Avery. Of course I planned to remain Carrie Singleton in my professional life at the library. When I told Dylan this, he simply said, "Whatever makes you happy."

That was typical Dylan and one of the reasons why I adored him. He never tried to control me or insist that I follow the "traditional" way of doing things. Whenever I found myself investigating a local crime that had somehow landed in my lap, he would tell me to be careful. He never ordered me not to get involved or tried to make me curtail my participation. Frankly, I couldn't live with a man who did, and I loved Dylan all the more for respecting me this way.

I turned onto the private Avery road; passed the white manor house where Dylan had grown up with his parents, now deceased; and drove on to the cottage where we lived. Though we both loved the cottage, we'd started house hunting last fall. The house model we liked the most was a five-bedroom colonial with a huge backyard that was scheduled to be built in a development a few miles away. So far, they hadn't broken ground yet, so if we went with this house, it would be more than a year before we could move in.

I unlocked the front door and released Smoky Joe from his carrier. As usual, he went straight to his bowl, as if he hadn't eaten all day. I fed him, changed into jeans and a T-shirt, then went outside to get the mail.

There was a packet from our travel agent. I ripped open the large envelope and thumbed through the papers inside. Dylan and I were honeymooning in Santorini and Mykonos. Ah, they wanted to know which day trips we wanted to sign up for, noting that we could do that online. And there was a note about a room change in our Mykonos hotel. We needed to contact them ASAP.

This should be the biggest problem we have to deal with, I thought as I went back inside to start dinner. I wanted to buy a few more items of clothing for our honeymoon, firm up our decision regarding the desserts at our reception, and give the musicians a playlist of our favorite songs. The day after our wedding, we were flying off to Greece! I hoped no major catastrophe would arise in the next two weeks to upset our plans.

Chapter Two

Over dinner, Dylan and I chatted about our workday. Dylan, who was a private investigator, was glowing because after interviewing the employees of one of his clients, he was pretty sure he now knew which one of them was stealing supplies. I told him about the article Sally had all but ordered me to write. And then, as usually happened in the past several months, the subject of our wedding took over.

"My cousin Judy Reiner RSVP'd to say she and her husband are coming," I said.

"And now that Bosco's cousin Willie is out of the hospital and can make it, we have a full table of Singletons," Dylan said.

"Looks that way. Let's take care of the table arrangements this weekend."

"Okay, and I'd like to stop over at Victor's tomorrow to decide the best way to arrange the chairs for the ceremony," Dylan said.

"Let's do it in the afternoon. The seamstress at the wedding store finished the alterations on my gown and Angela and Julia's dresses. We're meeting at eleven for a final fitting, then I'm treating them to brunch."

"Sounds like a plan."

I cleared the table and dished out ice cream for our dessert. Dylan brought his into the living room to eat while he looked through the packet of information our travel agent had sent us. He returned to the kitchen and placed his empty dish and spoon in the dishwasher as I was wiping down the table.

"For some reason, they no longer have the room we requested. But looks like we'll be getting an upgrade for the same price."

"That's fine with me." I gave him a quick kiss. "All done here. Next, I'm starting that article about Verity Babcock."

"Such efficiency," Dylan said, hugging me close.

"See you when I'm done."

Smoky Joe followed me into the guest room and settled himself on the bed while I sat down at my laptop. My plan was to whip up a rough copy and edit it afterward. I thought a minute, then began typing.

Though my family has lived in Clover Ridge for generations, I had never heard of Verity Babcock or knew of the terrible miscarriage of justice that ended her life in 1652. It was only after the recent expansion of our library, when I was helping Norman Tobin, our reference librarian, put the pamphlets, papers, and artifacts of our new and larger Historical Room in order, that I came upon Verity Babcock's diary. We have no record of how or when the diary arrived at the library, but we assume that one of her descendants must have donated it many years ago.

In it, Verity recorded her growing terror as friends and neighbors accused her of witchcraft, of which she had no knowledge.

I paused to allow the emotional impact of Verity's diary sweep over me. Since I'd read it, the details had been branded in my mind.

Verity had been widowed at an early age and left to support her son and daughter. Verity's mother had taught her how to heal illnesses, wounds, and insect and animal bites with herbs, and thus she was able to feed her small family and look after their livestock. Both children married and moved to other communities.

When one of her patients, her neighbor, died of pneumonia after ingesting the herbal potion she'd prepared for him, his widow spread the word that Verity was consorting with Satan and had poisoned her husband. Verity's terror grew as more townspeople claimed that her herbal remedies had made them or their livestock ill instead of improving their health. Finally, the matter was brought before the local magistrate. The diary ended there.

I'd done my research and learned that Verity's case had gone before a higher court, then to a grand jury for indictment and finally to a trial by jury. Witnesses came forth with supposed evidence that her remedies had brought them close to death. A townsman, who had often tried to cheat her when she shopped at his store, claimed she had poisoned his chickens. Verity knew he was lying, as was the neighbor who insisted his cow had died after eating her herbal cure. She was found guilty of witchcraft and hung soon after her trial.

I decided to add a few quotes that I'd copied from the diary, because they best illustrated Verity's emotional state as the accusations piled up, as well as the preposterous allegations that the court and the judge accepted as factual. One neighbor said Verity had caused her to have cramps, and two young girls swore they'd seen her dancing naked on the Green with a goat.

To think that people who had lived in a small village would make up such awful stories about one of their neighbors! Of course, some did it out of malice and in hopes of gaining the victim's property for themselves. For others it might have been a form of group hysteria. The laws and religion of Colonial America were rigid and strict, and anyone who didn't toe the line might be considered evil. And so many innocent people had been victimized. Some, like Verity Babcock, had even lost their lives.

I typed this up, saved the document, and turned off my computer. I planned to go over it tomorrow, then send it to Chuck Ryland and cc Sally. As I went to join Dylan in the living room, where he was watching TV, I wondered why I'd made such a fuss about writing the article when this case of injustice inflicted on a woman centuries ago made my blood boil. Thank goodness it had little relevance to anything that might happen today.

* * *

Saturday turned out to be another beautifully sunny day. I found a note from Dylan telling me he'd gone to the gym. I took my time over breakfast, then put my wedding shoes in a tote bag and drove to the wedding store in the mall. Angela and Julia had gone there with me back in December. Maisie, the petite saleswoman, who couldn't be more than twenty-three, had brought out several gowns, all of which were too froufrou for my taste, or included enough yards of satin to make a very long table cloth.

And then she'd showed me the gown I'd chosen. Angela, Julia, and Maisie all agreed it was *the one*. It had a strapless bodice, off-the-shoulder appliqués, and a beautiful fall of lace over a satin A-line skirt. It fitted me perfectly except that the skirt needed to be shortened.

Maisie spotted me the moment I entered the shop. She hurried over. "Miss Carrie, your gown is ready. Do you want to try it on now?"

"I'd love to." I followed her to a cubicle at the back of the store. "Angela and Julia should be arriving any minute now."

"I'll tell them you're here. And I'll get their dresses as soon as I bring you yours."

She returned soon after, my wedding gown draped over her arm. "Would you like me to help you into your gown?"

"Why don't I call you when I have it on so you can zip me up?"

"Will do," she chirped, and left as quickly as she'd appeared.

I peeled down to my underwear and stepped carefully into my wedding gown. Holding the top against me, I peered out the curtain and called to Maisie. She came quickly, a broad grin on her face.

"Your two attendants have arrived."

I turned around so she could zip me up. Then I slipped into my white satin strappy shoes and stepped outside the cubicle, to stand in front of the three-way mirror. Angela and Julia began to clap.

"You look stunning!" Maisie declared. Her glance fell to my hem. "And the length is perfect.

Angela handed me the veil she'd worn at her wedding a year ago. "Put it on. Let's see how it looks."

Maisie dashed off to get a few bobby pins as I fiddled with the veil. It was short and lacy and a perfect match for my dress. Maisie returned and adjusted the veil with a practiced hand so it draped just over my forehead. She placed two bobby pins in and stood back. "Voilà!"

Angela and Julia clapped again.

I grinned at myself in the mirror. I looked pretty damn good if I had to say so myself. Back in my cubicle, Maisie unzipped my gown. I removed my wedding attire and got back into my normal clothes. Maisie carried the gown and the veil to the front of the shop while I waited to see my matrons of honor in their dresses.

My wedding colors were lavender, teal, and gold. Both Angela and Julia had chosen lavender dresses that only required minor adjustments. Angela's was a pale satin sheath with a V-neck bodice and side cutouts that showed off her tall and willowy figure. Julia's chiffon dress was a darker shade; its sweetheart neckline, beaded bodice, and flowing skirt flattered her curvier lines. Tacey's satin flower-girl dress was teal and fitted her perfectly.

My attendants looked spectacular in their dresses and were pleased with the alterations. So was Maisie. Young though she was, she certainly knew how wedding dresses were supposed to fit.

We gathered up our finery, and Angela and Julia followed me in their cars to the Inn on the Green. The Inn was several hundred years old and faced the side of the Green adjacent to the library. While I'd eaten here several times, I'd never had the chance to try their weekend brunch. I'd heard the selections were varied and delicious, and I was eager to sample them for myself.

We were seated at a square table next to one of the large windows that looked out on the Green. Our server, an elderly gentleman, asked if we'd like a Bloody Mary, mimosa, or champagne. We all opted for champagne.

It was pure heaven, starting with breakfast-style food like waffles and omelets, then salads and pastas, and finally seafood and meat dishes. I had to remember to take only a small amount of each delicious offering, or I'd never manage to eat any of the Inn's famous cakes and their outstanding bread pudding.

We chatted in between bites of food—about my upcoming wedding, about Tacey and Mark, and about Scampi, Angela and Steve's little Maltipoo. Though I was literally half a block from where I worked, I felt as though I were on vacation. Here we sat, three women sharing a leisurely meal, something we rarely had time for in our busy schedules.

"Did you make any headway with that article Sally asked you to write?" Angela asked. We were drinking the last of our coffee over half-eaten desserts.

"I wrote it last night," I said. "I'll go over it later or tomorrow, then send it to Chuck Ryland at the *Gazette*."

Angela patted my shoulder. "Good for you, Carrie. I knew you'd get it done."

"Once I got started, it practically wrote itself. I fume every time I think about how that poor woman suffered." I grimaced. "It's Sally's high-handed attitude that irks me when she orders me to do something that's not in my job description."

Angela laughed. "She knows you're more than capable of writing an article for the newspaper."

"What are you talking about?" Julia asked. "What article have you written for the newspaper?"

"While putting the new Historical Room in order, I came upon the diary that Verity Babcock wrote before she was hung as a witch."

"I remember learning about Verity Babcock," Julia said. "I wrote an essay about her in high school."

"Did you?" I said, suddenly interested. Julia had grown up in a town about twenty miles north of Clover Ridge.

"Oh yes. We learned about the Connecticut residents who were hung as witches in my ninth-grade social studies class. You would think she'd have been exonerated by now."

"She never was?" I asked, wondering why I'd never looked into this myself.

"None of the people who were hung as witches were," Julia said. She glanced at her watch. "Oh my! It's twenty to two. I really have to get going."

"Me too," Angela said. "I told Steve I'd go shopping with him. There's a sale on tools, and he wants to buy a few."

"I need to head out as well," I said. "Now that we have our final number of guests, Dylan wants to drive over to Victor's house to figure out how best to arrange the chairs for the ceremony."

"Are Victor and Babette still an item?" Angela asked.

"Most definitely. Right now he's away on a business trip and flying home on Tuesday."

I settled the bill and we walked outside into the bright sunshine.

Julia hugged me. "Carrie, thanks so much for this delightful brunch. I enjoyed it immensely. I'm honored to be one of your matrons of honor."

"The honor is mine, cuz."

Angela seized me in a bear hug. "I'm so happy you're getting married."

I hugged her back, blinking back tears. Angela had been the first person to befriend me when I came to work at the library as an aide, doing whatever low-level tasks needed to be done. Since then, the many adventures we'd shared had only drawn us closer.

"I love you, BFF," I said.

"Back at ya!"

* * *

I drove home slowly, reflecting on my life and how lucky I was. I was marrying the man I adored. I had wonderful friends and relatives, and a job I really loved. I had my wedding to look forward to, followed by a honeymoon in Greece. An abundance of riches!

Dylan was waiting for me when I got to the cottage. I put away my wedding finery in the guest room closet and gave Smoky Joe some attention and a few treats. Then we climbed into Dylan's BMW and set out for Victor's house.

"Right now we're seventy-eight people, including us and our wedding party," Dylan said as we drove past the manor house. "Victor's living room can easily accommodate that number once all the furniture is removed. Today I want to figure out if the chairs should face the large bay window or the den."

"I always thought the bay window was the best place for the altar."

"It certainly is the most dramatic," Dylan agreed. "But arranging the chairs the other way may give us more room so our guests won't feel cramped. We'll have a better idea when we're at the house and can measure how much space each chair will take up after we figure in the aisle."

"Yes. The aisle has to be wide enough to allow our matrons of honor and groomsmen to stand as my dad walks beside me." I thought a minute. "Eight or nine rows of seats should do it."

"I also want to check out the deck, where we'll be having appetizers and drinks after the ceremony. Decide on the best place for the bar."

"And how many small tables we can fit in."

"Victor texted me this morning," Dylan said. "He's still planning to fly home from Bruges on Tuesday unless something comes up."

"How nice that he gave us the key to his house so we can stop by when he's not there," I said.

"And how happy it seems to make him that we're getting married in his home, when he's the one doing us the biggest of favors."

"I know," I agreed. "In the past few months he's become one of our closest friends."

We drove onto the semicircular driveway and parked in front of the door. The house was both elegant and well proportioned, but cozy at the same time. I mentally compared it to the houses Dylan and I had looked at and considered buying, but none came close to its appeal. Dylan unlocked the front door and disengaged the alarm system. It felt strange coming here without Victor to welcome us with Raspie—Rasputin, his borzoi—at his side.

Since Victor's home was complete with motion sensor lighting, the hall brightened as soon as we stepped inside. As usual, I admired the array of paintings on the walls and the pre-Columbian figures on their stands.

Dylan and I headed straight for the living room. He'd brought along a tape measure and quickly measured the length and width of the room. We brought in two kitchen chairs and measured how much room each took up, as well as the necessary amount of space that allowed for each guest's comfort and the requisite aisle. Since it was apparent that we could arrange the chairs either way, it was a no-brainer to have them face the lovely bay window. That accomplished, we walked along the hall to the kitchen and unlocked the back door leading to the deck.

The floor consisted of gray wooden slats set diagonally across an expanse as long as the kitchen it backed, and twenty feet wide. It was certainly large enough to accommodate almost eighty people and perhaps nine very small round tables. Not enough seats for everyone, but a wooden bench ran along the deck's railing for a good part of the deck.

I made a mental note to rent long pads for the bench so my guests wouldn't snag their clothing. I was glad to see that the fuchsia New Guinea impatiens, in pots every ten feet or so around the parameter, were in full bloom. Clearly, Victor had arranged for his gardener to water the plants while he was away.

Dylan came to stand beside me, and we gazed out at the spectacular scene before us. Three steps down from the deck was the expansive lawn, which stretched out the length of a football field before sloping gently down to the Long Island Sound. Tall oaks and lilac bushes bordered both sides of the property while rose bushes thrived in the garden to the left of the steps.

"Lovely, isn't it?" Dylan said as he slipped an arm around my waist.

"So peaceful."

"Would you like to live in a house like this?"

"Maybe one day. In the near future I'd rather live in a development filled with kids that's close to a school."

The gazebo below caught my attention. "Though I'd love to have a gazebo in our backyard."

Dylan laughed. "I don't know about that. After we put in an inground pool and a swing set, there probably won't be room for a gazebo."

"The kids might want a trampoline," I said. "Julia and Randy just got one. Mark and Tacey are crazy about it."

"Who knows what fad will be popular when we have kids their age," Dylan said.

We grinned at each other. Something to look forward to and find out.

I noticed a long object on the ground a few feet from the gazebo. It was difficult to make out what it was since it was lying where the lawn began to slope down, and the sun was shining in my eyes.

I grabbed Dylan's arm. "What's that?"

Dylan took off down the steps. I chased after him. When I caught up with him, he was crouching beside the body of a man in his mid-twenties, who lay stretched out on his back, an expression of pain on his face.

I gasped. "Is he dead?"

"Very." Dylan had his phone out and was making a call.

I stared at the large hole in the lawn and the shovel a few feet from the body. What was this all about?

"Hi, John—it's Dylan. Carrie and I just came upon a corpse on Victor Zalinka's lawn." Dylan listened a minute, then snapped a photo of the body. "I'm sending it to you now."

Chapter Three

While Dylan and I waited for Lieutenant John Mathers outside the front entrance of the house, Dylan called Victor to tell him what we'd discovered.

"Oh my God! Dead?" I heard Victor exclaim from across the Atlantic. "What was he digging up on my property?"

They spoke a few minutes more. Finally, Dylan promised to keep Victor updated and ended the call. He turned to me. "Victor said that unless his presence is demanded here, he'll be flying home Tuesday, as planned."

"I can't see why John would insist that Victor cut short his business trip," I said. "That poor man was probably murdered in the past day or two, when Victor wasn't even in the country."

"After touching his cheek, I'd say it happened no earlier than last night," Dylan said.

I shuddered. "How was he murdered?"

"I didn't see any bullet wounds or wounds of any kind, so whatever the weapon was, the damage must have been to the back of his head or lower body."

I nodded. "Meaning the killer snuck up on him."

"While he was digging."

We paused to consider all this. Who was the victim? Who was the murderer? And what were they after?

I let out a scream. Dylan drew me close. "What is it, Carrie?"

"Our wedding! How can we go ahead with our plans to get married here where a murder just took place?"

Before Dylan could answer, a police car drew up, its colorful lights spinning. Lieutenant John Mathers and Officer Danny Brower stepped out and walked toward us.

"So, Carrie, looks like you've found us another homicide victim, and this time you brought Dylan along," John said in greeting.

"We both noticed the body," I corrected him. "Believe me, this is very distressing."

"I know it is," John said, his tone considerably softer. John and his wife were good friends of ours, and he knew I must be freaking out—coming upon a corpse on the property where Dylan and I were getting married in two weeks' time. "Shall we?"

Dylan led the way around the house and across the lawn to where the body was lying.

"The technicians and the ME are on their way," John said as we walked.

The four of us stood around the corpse. I watched John survey the scene. He took in the gazebo; the freshly dug hole about two feet deep and three feet wide, and the shovel beside it.

"Looks like he was digging for something," Danny said.

"There's no way of telling if he found what he was looking for or if the killer took off with it," John said. He glanced at Dylan and me. "And the two of you happened to be here because . . .?"

"We came to decide on the best way to arrange the seating for the wedding ceremony. Victor's abroad until Tuesday, but he gave us the key," Dylan explained.

"Did anything seem amiss in the house?" John asked.

"Nothing," Dylan answered. "Of course we were only down-stairs, but Victor has a top-of-the-line security system because of his art collection. We would have noticed if there had been a break-in."

John thought a minute. "At this point I've no reason to extend our investigation to include Zalinka's house. I'm aware of his valuable art collection, and I don't want to bring officers into the home unless it becomes necessary. You say he's expected home on Tuesday?"

"Yes," I said. "He flew to Europe last Wednesday."

"I'll speak to him when he's back home," John said. "I'm no pathologist, but I'd say this poor soul was murdered in the past six to twenty-four hours."

I gasped. If we'd come that morning, we might have witnessed the cold-blooded killing.

"In that case, I'll set the alarm in the house, and we'll be off," Dylan said.

"Talk to you soon," John said, looking grim.

I started to shake as soon as I slid into the car. Dylan wrapped his arms around me. "Delayed reaction," he murmured.

I held him close. "How can this be happening?" I burst into tears. "Why can't we plan our wedding without someone getting murdered? And poor Victor. He was a suspect in another murder case. John has to see that he has nothing to do with this one."

"Of course John doesn't like Victor for this homicide. You heard him say the murder was recent. Victor's been gone for days. As for our wedding, it's two weeks from now. Plenty of time to find out why the victim was digging in Victor's backyard and who murdered him."

I sniffed. "And what if it doesn't play out that way?"

Dylan shrugged. "We'll get permission to hold the wedding on the Green and have the reception in the library."

I smiled. A farfetched idea, but my dearly beloved was just resourceful enough to pull it off.

Dylan pulled a tissue from the box he kept in the back seat and handed it to me. "Cheer up and dry your eyes. I promise we're getting married, regardless of that poor fellow we discovered today."

* * *

When we got home, Dylan made tea. We sat at the kitchen table, sipping it and saying very little. I was glad we hadn't made plans for the evening.

"Feeling better?" Dylan asked as he put our empty mugs in the sink.

I nodded.

He went into the spare bedroom to do some paperwork. I stretched out on the living room sofa with a mystery novel, but found I kept on reading the same paragraph over and over again. The phone calls began minutes later. The first was from Babette Fisher. Babette taught art at the local high school and served on the town council with me. For the past six months, she and Victor had been in an intense relationship.

"I just spoke to Victor. He said you and Dylan discovered a dead body on his back lawn. Another homicide, Carrie?" Babette sounded both apprehensive and excited, the blend I'd become all too familiar with when people got news that someone had been murdered.

"Yes, unfortunately. He hasn't been identified yet. We waited until John arrived and left before the CSI techies came on the scene."

"Please let me know when you hear anything. Victor asked me to keep him informed." She paused. "Does Lieutenant Mathers imagine Victor had anything to do with this?"

"I don't think so. I'll call if I learn anything."

"Thanks, Carrie."

I turned on the TV and caught the tail end of John being interviewed by a reporter. This time my cell phone played its jingle. Angela.

"I can't believe someone was murdered on Victor's back lawn, of all places!"

"I know."

"You don't sound surprised. Don't tell me—"

"Yes, Dylan and I were at the house when we noticed the body and called John."

"Oh no! You and Dylan discovered it!"

I was grateful that Angela didn't berate me for not telling her about the corpse, though I knew she wanted to.

"I'm worried, Angela. What was some strange guy doing, digging up Victor's lawn? What if the killer didn't find what he was after and decides to break into the house? How can we get married there if a killer's roaming free?"

"I'm sure John will give this case his full attention. And if you join the investigation, you'll speed things up and catch the killer before your big day."

"Really? Investigate when I still have lots of wedding stuff to deal with? Besides, I saw the victim, and I have no idea who he is. I wouldn't even know where to begin."

"You'll find a way. You always do."

Julia called, then I heard from Sally. And from Marion, the children's librarian. An hour later my father called, very concerned about my emotional state. I was touched but at the same time amused. Jim Singleton had not been around for most of my growing-up years. And now that I was thirty-one, I found myself dealing with a helicopter dad.

After our eventful day, Dylan and I decided to eat out, after all. We hopped in his car and went to the next town for pizza and Cokes.

John called us on Dylan's phone as we were driving home. Dylan put the call on speaker.

"The victim's name is Billy Carpenter. Turns out, his aunt and uncle owned the house for more than thirty years before they sold it to Victor Zalinka three years ago."

"Oh," I said, relieved that this couldn't possibly have anything to do with Victor.

"He served four years of a six-year prison sentence for a bank robbery. Never gave up his accomplices, and the cash was never recovered. But he behaved himself and got off early. He was released earlier this week."

"So he must have buried the money on the lawn. Someone followed him, killed him, and took off with the dough," Dylan said.

"Sure looks that way," John agreed.

"How was he murdered?" I asked.

"Shot twice—in the head and the neck—with a small-caliber weapon. We spoke to the neighbors on the block, but so far only one person heard what sounded like shots around four in the morning."

"Do you have any leads?" Dylan asked.

"Carpenter had two close pals who we think were in on the robbery, though he never gave them up. Also, Carpenter's cellmate got released a few days after he did. There's a good chance Carpenter told him about the money, and the guy stalked him. Or his pals did."

"Does this mean you'll probably be arresting someone soon?" I asked.

"I sure hope so, Carrie. I know how upsetting this must be for both of you. Believe me, I'll do my best to arrest the bad guy—or guys—but everything has to be done by the book or the case gets thrown out before it goes to court."

"I know," I said.

I must have sounded as down as I felt, because John said, "Carrie, I don't want you getting mixed up in this investigation. Try to stay calm and leave the sleuthing to my department. We have some good leads to start with, so hopefully we'll catch whoever killed this guy soon."

"I wouldn't dream of getting involved this close to our wedding," I said.

But the wheels were already spinning in my head. John had just told us who the obvious suspects were—Billy Carpenter's two good friends and his cellmate. I could google them, maybe talk to people who knew them, and help solve this homicide ASAP.

Chapter Four

I was glad I was scheduled to work on Sunday, figuring that being around people would help distract me from the previous day's unsettling experience and stop me from seeing the victim's face every time I closed my eyes—his dark stubbly beard and the pain etched in his features. Unfortunately, that wasn't exactly how it played out.

Somehow word had gotten out that Dylan and I had discovered the body, and everyone I ran into insisted on asking how I felt about finding a body where I was getting married. You'd think people would be more tactful, but human beings are inquisitive by nature and can't help asking questions.

Still, that didn't mean I had to answer them. I hurried off to check on the few ongoing programs, then took refuge in my office, determined not to step outside until two o'clock, when I was obliged to introduce a wonderful musical group scheduled to sing a medley of show tunes in our new stadium-seated auditorium.

I'd no sooner turned on my computer than Evelyn appeared, wearing a shirtwaist dress—white with a pattern of small sprigs of flowers—and black patent leather heels. The epitome of spring.

"So," she said when she'd perched on the corner of Trish's desk, "tell me everything you found out about the dead man."

"Not you too," I grumbled.

Evelyn frowned as she walked toward me, remembering just in time not to get too close.

"Carrie, dear, I only want to help you solve this murder so you can go ahead with your wedding. Isn't that what you want?"

"It is. Sorry to be grumpy, but of all the places for a body to turn up, this couldn't be worse."

"I agree," Evelyn said. "So let's work on this together."

I nodded. "His name is Billy Carpenter. His aunt and uncle sold the house to Victor. Did you know him?"

Evelyn crossed her legs and thought. "Billy used to come into the library and take out books about electrical inventions. That stopped when he was about fifteen. His parents had just divorced, and his father left town. Billy started to hang out with the problem kids in high school. In fact, he left school before graduating."

"Was he close to his aunt and uncle?" I asked.

"He lived with them off and on because his mother had custody of him and his sister, but she couldn't control Billy."

"A few days after he was released from prison, he went to dig up the money from the robbery," I told her. "John said he probably had two partners, but from the looks of things, Billy never split the money with them."

"So we can assume that one or both of his partners followed him, saw him digging up the money, and killed him for it," Evelyn said.

I nodded. "Or his prison cellmate did it. John said word from the prison is that he and Billy were pretty close."

"Thick as thieves," Evelyn said.

I rolled my eyes.

"Sorry. I couldn't resist. The next step is to figure out who Billy's partners were."

"John said he had two close friends: Luke Rizzo and Tino Valdez. They used to get into trouble together, so there's a good chance they were both in on the robbery five years ago."

"Of course—those were their names!" Evelyn said. "And now I remember the robbery. Luke had moved to Hartford to live with his father. He got a part-time job working for a store owner on the same block as the bank that was robbed. How coincidental is that? Of course the police questioned him, but Luke never admitted to being in on the heist. Billy was caught on camera, and he was arrested later that day. He never named his partners."

"I'm going to google the robbery and Billy's trial to see what else I can learn."

"Good idea. I'll stop by later to hear about your results," Evelyn said, and disappeared.

There were several articles about the robbery and trial in the Hartford and Clover Ridge local papers, but they revealed little more than what Evelyn had just told me. Dylan called me to see how I was feeling. He told me he'd spoken to Victor, who was mainly upset on our behalf.

"Oh, he's so sweet," I said. Then my desk phone rang. "I have to go."

"See you at home."

"Carrie, dear, how are you?" asked my great-aunt Harriet when I answered the other line.

"I'm okay. I suppose you heard that Dylan and I discovered a body on Victor Zalinka's lawn."

"We did. Your uncle and I didn't want to bother you yesterday, but perhaps you and Dylan would like to come to dinner tonight. It won't be anything fancy."

"I'd love that," I said. "Let me check with Dylan."

"It's okay with Dylan. I just spoke to him. He said it was up to you."

"Oh."

"Shall we say six o'clock?"

"Perfect."

I disconnected, thinking about how close Dylan had grown to my relatives. Of course he'd known Harriet and Bosco when they owned the Singleton Farm, and he often spent time there, even when my older brother Jordan and I weren't visiting. Dylan had also formed a close bond with my father. Jim now worked in Atlanta with Mac, Dylan's partner in the investigative agency, putting everything he'd learned during his life of crime to good use, catching bad guys.

Feeling calmer than I had hours earlier, I walked over to the library's coffee shop and bought a cheese and tomato sandwich and a cup of coffee, which I brought back to my office. I found Smoky Joe waiting to be let in for a quick meal and a pit stop.

I looked in on the one o'clock movie in the old meeting room downstairs, then returned to my office. Since I had almost an hour with nothing pressing that required my attention, I decided to polish the article about Verity Babcock.

I turned on my computer and read what I'd written. Except for a few minor edits, I thought the article read well. But something was missing. Where was the anger? The outrage that an innocent woman had been put to death because of the hysteria and ill will that had blazed through her community? I remembered Julia saying that Verity and the other victims had never been exonerated. How awful that after all these years the state had never rectified this wrong. I had to include this in my article.

I bit my lower lip as I began another paragraph, berating our town officials for failing to declare Verity and the others who had been hanged as witches innocent of all charges. I ended by stating their pardon was long overdue.

Pleased with my handiwork, I smiled as I emailed the article to Chuck Ryland at the *Gazette* and sent a copy to Sally.

* * *

Dylan and I set out for my aunt and uncle's at a quarter to six. Dylan had retrieved a bottle of Uncle Bosco's favorite wine from his seemingly endless supply that he stored in the manor house. I brought over a batch of low-calorie brownies I had in the freezer. They weren't as rich as my double-chocolate brownies, but Uncle Bosco declared them an okay substitute. I was proud of him for sticking to his diet, for the most part, since his heart attack eight months earlier and for continuing to exercise three times a week with a personal trainer.

My great-aunt and -uncle lived in a centuries-old home across the Green from the library. They'd moved there about ten years ago, after selling the Singleton Farm to Dylan's parents. Now Dylan's parents, whom I'd never met, were both deceased, and the farm, which the Averys had sold at a profit, was a successful B&B.

After a flurry of hugs and greetings, Uncle Bosco asked what we'd like to drink. We all opted for wine—red for Dylan and Uncle Bosco, white for Aunt Harriet and me. While Uncle Bosco and Dylan uncorked bottles, I helped Aunt Harriet carry platters and serving dishes of food to the dining room table.

We sat down and passed the serving dishes around, and for a few minutes we were too busy eating to speak. Uncle Bosco was the first to finish his food. He was treating himself to seconds under Aunt Harriet's watchful eyes when he said, "Carrie, my dear, I hope you've recovered from that fright you had yesterday."

"I've calmed down now," I said.

"The TV reporter said the victim had recently been released after serving a sentence for a bank robbery in Hartford. I seem to remember that. From the pictures they showed us, it's assumed he was digging up the money he'd buried in the ground close to the gazebo."

"The latest I heard is the police are questioning his former cellmate since he was released a few days after Carpenter," Uncle Bosco said.

"I'm glad Victor was away when Billy Carpenter was murdered," I said. "I'd hate to think of what might have happened if he'd heard voices arguing or a gunshot. Or if Raspi heard something and dashed out into the night."

"Who's Raspi?" Aunt Harriet asked.

"Victor's Borzoi." I turned to Uncle Bosco. "By the way, I finished my article about Verity Babcock and sent it off to the *Gazette*."

Uncle Bosco frowned. "Again, my apologies for not trying to stop it from being foisted on you so close to your wedding."

"No problem," I said, "Turns out it didn't take me very long. But why the sudden change of heart about telling the public we'd found the diary?"

"Somehow the *Gazette* heard about your discovery. Chuck contacted Sally, and they both liked the idea of your writing the article. As I told you, the other board members were heartily in agreement, so there wasn't anything I could do to change their minds."

"I'm curious, why did the library board want us to keep news of finding the diary under wraps in the first place? Verity died so many years ago."

"We wanted to find out if the state had changed its policy regarding those people charged under the crime of witchcraft, before releasing the news about your discovery. Hanging people for witchcraft is a shameful period in our state's history. Over the years, attempts have been made to have the victims officially pardoned, but so far Verity Babcock and the other poor souls haven't been exonerated."

"So I've learned," I said. "Totally shameful. At first I wished I hadn't been coerced into writing the article, but now I'm glad that I wrote it."

We finished our main course. I helped Aunt Harriet clear the table and bring out a fruit platter and my brownies. Our conversation moved on to our wedding, and Dylan mentioned the small change in our honeymoon arrangements.

"Have you decided to place a down payment on a house in the new development you visited last weekend?" Uncle Bosco asked.

"Not yet," Dylan said.

"We like it, but there's another development going up a few miles north of it that we want to look at," I said, "though so far there's not much to see."

My aunt and uncle exchanged glances. What were they up to?

"Are you set on buying a brand new house?" Uncle Bosco asked. "You know, an old house has charm that only comes with age."

"And lovely trees and shrubbery that will take years to grow in a new development," Aunt Harriet added.

Dylan laughed. "Along with all sorts of repair problems. Not that a brand new house comes without any issues."

I looked at my aunt and my uncle. "Do you have a particular house in mind?"

"We do, as a matter of fact," Uncle Bosco said.

"It's about half a mile from where our family farm used to be. On Old Willows Road," Aunt Harriet said.

"Really?" I smiled. "That's such a pretty road, with lovely homes."

"This house is a real beauty—on over an acre of land, some of it wooded, with a little brook than runs through the back of the property," Uncle Bosco said. "It has four bedrooms and a large kitchen that was recently remodeled. All of the appliances are top of the line."

"When did it go on the market?" I asked, suddenly suspicious.

"Oh, some time ago." Aunt Harriet waved her hand as if my question were trivial.

"What's 'some time'?" Dylan asked.

"A year or two," Uncle Bosco said. "Certainly no more than three years total. Right, Harriet?"

"Definitely," my aunt agreed.

"Three years!" I exclaimed. "That's a long time for a house to be on the market."

"It was nearly sold a few times, but somehow the sale never went through," Aunt Harriet said.

"But you needn't worry about the condition of the house," Uncle Bosco assured me. "We know the family that owns it. They've been very diligent about keeping it up and making sure it's in tip-top condition."

Dylan and I looked at each other. "So what's the catch?" he asked.

"There must be a good reason why this keeps happening," I insisted. "Aren't you going to tell us what it is?"

Uncle Bosco cleared his throat. "The potential buyers claimed they heard talking and laughter and saw moving shadows when they were in the house. It happened a few times, but never when the realtor was in the room with them."

I scoffed. "It sounds like the house is haunted."

"Of course it's not haunted," Aunt Harriet said. "Floorboards creak. Furnaces shut off and on. A strong wind can sound like a howling wolf. Isn't that right, Bosco?"

"Yes, dear."

Aunt Harriet shook her head as she tsk-tsked. "It's on the loveliest piece of property. The owners are selling it for a very reasonable price."

"And if you're interested, I'm sure they'll come down even more," Uncle Bosco added.

Intriguing, I thought.

"I suppose we can take a look," Dylan said.

I stared at my fiancé. Dylan knew I saw and spoke to Evelyn, even though he, like everyone but little Tacey, couldn't. But he had communicated with the ghost of his dead uncle, so he'd had that experience. Still, I found it surprising that he was willing to visit this house. "You really want to?"

"Why not, if it's all Harriet and Bosco claim it is?" He winked at me. "We can decide for ourselves whether the place is haunted."

"I guess we could check it out next weekend."

Aunt Harriet was already heading into the kitchen. She returned to the table a minute later and handed me a piece of paper. "Here's the Wolcotts' number. They'll be thrilled to hear from you."

"I'm sure they will," I said, wondering if I was crazy to even contemplate buying a house occupied by ghosts.

Chapter Five

"Why are you so interested in looking at that house?" I asked Dylan as soon as we were on our way back to the cottage.

"Why not? it sounds lovely. Reasonably priced. And I like the idea of living in a house with character."

I laughed. "Is a house with character a euphemism for a haunted house?"

Dylan shrugged. "I suppose."

We drove on. When we stopped at a red light, Dylan turned to me. "Since when do a couple of ghosts scare you off?"

"I'm no maven when it comes to ghosts since I've only met two—Evelyn and your Uncle Alec."

"They certainly aren't frightening or malevolent."

"They aren't," I agreed reluctantly since I didn't know where this was going.

"Don't you find it curious that the supposed ghosts in the house Bosco and Harriet think so highly of only appear when the potential owners are alone with them?"

"Kind of," I admitted. "Either the ghosts are deliberately scaring them off for some reason, or they don't want the realtor who might have known them when they were alive to discover they exist in ghostly form."

The light turned green, and Dylan merged onto the parkway. "But we might be able to figure it out." I reached for my cell phone and clicked on Google. I typed in the address of the house and, after chasing down a few links, finally got what I was searching for. "Yes!"

"Care to share?"

"According to this article, the house was built in the 1800s. The Wolcott family has owned it for a few generations." I stopped to read a few more lines that told me very little. "That's . . . it." I returned to Google and clicked on another link.

"Hmm . . . this gives more information. The house was built in 1843 by a young Englishman named Allistair Perry for his American bride. Twelve years later there was a fire, and their two little girls perished. His wife insisted that they sell the house and move."

"How sad," Dylan said.

I read on, "The house stood empty and abandoned until a shipbuilder bought it and rebuilt the damaged section. His family lived there until he and his wife died. The children sold it to another family, and the Wolcotts acquired it in the 1950s."

"Has any tragedy befallen them?" Dylan asked.

"No. Ted Wolcott grew up in the house and bought it from his parents a few years after he married Marjorie Harcourt. They did extensive construction in the nineties and gifted it to their daughter. She raised her family, got divorced, and died a few years ago. Neither of her two children wanted the house so they put it on the market. Their grandparents, Marjorie and Ted, are overseeing the sale since both grandchildren live out of state. Only they haven't been able to sell it."

"Fascinating story," Dylan said, "though it still doesn't explain why ghosts are driving potential buyers away. Shall we go and see the house for ourselves?"

"Let's. Now I'm curious to see it. Maybe we'll meet the supposed ghosts."

"I'll call the Wolcotts tomorrow and set up an appointment for next weekend. Meanwhile, I'll have Rosalind see what else she can dig up regarding the history of the house and the families that owned it."

"Good idea." Dylan's office manager was a whiz at ferreting out information regarding just about anything. There had to be a good reason why ghosts were suddenly haunting a house that was almost two hundred years old.

*　*　*

When we got home, I gave Smoky Joe some attention, then went into the living room, where Dylan was watching TV.

"We said we'd work on the seating arrangements this weekend," I said.

"We did," Dylan agreed, his eyes never leaving the TV.

"Do you want to do it tomorrow night? Oh, tomorrow's a late day for me."

Dylan reached for the remote and clicked off the TV. "In that case we'd better do it now. You never know what snags we might run into that will require our time and attention."

"Besides, I want to bring it to the printer as soon as we're done, so I can order the poster and the small place cards listing the names and tables."

I went into the guest bedroom-slash-office and returned with the guest list. Dylan and I studied it for a minute or two.

"It shouldn't be too difficult," I said. "Last count we were seventy-eight total. We can have tables with eight, nine, or ten seats."

"Let's start with work colleagues," Dylan said. "Since you've invited all your work pals and their mates, that will require two tables."

41

I thought a bit. "Do we put Angela and Steve with the library people or with her parents?"

"We'll think about it," Dylan said, reaching for a pad and pen. "That's question number one."

"And where should Susan and Ron sit?" I wondered. "With the library people or Clover Ridge neighbors?"

Susan Roberts had been my other part-time assistant until last November when she'd left to manage the Gallery on the Green and focus on her painting. Even before then she'd been in a romantic relationship with Ron Mallory, the gallery owner who was in his mid-sixties, forty years older than Susan. I was surprised they were still together. But then, as Evelyn had reminded me more than once, not all couples were the same.

"Hmm," Dylan mused. "That makes question number two."

An hour later, we had a list of questions we needed to address, and our table arrangements were far from complete. When Dylan yawned for the third time, I took pity on him.

"Let's finish this Tuesday evening," I said.

"Great idea."

Later, as we were drifting off to sleep, I said, "I never imagined that setting up table arrangements for a wedding could be so exhausting."

"Or so complicated."

* * *

Monday morning Chuck Ryland called me on the library phone to tell me how much he liked my article about Verity Babcock. I had met him briefly a month or two ago—a big, balding guy in his fifties with a booming voice—at an open town council meeting. He'd showed up to complain that the *Gazette* was on its last legs, and we council members weren't doing enough to encourage small businesses to take out ads in the paper.

"This is terrific, Carrie. Really terrific! Maybe it will finally get the state's General Assembly to pardon those poor victims of group hysteria who were hung as witches in the Dark Ages."

"I'm glad you like it," I said, feeling proud of myself.

"Just needs a few tweaks and it's good to go. Look for the article in Wednesday's paper."

"Thanks, I will," I said.

Sally stopped by my office around eleven to tell me she liked the article as well. "I knew you'd do us proud. And Chuck is singing your praises."

I shrugged. "Verity's a worthy cause. What I didn't like was being ambushed."

"Sorry about that. I'll keep that in mind next time."

"Next time?"

"Though we have our own newsletter and Facebook page, posting an occasional article in the *Gazette* is good PR." She winked. "Especially just before it's time to vote on our budget."

* * *

"Has John given you an update on the murder at Victor Zalinka's place?" Angela asked. It was five minutes past noon, and we were walking the three blocks to the Cozy Corner Café, where we often ate lunch when our schedules allowed.

"Not since he called to tell us the victim, Billy Carpenter, had gone to prison for robbing a bank. He was probably digging up the cash when either his cellmate or his partners shot him and took off with the money."

Angela sent me an amused glance. "You haven't done any sleuthing yourself?"

"Are you kidding? Between work and wedding stuff, I don't have a free moment."

Like spending an hour online that morning choosing gifts for her, Julia, and Tacey. I had finally decided on a lovely pearl necklace and bracelet set for each of my matrons of honor, and an adorable necklace with a tiny heart for my flower girl. All were scheduled to arrive the week of the wedding.

"What still needs to be done?" Angela asked.

"Dylan and I are trying to finish up the seating arrangements. Would you like to sit with the library crew or with your parents?"

Angela thought a moment. "Can the four of us sit with Fran and Sally and their husbands? My parents got to spend time with them at our wedding and really enjoyed their company."

"Sure. That can be arranged." I mentally added Marion's assistant Gayle and her boyfriend, making it ten people. One table done!

"Is everyone from the library able to come?" Angela asked.

"Pete's sorry he and his wife can't make it. They have long-standing plans—a family celebration. And Harvey simply RSVP'd that he wouldn't be attending."

"No loss there," Angela said. "I can't remember the last time Harvey cracked a smile."

"He certainly isn't the friendliest person."

We burst out laughing because Harvey Kirk, who oversaw digital services, as the computer section was now called, had to be the grumpiest person we knew. I'd only invited him because I'd extended an invitation to everyone who worked in the library, and I didn't want him to feel left out.

The Café was crowded, and we had to wait for a table, but after a few minutes Joe, the manager, led us to a table for two in the rear.

"We have soft-shell crab sandwiches and beet salad on the menu today. Both are going like wildfire."

"Good to know, thanks, Joe," I said as Angela, and I sat down.

Our waitress came over almost immediately, someone new who said her name was Betsy. We both ordered soft-shell crab sandwiches and an order of beet salad to share and something to drink. That done, Angela regaled me with her Maltipoo Scampi's latest antics. I asked her if she knew anything about the house that my aunt and uncle were so eager to have Dylan and me look at. Angela said she knew nothing about it but said she'd ask her mom. Though Angela knew about Evelyn, I decided not to mention that the house might be haunted.

Our orders arrived shortly after, and we dug in. We'd just finished eating when the wail of an approaching siren cut through the hum of conversation. Several diners got up to peer out the windows. A few even went outside.

"What's going on?" I asked Betsy when she refilled my coffee mug.

"I'm not sure. Something went down in an apartment building a block away. The police are there. An ambulance just drove by."

Angela and I exchanged glances. We asked for the bill and went up to the register to pay. Through the window I saw a TV van racing to the scene.

"Let's find out what happened," I said.

Chapter Six

A crowd surrounded a young female reporter who stood speaking into her mic as her cameraman filmed her for the TV audience. Behind her, yellow tape marked off the entrance of an apartment building as a crime scene while a police car's flashing lights spun round and round. I stepped as close as I could to the reporter, eager to hear what she was saying.

" . . . the body of Luke Rizzo was discovered minutes ago by his brother. Vinny Rizzo stopped by his brother's apartment during his lunch break to find out why he hadn't shown up at work. The victim had been stabbed multiple times. Judging by the state of rigor mortis, the estimated time of death is around midnight."

Angela and I both gasped. I finally managed to speak. "Luke Rizzo was one of Billy Carpenter's good friends and most likely in on the bank robbery five years ago. John's theory is that Billy Carpenter took off with the money and buried it in his aunt and uncle's backyard. His two partners knew he'd stashed the money someplace."

"So when he got out of prison they stalked him," Angela said. "They caught him digging up the money, killed him, and took the cash."

"And now Luke is dead," I said.

"Which means the remaining friend must have killed him," Angela said.

"Maybe. Maybe not."

I looked around and saw John in the distance, talking to one of the EMTs who had carried the body out of the building on a stretcher. There was no way I could make my way through the crowd to reach him. Besides, John was too busy handling the situation to talk to me. Though I hadn't known Billy or Luke, I was feeling sick about the whole business.

"I need to call Dylan," I said.

Angela nodded. We started walking back to the library. I dialed Dylan's number and was glad that for once he was at his desk in the middle of the day. I told him what had happened.

"So Luke Rizzo was murdered," Dylan mused. "Another of the trio of friends probably responsible for the bank job."

"Do you think Luke murdered Billy?" I asked. "Took the money he'd dug up, then Tino killed Luke for the money?"

"It's possible. Or maybe they both murdered Billy, argued over the money, and Tino killed Luke."

I shook my head in disbelief. "And they'd been best friends for years."

"Best friends who had no problem turning on each other, starting with Billy Carpenter."

"No honor among thieves," I said.

"Sure looks that way," Dylan agreed.

*   *   *

I listened to John's statement regarding the latest murder as I drove home from work. "I want to assure those of you who have been calling the precinct that this homicide is most likely the second murder in connection to a robbery that took place years ago, and not the work of a serial killer. We are in the process of interviewing several parties of interest. So far no arrests have been made."

Meaning he was questioning Tino Valdez and Billy's cellmate and so far neither had admitted he'd committed the murders. *Still,* I thought, *one of them has to be guilty.* It was only a matter of time before John got the murderer to confess.

Dylan came home a little after six, and we had dinner. Over coffee and brownies we managed to finish up the seating arrangements.

"I'm glad that's done," Dylan said as he leaned back in his chair.

"You still have to order gifts for Mac, Mark, and your two groomsmen."

"I did that today. I've ordered a set of really good crystal wineglasses for Mac, a pair of sunglasses for our ringbearer, and leather toiletry bags for Randy and Gary."

"Great! Now all we have left to do is our list of songs for the band."

"Not tonight," Dylan said, putting his dishes in the sink.

"Not tonight," I agreed.

"Time to veg out and relax."

Feeling virtuous because we'd managed to check off a few items on our to-do list, we stretched out on the living room sofa and switched on the TV. Smoky Joe strolled out of the bedroom and settled down between us.

* * *

Wednesday morning I woke up early so I could stop by a stationery store on the way to work and pick up a few copies of the Clover Ridge *Gazette.* I bought five and hurried back to the car, eager to see my article in print.

And there it was, smack in the middle of the paper, just as Chuck said it would be! I read it carefully, aware of a changed phrase in a few places and the elimination of a comma or two, but it was just as I had written it. I scanned the photos, not thrilled by how I looked in one of them, but the one where I was holding the diary had come out well, and Norman looked just like himself, a pleasant, nice-looking man in his forties who loved his job.

Sally was waiting for me when I opened the door to the library, a broad grin on her face. "Carrie, my dear, you did well! You and the library extension are the best things that have happened to this library in years!"

"Really?" I felt myself glow. While Sally had praised my work a few times since I'd become head of programs and events, she'd never said anything like this.

"Yes, really."

I released Smoky Joe from his carrier and dropped it off in my office, then hurried over to show Angela and Fran the article in the paper. Marion and Gayle joined us. So did Norman. Even Harvey Kirk stopped by the circulation desk and congratulated me before slinking away.

All morning patrons came over to congratulate me on the article. Many of them asked if the diary was in the library, and I directed them to the Historical Room. It made me realize how few people were aware of the many historical artifacts we had on display, and I made a mental note to write an article about our collection in an upcoming newsletter.

When Evelyn made an appearance, I showed her the article. She read it carefully, then beamed at me.

"Good job, Carrie. I was part of the group that tried to get a pardon for Verity some years ago. We weren't successful, but now that her diary has come to light, it's the perfect time to ask the state's Board of Pardons and Paroles to exonerate her posthumously."

"I'll keep that in mind." *When I'm back from my honeymoon.*

I spent an hour calling various presenters I wanted to book for August and September. I also had a long conversation with a director of a terrific acting group that put on plays they'd shortened to run no more than an hour and a half. The group was so popular, they had to be scheduled two years in advance. I only managed to get them for a Sunday in September because another library would be undergoing renovations then and had canceled their arrangement.

Chuck called to let me know that several subscribers had contacted him to say how much they loved my article and asking if there would be a follow-up. "I told them we were thinking about it."

"You are?"

"Well, if you're interested in doing it. Or if you come across another gem in the historical collection that reflects an important event that took place in our town's history. I'm always open to anything you care to write."

"Thanks a lot, Chuck," I said, meaning it. "When I get back from my honeymoon, I'll see if there's anything in the Historical Room that would appeal to your readers."

"If you do, shoot me an email to run it by me. You've got a nice writing style."

I called Dylan to tell him what Chuck had said.

"Just think, you can have another career if you like—Carrie Singleton-Avery, journalist."

When Trish arrived we spent the rest of the morning blocking out the next newsletter. We always worked a few months ahead, which meant we needed to schedule all activities in advance. That required a short paragraph from Marion and Harvey, both of whom always seemed to forget to send me their reports despite my frequent reminders.

Angela and I decided to have lunch at our favorite Indian restaurant. When I got back to my office, Trish said, "Someone left you a posh invitation."

I glanced at the glossy envelope on my desk. In beautiful calligraphy it said, *For Carrie Singleton, Personal.*

Interesting. "When did this arrive?"

"Sally asked me to take over the hospitality desk. It was here when I got back. Someone had slipped it under the door."

"I see." Curious, I opened the envelope. Inside, in the same calligraphy, was written:

You are invited to the June meeting of the Wise Women's Circle this Friday evening at seven thirty. Please do not share this with anyone except the person closest to you.

Our circle has been in existence for many years. Our purpose is to protect those women in need of protection. Because our work requires privacy and discretion, our circle is known to very few besides those closest to us.

We know you must have many questions. Feel free to ask Sally about our circle as she is a Wise Woman. If you agree to join us Friday evening, she will tell you where we will be meeting.

I looked up. *Wise Women? Secret circle?* My face must have revealed my confused state because Trish asked, "Is everything all right?"

"Y-yes," I stumbled. "It's just from—someone I know." I shoved the invitation into my pocketbook. I had no idea who had left it for me, as it wasn't signed. "I—er—need to talk to Sally. I won't be long."

"Okay," Trish said, seemingly not at all put out by my strange behavior. "I'll continue working on the newsletter till I leave."

"Sounds like a plan," I said, and scooted out of the office.

Sally was waiting for me, grinning from ear to ear. "Please close the door."

I did so and sat down in one of the two chairs across from her desk.

"You read the invitation."

I nodded.

"And you have a few questions."

"I don't know where to begin."

"I'm happy to answer your questions to the best of my ability and discretion, on the condition that you don't share what I tell you with anyone other than the person closest to you."

Dylan.

"If you tell Dylan, please instruct him not to share what I'm about to tell you with anyone."

"Got it. What is the Wise Women Circle, and why did I get an invitation to your meeting?"

"It's a group of women that helps women in trouble. It's been in existence for well over one hundred years."

"But why was I asked to join? And why is it secret?"

"Because of your concern regarding Verity Babcock's fate and your desire to see her exonerated. One of Verity's descendants created the Wise Women's Circle in 1910. It's been going ever since.

"The reason it started out as a secret group is because in those days a woman's first obligation was to her family—her spouse, her children, and her elderly parents." Sally laughed. "And because occasionally, in the service of helping women in distress, members did things not sanctioned by the law. So the circle thought it wise to remain discrete, if not exactly secret."

I nodded as I took in what Sally was telling me. Women who were abused or suffering were helped by other women who sometimes took matters into their own hands.

"So you're saying the circle sometimes does things that aren't legal."

"No one's obliged to do anything she's uncomfortable doing."

Like murder?

Sally laughed as though she were reading my mind. "Don't worry, Carrie. We don't resort to violence. Usually."

I did my best to quell my rising anxiety. "Who belongs to the circle?"

Sally shrugged. "About twenty-five women who live in or near Clover Ridge. You probably know some of them."

A secret group! The idea was both tantalizing and frightening. I didn't want to get into something I couldn't handle, but then Sally belonged, and she was a respected member of the community. "I'd like some time to think about attending the meeting."

"I understand, but please let me know what you decide by the end of your workday today."

"Okay."

"And if you come to the meeting, it's with the understanding that you're seriously considering joining the circle."

"Oh."

Sally chuckled. "No need to feel nervous. Like any group, we have nonactive members who support our mission policy by contributing whatever a victim might need rather than getting involved in resolving a delicate situation."

"Can you give me an example of how the circle helped a woman in need?" I asked.

"Certainly." Sally sank back in her chair. "There's Bella Travis. She died a few years ago. When Bella was in her mid-eighties, she was living by herself in a small house that needed a good deal of repairs. Her thirty-something grandson, who never held a job in his life, moved in with her. A friend of Bella's mentioned to a member of our circle that she hadn't seen Bella in months. The few times the friend stopped by Bella's house, the grandson told her that Bella wasn't up to seeing visitors. What's more, there were strange cars parked in the driveway and loud music coming from the house late at night.

"The friend began to worry that Bella was being held prisoner in her own home. The Wise Woman checked, and sure enough her grandson had taken over her house and her bank account." Sally grinned. "The circle convinced the scrounger it was time he moved on and left his grandmother in peace. He took their advice, and off he went."

"But couldn't you have gotten the same results by reporting the situation to the police?"

"Often that's exactly what we do. But in Bella's case, we decided it would be faster and more effective to handle it our way." Sally shot me a knowing look. "Very similar to what you often do yourself, Carrie Singleton."

"Me?" I asked, surprised.

"You've helped many women in trouble. For example, how many times have you sped up an investigation and saved someone from being wrongly accused of murder?"

"I never looked at it that way," I said.

Sally stood. "Belonging to the Wise Women's Circle is a noble cause."

I stood too. "I'll let you know my decision before I leave today."

Chapter Seven

I couldn't return to my office. Trish would ask me what Sally had wanted, and normally I would tell her, as that was the nature of our relationship. But I couldn't talk about our little chat because I'd been sworn to secrecy and, frankly I was too rattled to make up a convincing story.

As a woman, I knew well the perils that often beset my gender. Sally was right. I'd done my utmost to help several women in trouble. But the idea that a group like the Wise Women's Circle existed in Clover Ridge somewhat disturbed me. Sally claimed their intentions were good. They helped women in need of help, something I was all for, but she had chosen Bella Travis's story for a reason. She wanted me to know they had no problem resorting to intimidation.

How far beyond that did they go? Were abusive men roughed up? Had the group ever gone as far as murder?

Finally, I realized I felt betrayed, the way any of us would feel betrayed upon discovering that a friend belonged to a secret society we never knew existed. Sally was a member. Who else among my friends, relatives, and colleagues were Wise Women? Was Aunt Harriet? Was Sylvia Mather? Was Marion Marshall?

I stopped abruptly, having discovered that I'd wandered into the new section of the library. I peered into the art gallery and decided to go inside. I was relieved to find myself alone. There were two exhibits up: paintings of flowers and birds by a young Chinese woman; and scenes of children at various activities—girls playing at recess, a batter up at a softball game, a ten-year-old boy arguing with his mother—the work of one of our own patrons, a grandmother who had taken up painting two years earlier. I'd seen the show when it was installed a week ago, but this morning I took my time and studied each work of art. It helped calm me.

"What's gotten you so bothered that you're seeking solace in art?"

I turned to Evelyn. "A secret society of good Samaritans that helps women in trouble. They want me to attend their meeting Friday night."

"The Wise Women invited you to join them?" Was that awe I detected in Evelyn's voice?

"Yes, because of my article about Verity Babcock."

"And because of the women you've helped," Evelyn said. "Like my niece Michelle, who I've heard is doing well."

"Oh." I thought a minute. "But how do they know?"

Evelyn smiled. "The Wise Women know everything that goes on in Clover Ridge."

"Sally said the group was secret, but you seem to know all about them. Were you a member? You never mentioned them before."

"Yes. No. And the subject never came up."

A patron entered the gallery. We greeted each other, then I followed Evelyn down the hall to the auditorium. Finding it empty, we made our way to the front. I sat down in the first row while Evelyn perched on the edge of the stage.

She chuckled. "I'd venture to say most of us knew about the Wise Women and their handiwork by the time we were settling down in our adult lives. If we talked about their doings, it was in hushed tones. Not to be gossiped about, though just about any other subject was fair game."

"Did you know anyone who belonged to the circle?"

"Two of my friends were members, but I was never asked to join. They were activists and more civic-minded than me. I admired them both. It's an honor to be invited to join."

"Is it?" I said bleakly. "All this secrecy makes me suspicious of what they might resort to in order to achieve their ends."

Evelyn cocked her head. "You mean like killing an abusive husband?"

"Exactly."

"That's not their style. From the bits and pieces I've heard over the years, they're very effective in convincing an offending partner it's in his best interest to stop harassing the woman in question. They're quite successful."

I thought a moment. "Are there Wise Men as well?"

"They're not called that, but a few men have taken up the cause and joined the circle."

When I said nothing, Evelyn went on. "Carrie, you are the daughter I never had. As long as I've known you, I've felt free to give you unsolicited advice. I've even asked you to take on responsibilities regarding people I've cared for, and you've been kind enough to oblige. But you have to decide whether you want to join the Wise Women's Circle. It's a responsibility. It's a commitment. And you do more than your share when it comes to looking after the people of Clover Ridge, regardless of their gender."

Tears welled up in my eyes. "Evelyn, I wish I could hug you. That's the most beautiful thing anyone's ever said to me."

Evelyn rolled her eyes. "No need to get melodramatic. The people who love you have told you often enough that you're special. It's time you realized it yourself."

"I'll try," I said softly.

"Don't be afraid to give the Wise Women a go. If you decide against joining, well, then let them know."

I laughed as I remembered. "This reminds me of the first time you appeared and told me to tell Sally I'd think about taking the job. I was all set to say . . ."

But Evelyn had already disappeared, leaving me to reflect on how close I'd come to refusing the position of head of programs and events, and missing out on the life I loved so much.

* * *

I returned to an empty office. Trish had left me a note saying that Sally had asked her to cover the hospitality desk. Had Sally done that, I wondered, knowing that after our conversation I'd need my privacy? Yes, I decided. Aside from being my boss and a Wise Woman in the literal sense, she was my friend and wanted to ease the turmoil she knew the invitation was causing me.

I called Sally and told her I'd decided to attend the Friday night meeting.

"Good. I thought you might," she said, and gave me the name of the woman who was hosting the meeting, along with her address and phone number.

"I suppose I'll be seeing you there," I said.

"I'm planning to attend."

We disconnected and I discovered that, having made my decision, I was able to concentrate on library affairs for the remainder of the afternoon.

* * *

Over dinner, I told Dylan about my invitation to the Wise Women's meeting and everything that Sally and Evelyn had filled me in about the circle.

"I remember hearing about them over the years," he said when I'd finished. "Sounds like the kind of group you'd be interested in joining. They say it's the article you wrote, but I bet they've had their eye on you because of all the women you helped in the past year and a half."

Even if I weren't passionately in love with my handsome fiancé, I'd marry him because he understood me so well. Dylan never tried to stop me from doing something because it might be dangerous, though he never hesitated to tell me to be careful.

I kissed him hard on the mouth.

"What's that for?" Dylan asked when he could speak.

"For removing my last vestige of doubt about going on Friday."

"Oh."

"Now, let's clear the table so we can work on the playlist for our wedding."

* * *

I slept in the next morning since Thursday was a late workday. I ate a leisurely breakfast as I ran through my wedding to-do list. After emailing the playlist to our band leader, there was nothing we had to do until a few days before the wedding, when we would make last-minute calls to the caterer and the party rental place to give them our final numbers. Babette and Victor had offered to do this for us, but Dylan understood that I wouldn't relax unless we made these calls ourselves. Not that I expected to relax those few days before our big event.

However, I wanted to buy a few more items of clothing for our honeymoon in Greece. With this in mind, I decided to drive to a boutique in Merrivale I'd heard so much about.

"Sorry, Smoky Joe," I told my furry feline as he ran to the front door. "I'll be back in a few hours, then we're off to the library."

His plaintive meow expressed his displeasure.

It was another perfect sunny June morning. Trees, shrubs, and flowers were in bloom beneath a cloudless azure sky. I hummed as I drove along the private Avery road. So much had happened to me during the twenty months I'd lived in the cottage. Getting a meaningful job, falling in love with Dylan, making friends and settling into life in Clover Ridge. And now Dylan and I were getting married!

I thought about our appointment Saturday morning to check out the house that my aunt and uncle were so eager to have us look at. After hearing their description, I had a good feeling about the place. I grinned, wondering if the ghost or ghosts would make an appearance. After my close friendship with Evelyn, the idea of living in a haunted house was not a deal breaker. Also, I liked the idea of living close to the site of the old Singleton Farm. It had been a part of my family history, and I had fond memories of spending summer vacations there with Aunt Harriet and Uncle Bosco.

I spotted a stationery store in the strip mall coming up on my right, and stopped to buy a copy of the *Gazette*. My article in yesterday's paper might have inspired letters in response to the subject of Verity Babcock.

Back in the car, I turned to the Letters to the Editor section. Sure enough, there were a few letters commenting on the article, praising me for having revived the issue of a pardon for Verity Babcock. One writer said he planned to contact state officials and insist that they open up proceedings to issue her a pardon as well as an apology for having taken her life under the ridiculous charge of witchcraft.

Finally, there was a long letter from someone named Garrett Grimm. My fury grew as I read on. The writer contended that the charge of witchcraft was a legitimate crime at the time because those accused had caused the deaths of humans and livestock.

Grimm claimed to have studied Verity Babcock's life, the charges against her, and her ensuing trial. At the time she was the most knowledgeable herbalist in the area. He went on to write that information gleaned from letters and journals of the time revealed that Verity was a person with no close friends. After her husband died, she often quarreled with her neighbors, accusing one of letting his cattle graze on her land, another of extending one of his planting fields onto her property. Though she won both cases, a neighbor, John Whitcomb, died after ingesting her herbal remedies. So, he claimed, even if Verity Babcock wasn't a witch in our modern interpretation of the word, she was a murderer and deserved the sentence of hanging that she'd received.

He ended his diatribe by saying the discovery of the diary—or should he call it a *rediscovery* since the library seemed to have had no knowledge that they owned such an item—was of historical interest and should be made available to patrons. He also advised me to study my subject more thoroughly and objectively before suggesting that a pardon was in order. He finished with "After all, if our legislators considered this a worthy task, exoneration would have been offered years ago when the subject was first brought to their attention."

I howled with outrage as I shoved the newspaper aside. How dare he? Where was Garrett Grimm getting his information? Of course Verity must have quarreled with her neighbors if they were taking advantage of her widow status. The fact that she'd won both judgments against them spoke volumes.

I'd read Verity's diary a few times. Her explanation regarding the death of her neighbor rang true each time I came to that section. John Whitcomb had been ill for several days before his wife asked for Verity's help. After examining the sick man, Verity told his wife that she'd waited too long to call her in, and now she doubted that any herbal remedy she might offer could bring about a cure. But John's wife, Hester, had cried and pleaded until Verity agreed to treat John.

John revived after one dosage but died the following evening. In her grief, Hester claimed that Verity was a witch and had poisoned her husband. Verity wrote about her growing terror as more charges were mounted against her and her trial date grew near. What was Garrett Grimm's agenda? Why was he so set on besmirching poor Verity's reputation, labeling her a murderer if not a witch?

The boutique in Merrivale had a wonderful array of clothing, and I soon forgot about Grimm's attack on Verity Babcock as I tried on summer dresses and shorts and tops. My young saleswoman was most helpful, and an hour later I left the store laden down with additions to my summer wardrobe. I hummed as I drove home, thrilled with my success.

Back at the cottage, I fed Smoky Joe, made myself a salad for lunch, and drove to the library. As soon as I released Smoky Joe from his carrier, I stopped by Sally's office to tell her about Garrett Grimm's letter in the *Gazette*.

"I read it." She dismissed my concern with a wave of her hand. "Don't let Garrett's rant upset you. The man's a troublemaker. He doesn't have an ethical bone in his body."

"But why does he insist that Verity murdered John Whitcomb and deserved to be hung?"

"He thrives on attention," Sally said. "And he's one person who should keep a low profile."

"Why?"

"Garrett's a wheeler-dealer. Always making deals as crooked as a boomerang. He's been arrested a few times, but somehow the charges never stick. And if that old lime-green jalopy he drives around in is any indication of his success or lack thereof, I'd say he's a loser all around."

"So his letter in the paper didn't upset you?" I said.

"Carrie, dear, focus on all the positive feedback your article has received. I was delighted that so many people have come out in support of a pardon. Maybe we'll be successful this time."

Heartened by Sally's reaction to Garrett Grimm's letter, I was calmer when I sat down at my computer to compose my own letter to the editor. I began by thanking the many people who had written in support of exoneration for Verity Babcock. I then set about refuting every negative comment that Garrett Grimm had written about her. Yes, she was an herbalist, but no, she wasn't a witch. She had brought many of her friends and neighbors back to health. She had won both cases against her neighbors because they were in the wrong, and finally, there was no proof whatsoever that she'd ever murdered any person or animal.

I quoted a few lines from her diary that made it very clear she'd been terrified by the lies and stories neighbors had made up about her. I ended by writing:

"That a few neighbors tried to take advantage of her status as a widow is apparent when you consider the judgments ruled against those neighbors and in her favor. Verity was a healer. She was not responsible for the death of anyone she tried to help. John Whitcomb was ill with a bad case of pneumonia when his wife begged Verity to cure her husband. Even today, people die of pneumonia, whether or not they take medicine. It's sad that anyone living in the twenty-first century may believe that Verity deserved her fate."

I closed my missive with

"I think it's safe to say that while the charges of witchcraft were bogus, the reason for the charges were all too real. I remind Mr. Grimm that fear, envy, and resentment were often the impetus for one neighbor to accuse another of witchcraft in the mid-1600s. An accuser often gained recompense for what he or she supposedly lost, and the recompense was taken from the so-called 'witch's' pocket."

Satisfied with my response, I pressed "Send" and off it went to the *Gazette*.

Chapter Eight

My pulse raced with nervous anticipation as I set out for the Wise Women's meeting. According to my GPS, the address Sally had given me was on a street Dylan and I drove past when we visited Victor, so there was no chance of my getting lost.

I rapped the bronze knocker on the front door and stepped back to admire the colonial-style brick house. There was a bay window on either side of the door and shutters on the upstairs windows. The mulched flowerbeds were filled with pink and fuchsia annuals in bloom.

A pleasant-looking woman in her sixties greeted me in the hall with a smile and a handshake. "Hello, Carrie. I'm Winifred Thompson—Winnie to my friends. Please come inside and meet everyone."

A young man who looked to be in his early twenties shuffled down the stairs from the floor above. Dressed in baggy jeans and a T-shirt, his straggly hair was unkempt, as if he just had woken up. His dazed expression added to that impression.

"Leslie!" Winnie said, clearly embarrassed by her son's unexpected appearance. "I thought you went out for the evening."

He laughed as if she'd said something funny. "I decided to take a nap instead. What's for dinner?"

"I'm sure you'll find something in the fridge. And please eat it in your room. As I told you earlier, I'm hosting a meeting."

"Oh, you're hosting a meeting," he echoed sarcastically as he ambled into the kitchen—barefoot, I now noticed.

"Sorry about that," Winnie apologized to me. "My son is twenty-five, but he sometimes acts like a teenager."

She led me into the family room, where about fifteen women were seated in a circle. They appeared to range in age from early thirties, like me, to their eighties. Sally waved at me, which helped take away some of my anxiety. A few others called out friendly greetings.

I gave a start to find Reggie Williams's wife, Marissa, grinning at me. And let out a gasp when Sylvia Mathers gave me a thumbs-up. So there were women here whom I knew! A few others looked familiar, but the rest were strangers.

Winnie led me to the one available seat, a chair beside the long sofa where Sally was sitting.

"Wise Women, this is our guest, Carrie Singleton."

Everyone clapped. When the applause died down, I said, "Thank you for inviting me here tonight."

"It's our pleasure and our honor to have you as our guest. As I've told you, I'm Winnie Thompson. I'm a recently retired family court judge, and I've lived in Clover Ridge all my life. I'm a descendent of the Carrington family, the same family Verity Babcock was born into. One of my great-great-great aunts started the Wise Women's Circle in the early twentieth century. We have done our best to keep the circle going.

"Now each Wise Woman will introduce herself in turn, though you already know a few of us. We don't expect you to remember everyone's name, so don't feel bad if you forget who we are."

This brought on laughter and smiles, which removed the last bit of my anxiety. I'd expected a formal atmosphere and instead was finding only friendliness and ease.

Each woman stated her name, how long she'd been living in Clover Ridge, and what type of work she did. The jobs varied, from caterer to college professor, to housecleaner. Two of the younger women were stay-at-home moms. I smiled at each one in turn.

When everyone had spoken, Winnie said, "We held the business part of our meeting before you arrived, and now we're ready to talk about new business and why we've asked you to join us. I hope you'll tell us a little about yourself."

I cleared my throat. "My name is Carrie Singleton. I'm the head of programs and events at the Clover Ridge Library. I also serve on the town board, at least through November of this year.

"My family has lived in Clover Ridge for four generations, but I never heard of the Wise Women's Circle until a few days ago, when I received your invitation."

"We try to keep it that way," a short, dark-haired woman named Norma called out.

"And I'm getting married in two weeks."

The room burst out in applause.

Sylvia raised her hand, and Winnie acknowledged her. "Carrie is too modest to mention that she's helped my husband solve a number of homicides."

"I think we're all well aware of that," Winnie said, "and it's the reason why we sleep more easily in our beds. Though we have had a few recent murders, and so far no suspect has been apprehended."

"Lowlifes killing one another," Beverly, a retired professor in her eighties commented. "We've nothing to fear from them."

Other Wise Women chimed in, expressing their opinions, until Winnie held up her hand. Immediately the conversation came to a halt.

"I'd like to get back to the subject of tonight's meeting. Verity Babcock is very dear to my heart, as she is to all Wise Women and members of my family. We have made several attempts to have her exonerated for the ridiculous and cruel charge of witchcraft that took her life all those years ago."

"Yes!" members shouted as they raised fists into the air.

"We've been told there is no existing state law that would allow Verity to be pardoned. Nor is there any record of the evidence that led up to her trial that sent her to her death."

Winnie beamed at me. "But the discovery of Verity's diary throws light on her state of mind while she was being hounded by those accusing her of having caused illness and death."

I cleared my throat. "I'm glad I discovered Verity's diary hidden away among the various pamphlets, books, and papers in the library's Historical Room, but I fail to see how that will help get her exonerated."

"If I may, Winnie," Marissa said. Reggie Williams's wife, a stunning Black woman who was a research lawyer, stood. "As our circle's archivist, I am constantly searching for articles about Verity Babcock and the crime of witchcraft. I also keep my ear to the ground to find out which women living in our area might have need of our services, though this is something all Wise Women do."

Marissa smiled at me. "For example, last year I learned about Michelle Davis Forbes, a young woman who lived her first sixteen years in Clover Ridge, moved away, then returned with her husband a few years ago. He soon abandoned her. Depressed and unemployed, Michelle was in a bad way. I was about to bring up her situation at a circle meeting, when I discovered that Michelle was receiving assistance from you, Carrie Singleton. And now she's thriving in her new life."

My ears grew warm as the other women applauded. Evelyn had asked me to help her niece, Michelle, who was sad and downhearted after her husband had left her. All I'd done was introduce her to my lawyer and help her find a job.

"Another big reason why we've asked you here tonight," Winnie said, beaming.

"Getting back to Verity's situation," Marissa said, "as soon as we learned that Verity's diary was in the library, I went there hoping to read it from cover to cover, but I was informed that no one has access to the diary—at least not until a forensic expert examines it and decides the best way to make it available to the public.

"However, I delved into every historical paper I could find that dates back to the witch trials and made a list of every name I came across, then spent hours studying family trees to find out which current Clover Ridge residents are related to any of Verity's accusers."

"Anyone related to Judge Robert Haverford?" someone asked. "From what I heard, he was happy to prosecute witches."

"No, but I discovered something interesting," Marissa said. "Garrett Grimm is a descendent of John Whitcomb, the neighbor Verity was accused of poisoning," Marissa said. "He's a distant cousin on his mother's side."

The Wise Women shook their heads and made scoffing sounds.

"His letter in Wednesday's *Gazette* took me by surprise," Sylvia said, "Garrett doesn't usually take an interest in anyone besides himself. And now we know why. He must think that arguing against a popular cause makes him look important, when it only makes him look like more of a fool."

Marissa turned to me. "Carrie, from what I've read in your article, Verity's diary reveals the horror and abuse she had to endure from the moment she was accused of witchcraft. I think that sending a copy of the diary to the appropriate branch in Hartford will go a long way in starting the procedure to gain exoneration."

"Hear! Hear!" the Wise Women chanted.

"Verity was an early #metoo victim," Beverly said. "Victimized because she was a literate woman and an herbalist. I'm proud to defend her now that she can't defend herself."

"Hear! Hear!" chanted the chorus again.

"I was glad to be of help," I said.

Winnie stood. "Thank you, Beverly and Marissa. As we discussed earlier, a few of us will meet next week to compose a letter to the powers that be."

The conversation moved on to the discussion of a few "Millie's" they'd helped recently. Winnie explained that recipients of their aid were called this in honor of Millie Rossiter, the first woman the Wise Women had rescued from an abusive marriage. She didn't offer details, and I didn't ask to hear them.

Forty-five minutes after I'd been introduced to the group, Winnie said it was time for coffee and dessert. Someone's hand shot up and put it to a motion.

"I second it," Marissa said.

We all traipsed across the hall to the dining room, where platters of cookies and cakes were set out on the table, along with plates and utensils. Next to it was a large coffee urn and a smaller urn filled with hot water for tea. There was a selection of teabags beside the sugar and creamer.

Relieved to have made it through the meeting without hearing anything I could object to, I poured myself a cup of coffee, then studied the several desserts. I decided I'd have a slice of pecan pie. The whipped cream appeared to be the real McCoy, so I spooned a dollop on top.

"So, what did you think of the Wise Women?" Sally asked.

"They all seem very nice and—caring," I said, knowing it wasn't the answer she was hoping for, but nothing else came to mind.

"That we are. Will you be joining us?"

"I have to think about it."

"Of course." Sally noticed that Sylvia had gotten close to us. She gave her a quick smile and moved away.

"So," Sylvia drawled, "what do you think of our little group?"

"Nice. Friendly." I lowered my voice. "Is John okay with your belonging to the Wise Women? I mean, some of their tactics aren't exactly legal."

Sylvia burst out laughing. "John hasn't approved of a number of things I've done during our married life, but when the circle gets involved in something not sanctioned by law, I bow out of that project."

"I see." For the first time it dawned on me that being married to the chief of police had its complications, even if Sylvia weren't a Wise Woman.

"Don't let anyone bully you into deciding whether or not you want to join," Sylvia said, her voice barely above a whisper. "You're the catch of the decade, and they'll pressure you to become a member. Take as much time as you need. I debated for six months."

"Oh. Thanks for the tip. How long have you been a Wise Woman?"

"Barely a year. It took me a while to decide. I'm glad I joined." She shot me a warning glance. "Oh, hello, Winnie."

"I hope you didn't find your first meeting with the Wise Women overwhelming," Winnie said.

"Not at all," I said. "Everyone's been very kind. And this pie is outstanding."

"I'm glad you're enjoying it."

Why did that simple sentence strike me as ominous? And why had Sylvia left?

"Carrie, your values and beliefs are aligned with those of the Wise Women. I'm delighted to extend an invitation to join our circle."

Her official offer caught me by surprise. I took a few deep breaths. "Thank you for asking me. It's a great honor, I know, but with so much going on in my personal life, I can't give you an answer right now."

"Can you see yourself becoming a member? Of course, becoming a Wise Woman requires a strong commitment."

"Yes, it does, which is why I have to think long and hard about joining. And I will, when I return from my honeymoon."

Winnie waited, hoping I'd say more, but I remained silent. She gave a little laugh. "Of course, I didn't expect you to give me your answer tonight. But please think about it and let me know when you have reached your decision."

"I certainly will."

She smiled. "I'd like to ask you a question regarding another matter."

"Yes?"

"I can't but wonder—who donated Verity's diary to the library?"

I thought a minute. "I have no idea. So many of the items donated to the Historical Room arrive without notes or means of identification. As I've said, I found the diary in a pile of papers and pamphlets while putting our new Historical Room in order. Once I realized what it was, Norman Tobin, our reference librarian, and I searched high and low for an accompanying note that would tell us who had donated it. But we found nothing."

I smiled. "As a descendent of Verity's, I can imagine you'd like to have that information. I promise that, should we come across it, I'll let you know immediately."

"That's very kind of you, Carrie." The ominous note was back in Winnie's voice. "I find it interesting that no one ever came upon the diary in all the years it's been hidden away in the library. And I wonder why there's no record of who donated it to the library or even if that person had the right to donate it."

I stared at her. "What are you implying?"

Winnie drew back her shoulders. "It seems to me, that as Verity's closest relative, I am the lawful owner of the diary. It's only right that it remain in our family."

Winnie's unexpected and unreasonable demand regarding Verity's diary cast a somber shadow on the evening. *Time to leave,* I decided. Once outside, I halted. Something compelled me to glance back at the house. When I did, I saw that Leslie Thompson was staring down at me from an upstairs window.

Chapter Nine

"I told Winnie that while I understood she'd love to own the diary, it belonged to the library."

I was sitting with Dylan in the living room, telling him how my evening had gone.

"Hmm, how did she take it?"

"Not very well. She asked me how I knew it was a relative who had gifted it to the library and not someone who had stolen it when Verity was forced from her home."

"Still, the library owns it, and while 'possession is nine-tenths of the law' isn't really the law, it does give the edge to the possessor," Dylan said.

"Most of the items in the Historical Room don't have provenance. We aren't an art gallery trying to prove the historical and authentic origin of every piece of paper that patrons donate."

Dylan put his arm around me. "Babe, don't let her get to you. You have more important things to look forward to. Like our wedding. And checking out that haunted house tomorrow."

"But why say it to me and not to Sally?" I asked, unable to leave the subject alone. "Sally's the library director and a fellow Wise Woman."

"How do you know she hasn't?"

"Because I asked Winnie. She simply shrugged her shoulders and left me standing there."

Dylan nodded knowingly. "That figures."

"What?"

"I bet she brought it up to Sally, and Sally shot her down. Sally may be a fellow Wise Woman, but she's dedicated to the library. She wouldn't give up the diary, come hell or high water."

"You're right. She wouldn't," I agreed. "But what made Winnie think I would?"

"It was worth a try."

I nodded thoughtfully. "The circle wants to see Verity exonerated, but Winnie has her own agenda. She wants the diary to glorify her ancestor."

"I agree," Dylan said. "Now can I get back to the game? The bases are loaded and the score's tied."

I kissed him. "You can."

* * *

Since Saturday turned out to be such a beautiful day, Dylan and I decided to take a long walk in the Seabrook Preserve instead of hitting the gym. We came home to shower and change, then drove to the Haverford Inn for our lunch date with Babette and Victor, whom we hadn't seen since he'd returned home from Bruges on Tuesday.

The Inn, which had been built as a grist mill in the 1800s, was a fifteen-minute drive from Clover Ridge. Victor had been trying to get us to eat there for months, but with all his traveling and our busy schedules, we hadn't managed to arrange a date until today.

"It looks kind of shabby," I commented as we pulled into a parking spot in front of a weather-beaten one-story building. A few roof shingles were missing, and judging by the cracks, the parking area hadn't been paved in years.

Dylan chuckled. "I agree, but Victor claims it has the best burgers and crab cakes for miles around."

A dark, narrow hallway beneath a low ceiling, its floor the original uneven wooden planks, led to a wood-paneled room, most of which was taken up by the bar. Though it was only a few minutes past noon, most of the ten stools ringing the bar were occupied, as were the four tables.

"I guess they're not here yet," I said.

A door at the rear of the room swung open, and Victor came forward, his arms outstretched, to greet us.

"I saw you drive by," he said before embracing me in a bear hug, then doing the same to Dylan.

"Come," he said, opening the door. We followed him into a large, airy room, to a table beside a window. The only other occupied table was on the opposite side of the room.

Babette stood to hug Dylan and me. She looked pretty in a white peasant blouse and colorful skirt. Her blonde hair had been styled to frame her face most attractively.

"I hope you haven't been waiting long," I said as I sank into a chair that, though wooden and without a cushion of any kind, was surprisingly comfortable.

"We only arrived five minutes ago," Victor said, grinning at me from across the table.

"It's so good to see you both," I said, meaning it.

And we were off, chatting about everything and anything. The four of us had become very good friends over the past six months. I'd been immediately drawn to Victor—a warm, handsome widower from Slovenia, in his fifties, who owned a lucrative import-export business and was an avid art collector—as soon as we'd met.

I'd known Babette before she and Victor were a couple because we both served on the town board. I wouldn't say we'd butted heads, but we weren't especially friendly. Babette had sought attention in odd ways, and it bothered me that she often had a personal agenda when it came to making council decisions. But since she and Victor had fallen in love, Babette had let down her guard. Now she was more approachable and fun to be with.

"Carrie and Dylan, I want to give you this before I forget and bring it back home again."

Victor picked up a large paper shopping bag and brought it over to Dylan and me. I reached inside and pulled out a medieval tapestry and a large box of Belgian chocolates.

"Oh!" I said. "How wonderful!"

Victor grinned, delighted by my show of joy. "I know you both prefer dark chocolate, so that's what I got you. As for the tapestry, if you don't like it, I can—"

"I love it!" I exclaimed as soon as I caught sight of the scene—a stone house beside a bridge over a narrow body of water.

"We love it," Dylan said, unfolding it to its full extension. "Thank you, Victor. Our first new item for our new home."

"It's a tapestry of medieval Bruges, a city you must visit very soon," Victor said.

"Thank you so much!" I kissed Victor's well-shaven cheek, and he returned to his seat.

Our waitress, a middle-aged blonde woman whose name badge said "Nadia," placed four huge menus on the table. She returned a minute later with a basket of assorted rolls with butter and other spreads. I tried one that was made with eggplant.

"Delicious," I said.

"So, how are the almost newlyweds?" Babette asked as she buttered a roll.

"Fine," I said. "Pretty much on schedule."

"I'm so sorry you encountered a dead body on the lawn while I was gone," Victor said.

"It was upsetting, finding him lying there next to the gazebo," I admitted. "How strange that he buried the money he'd stolen in his aunt and uncle's backyard. At least, that's what the police think."

Victor nodded thoughtfully. "The Wilsons talked about their nephew. I got to know Martha and Stan pretty well from my visits before I bought the house. Billy was Martha's sister's son. He was closer to his aunt and uncle than he was to either of his parents, whom he hardly ever saw."

"Did she mention that he was in prison?" I asked.

"Not at first. She said he was living out of state. The way she put it got me wondering. So I wasn't surprised when they told me about the robbery and Billy's trial the last time we talked. They opened up, and I got the definite feeling it was the first time they were sharing their anguish about Billy with someone besides each other.

"Stan insisted their nephew was a good kid, but after his parents' divorce Billy had grown sullen and angry. He'd given up on the idea of going to college, and never managed to keep a job for very long. He'd taken to staying with them for weeks at a time. Martha said they felt bad about leaving him on his own, but they needed to move south for their health."

"Did they ever mention Billy's two friends?" I asked. "The police think they were in on the robbery."

"Wasn't one of them murdered a few days after Billy?" Babette said.

"Yes," Dylan said. "Luke Rizzo was his name."

Babette scoffed. "I wonder if he robbed and killed Billy, then someone robbed and killed him for the loot."

"Stan and Martha knew Luke Rizzo and Tino Valdez because the boys sometimes hung out at their house when Billy was staying with them," Victor said. "Stan and Martha thought they were a bad influence on Billy—often getting drunk and disorderly, without any plans for life after high school. But since they were their nephew's only friends, they gave them the occasional meal when they came by."

Victor squinted as he remembered something. "They said a few weeks before the robbery, Billy acted kind of hyper and once said he was finally going to do a job that he was good at. When they questioned him further, he said they'd find out about it when the time was right, and not before. They thought it best not to press him and ask what he meant.

"Weeks later, Billy was arrested for robbing the bank. When Martha asked him why he didn't take the job he'd been offered, Billy told her he didn't know what she was talking about."

"Interesting. His aunt thought it was a job-job. But Billy meant a—" I said, then broke off because Nadia had returned.

Victor recommended the lamb burgers. Since I didn't feel like reading through the extensive menu, I went with his suggestion. We all did, as it turned out.

"And two cheesy stuffed baked potatoes and a popcorn shrimp dish for us to share as appetizers," Victor said. He turned to Dylan and me. "Trust me. You have to taste these."

Nadia jotted it all down. As she was walking away, Victor called out, "And an order of marinated mushrooms for the table."

Dylan and I exchanged glances. This sounded like a lot of food, but we were willing to let Victor call the shots.

Victor beamed at us. "I'm so happy to see you both."

"We're happy to see you too," Dylan said.

"I've arranged to have the cleaners come the Thursday before the wedding, so the house will be spotless for your guests. And of course all the furniture will be removed from the living room, so the chairs for the ceremony can be set up Friday morning in time for the rehearsal that afternoon."

Our appetizers arrived—generous portions of everything. I had just about reached my lunch maximum when we were served our burgers, along with bowls filled with potato salad, cole slaw, and mini pickles.

"This is delicious," I said after my first bite of the lamb burger.

"Of course it is. And what you can't finish, you'll take home."

Which was most of our burgers since we'd already eaten so much. I was glad Dylan and I had had the foresight to keep a few thermal insulated bags in the car trunk since we weren't going straight home from the restaurant.

None of us wanted coffee or dessert, but we went on talking for a while. Finally, Dylan glanced at his watch and said we had to leave. He reached for his wallet, but Victor had already alerted Nadia that he was to receive the bill.

"This is too much," I told him. "You've given us the use of your home for our wedding, and now this wonderful lunch. Let us treat you and Babette."

"Please, Carrie. I've been wanting to bring you and Dylan to this place for months. Don't you realize that you two are family to me?"

There was a vulnerability in his expression I'd never noticed before. Something made me glance at Babette. Her nod was almost imperceptible, but I caught it in time. She knew this was important to the man she loved. And so I hugged Victor and thanked him profusely. Dylan hugged him too.

Babette and I kissed each other's cheeks, then she moved to put her arm around Victor's waist. "Let us know what you think of the house."

"Will do," I said.

When we were inside the car, Dylan shook his head, "And I was planning to pay for lunch."

"There was no way he was going to let you do that," I said. "Babette made that clear to me."

"So I noticed."

I chuckled as Dylan backed out of the parking space. "Of course you noticed. I should realize by now there's not much that you miss."

"Hey, I'm an investigator, remember? I've been trained to notice."

I thought a moment. "Victor said we're family to him. I suppose that's because he lost his wife a few years ago. And he's never mentioned children."

Dylan didn't say anything as he turned onto the road that would take us to the haunted house. When I glanced over to see if he'd heard me, I realized he was trying to decide how to answer me. Finally, he asked, "What do you know about Victor's life before he moved to Clover Ridge?"

"Only that he was born in what was then Czechoslovakia and lived in Croatia for several years before moving to the States."

"His wife, Hanna, was from Croatia—"

"I thought his wife's name was Dusana," I interrupted. "She died a few years ago, and he donated money to the hospital in her name."

"Dusana was his second wife, and they'd been married for over twenty-five years. But Victor met his first wife when they were both attending Charles University in Prague. Hanna was Croatian, so they settled in Croatia. They had two small children—a boy and a girl—when the Bosnia-Herzegovina War broke out." Dylan cleared his throat. "While he was fighting for the Bosnian Croats, his family died in a bombing."

"Oh. How awful. I had no idea." Stunned, I fell back against my seat. "When did you find this out? Why didn't you tell me?"

A minute later, we stopped at a red light. Dylan turned to me. "Believe me, I wasn't keeping it to myself, but I never found the right time to tell you. There's so much going on in our own lives. Then we found Billy Carpenter's body—"

"When did Victor tell you about his wife and children?"

"A few weeks ago. It was the night of the last board meeting. Since both you and Babette were out for the evening, Victor suggested he and I go out for dinner. That's when he told me."

I thought back to that evening. I remembered being all churned up about the board's heated discussion regarding the site of an abandoned gas station a few blocks from the high school; I'd brought that news home and shared it with Dylan. Dylan had listened and been supportive. Still, there must have been other times when he might have told me something this important. Unless he was reluctant to tell me because it was so very sad.

Which was why I didn't make an issue of it. Victor had found a second love, and eventually lost her too. How much could one person suffer?

Dylan's hand covered mine as the light turned green, and we drove on. "Sad, isn't it? I hope we never have to go through anything like it."

"How did the subject come up?"

"I think we were talking about Babette, and Victor was telling me how happy he was to have found her." He chuckled. "I told him about our history, going back to when we were little kids and I used to play with your brother Jordan. So he started telling me about his life. And losing his family."

"How does someone go on after that happens?"

"I asked him that. He said for a few years everything was gray. Then he decided he had to move on. So many people he knew had died in that war. But he was alive and he had to make something of his life. Which was when he started his import-export business. Which is how he met Dusana." Dylan smiled. "Eventually they fell in love and married. She couldn't have children, but they were very happy, he said."

"Second chances," I murmured.

"And third," Dylan said. "For some reason, you and I come as a package with Babette."

I laughed as I remembered when their relationship had begun. "That's because Babette desperately needed a judge for the kids' art contests at the Thanksgiving Eve festival. I brought Victor over, and it worked out. They'd known each other, but that night things took a turn. And don't forget we helped prove that Victor wasn't guilty of committing a murder."

"He sees us as family, Carrie. I suppose we're about the age his son and daughter would have been."

"I'm happy to be Victor's family," I said.

"Me too."

Chapter Ten

We pulled up in front of the Haunted House a few minutes before two thirty. A red SUV stood in the driveway. Dylan and I remained in the car as we studied the scene before us.

The pale yellow house stood on a rise set back from the road. Its two stories were topped by a steep roof with a forest-green gable the same color as the front door and shutters. I'd learned from my reading that Ted Wolcott and his wife had added extensions to both sides of the house about thirty years ago.

When I'd stayed at the Singleton Farm during childhood summers, I often rode my bike here to stare at this lovely home nestled among flowers and bushes, bounded by a dense row of evergreens on both sides of the expansive lawn. Though I'd never seen anyone enter or leave the house, I'd spent many hours imagining the lucky people who lived inside.

"It looks like it's been well cared for, that's for sure," Dylan said as we started up the walk.

"I agree. The exterior is freshly painted, and someone's put down mulch and planted annuals around the front of the house."

"Oh, look!" I exclaimed when I caught sight of the weeping willow and the brook running past it at the rear of the property.

As we approached the front door, it opened, and an attractive woman in her forties came outside to join us. "I see you found the house with no difficulty." She smiled as she extended her hand. "I'm Terri Leoni from Gallison Realty."

"I'm Carrie Singleton. This is my fiancé, Dylan Avery." We shook hands.

"Well-known Clover Ridge names. So nice to meet you, Carrie and Dylan." Terri grinned at me. "Especially since the former Singleton Farm was just down the road."

"That my parents bought and sold. The farmhouse is now a B&B," Dylan said wryly.

"Houses often change hands," Terri said. "We Americans move about for various reasons. Children rarely feel the need to keep up the old homestead. This house, for example, has had several owners."

"Yes, we're familiar with its history," I said, suddenly not wanting to hear it repeated.

Which was fine with Terri. She winked at me and said, "In that case, come inside so you can see it for yourself."

She opened the door, and we stepped into the hallway. I looked about, struck by the light and airy feeling created by the skylight above. I was surprised at how modern the interior was and how the rooms flowed, one into the other. The living room and dining room were on either side of the staircase that led up to the bedrooms. Behind the stairs were a small bathroom and stairs leading down to the basement. The kitchen and family room stretched across the back of the house. I realized that one of the side additions was a two-car garage. The other was a room off the living room with windows on three sides.

"Perfect for an office," Dylan murmured as he followed my gaze.

Terri said little until we reached the kitchen, which was large enough to include a center island and a comfortable eating area, and was outfitted with up-to-the minute stainless steel appliances. The refrigerator had glass doors, which had always intrigued me.

"The kitchen was updated three years ago," Terri said, "Shortly after, hardwood flooring was put down throughout the entire downstairs area."

"Why?" I asked.

Terri shrugged. "The owners hoped it might encourage one of their grandchildren to come back and live here."

A window above the sink looked out onto the stone patio and the spacious lawn beyond that ended in a small forest of trees. Once again the weeping willow and the brook caught my attention.

"The size of the property is just under three acres. There are houses on either side and a farm behind those trees." Terri pointed to the back. "The field that abuts the property has been used to grow corn for the last several years."

"Nice and quiet," I said.

"The back yard is large enough for a pool," Dylan said.

"And a vegetable garden," I said.

"Why don't we take a look outside after I show you the basement and the bedrooms?"

We followed Terri down to the finished basement, which would make a great playroom. We peeked into the furnace room, all clean and tidy; then we headed back upstairs. I was pleased that the staircase leading to the bedrooms stopped midway, with a resting spot and a window of its own.

Upstairs, the three smaller bedrooms were situated close to a bathroom. At the other end of the short hall was the master suite—an oversized bedroom with two walk-in closets and a huge modern bathroom. I could barely contain my grin. Dylan and I looked at each other. I didn't want to say anything in front of Terri, but both of us were hooked.

"You like?" she asked.

"It's lovely," I said, trying to sound noncommittal.

"Why don't you go through it again on your own, and then we can meet out on the patio and talk some more."

"Sounds like a good idea," Dylan said.

I held my breath until Terri's footsteps descended to the ground floor.

"So?" Dylan said.

"I like it."

"I do too."

We went through the upstairs rooms again. Dylan studied the registers on the floors and the walls. "We need to ask her about the heating/air conditioning system." He made a note on his iPhone.

Downstairs, I examined the kitchen appliances again, then went into the small room next to it to inspect the washer and dryer. "These are quite old. They'll need to be replaced," I said.

Dylan added that to a list on his iPhone.

"No sign of any ghosts," I commented.

"No sign," Dylan agreed.

We peered into the supply closet between the laundry room and the kitchen, then moved on to the living room and stood in front of the brick fireplace.

I glanced up into the blackened flue. "Ugh! I wonder when the chimney was last cleaned."

"Not in several years," a young child said.

I stood frozen except for my eyes, which darted around the room. I didn't see anyone, but that meant nothing. When I found my voice, I said, "Thanks for letting us know."

I heard giggling, then: "Anything else you want to know about the house?"

"Whatever you care to tell us."

Dylan made a gurgling sound as the transparent image of a girl about nine years old appeared in the corner of the room. A minute later a younger girl joined her. They wore long dresses with full skirts.

"It's a lovely house," the younger girl said.

"I think the new people made too many changes. Unnecessary changes," the older one said. She shrugged. "But that's what people do, I guess, when they buy someone's home."

"Was your father Allistair Perry?" I asked.

"Yes," said the older girl. "He had the house built when he and our mother married. My name is Abigail Jane Perry."

"I'm Lucy," said her sister.

"Nice to meet you both," I said. "My name is Carrie Singleton and—"

"Oh! Like the farm!" Lucy crowed. "The Wolcotts used to go there for corn and eggs."

"Lucy," her sister cautioned.

"Sorry." Lucy lowered her head.

"She's not used to having people to talk to besides me," Abigail explained. "Usually the minute a stranger hears us, they go flying out of the house." She eyed me cautiously. "But you're different."

Dylan laughed. I was glad to see he'd regained his composure. "That's because one of Carrie's best friends is a ghost. I'm Dylan, by the way—Carrie's fiancé."

"It's a pleasure to meet you, Dylan," Abigail said.

"We are ghosts, aren't we?" Lucy said, looking sad.

Abigail put her arm around her sister. "Don't feel bad, Luce. We'll get to where we're supposed to go—one day."

I decided to be up front with the two ghost children. "Dylan and I heard that a few potential buyers were frightened away when they heard you girls."

Abigail waved her hand. "Pshaw! Scaredy cats! They weren't right for the house."

"What about the people who lived here after the fire?" I said. "Did they know you were still here?"

"Not the first family that came after the house was repaired. We were afraid to make any noise and scare them away. But the Wolcotts were different. They heard us talking one day, and after they got over their shock, they became our friends."

"Interesting," Dylan said.

"They kept it a secret," Lucy said. "You won't tell anyone, will you?"

"Of course not," I said.

I gave a start at the sound of the sliding door being opened. "Would you like to come outside and look over the property?" Terri asked.

"We'll be right there." I said.

"After we look around inside a bit more," Dylan added.

"Okay. Whenever you're ready."

"Are you going to buy the house?" Lucy asked when Terri had closed the door behind her. "I hope you will."

Dylan and I burst out laughing. "There's a good chance we'll be doing just that," Dylan said.

"Oh goody," the girls said together and disappeared.

* * *

Dylan and I walked around the grounds and viewed the interior of the house once again, this time shooting questions at Terri: How much were the school taxes? How old was the furnace? And anything else we could think of. Though we tried to act nonchalant, our interest in buying the house came through loud and clear, and soon she was pressuring us for a commitment.

"This is the first time Carrie and I have seen the house. Sure, we like it but we need to talk it over," Dylan said as the three of us stood around the center island in the kitchen.

Terri told us what the Wolcotts were asking for the house. "If it's within your price range, I suggest you make an offer. You seem to love the house. I'd hate to see you lose it to someone else."

Which someone else? we were kind enough not to ask.

"We'll be in touch," Dylan said firmly. We thanked Terri and left.

We discussed finances as we drove home, comparing the amount we'd been willing to spend on the unbuilt house we'd been considering and the one we'd just seen. The cost of the new house was much lower than the asking price of the ghost house, but it didn't include landscaping and other expenses that were sure to crop up.

"Let's offer the amount we would pay if we bought the house in the development," Dylan said.

"Really? Will they go for it?"

"We'll find out soon enough."

We'd been home all of five minutes when Terri called us on our landline. I reached for the phone.

"Have you thought about offering a bid?" she asked.

Dylan nodded and I gave her the low-ball amount we'd decided on.

"Are you serious?" She sounded disappointed.

"That's our offer. Please present it to the Wolcotts."

She called back ten minutes later. "They've accepted your bid."

"Thanks for letting us know."

I was too excited to listen to Terri's follow-up instructions.

"We'll be in touch." I hung up and screamed.
Dylan and I hugged each other tight.
"We're buying our house!" I said.
"Our haunted house."
I grinned. "I'm so happy."
"So am I, babe. So am I."

Chapter Eleven

I hummed as I drove to work Monday morning. Dylan and I had found a house that we loved! It had come about so suddenly, but I could see us living there all our married life. It was spacious yet cozy, and had everything I'd ever wanted. There were stores close by, and the elementary school was a five-minute drive away.

Aunt Harriet and Uncle Bosco were thrilled when I called to tell them we'd put a bid on the house, and it had been accepted.

"I hope you remembered that we said the Wolcotts would come down in price," Aunt Harriet said, sounding a bit worried.

"Oh, they did," I said. "Immediately."

When I told her what we were paying, she whooped. "You and Dylan are savvy consumers."

I called my parents and Angela and Steve. And Julia and Randy. And Victor and Babette.

As soon as I got to the library, I shared our good news with my colleagues. They were thrilled for Dylan and me.

"When do you think you'll move in?" Angela asked.

"I have no idea. The house doesn't need much work, but I want to go over it carefully and see what needs attention before moving in.

We'll need a new washer and dryer. And though it's in good condition, I'd like to paint the interior, change the carpet in the bedrooms and on the stairs, and find out if the hardwood floors require special care or treatment."

Marion grinned at me. "Listen to her!" she teased. "A house-proud homeowner."

"Maybe you'll adopt a dog after you move in," Angela said.

"Maybe," I said.

Evelyn was delighted with my news. She nodded her head thoughtfully when I told her about Abigail and Lucy.

"Dylan and I don't mind sharing our home with two little ghosts, but Lucy is unhappy because they haven't moved on."

Evelyn nodded. "I can help you help them with that."

"Thank you," I said solemnly. "I was hoping you would."

She cast me a sideways glance. "I'm impressed by how quickly you and Dylan made up your minds to buy this house."

"It's beautiful."

"It's more than beautiful. It's the right place for you and Dylan, and you both knew it immediately."

"And I wasn't afraid to act on it," I murmured.

"Indeed you were not."

I knew Evelyn was thinking how much I'd changed from the person she'd first met, who had balked at the first sign of commitment and long-term plans. Because I was remembering that person too.

Evelyn faded away and I settled down to see what required my attention. But focusing on library work was difficult. Dylan called to tell me that he'd arranged to have an engineer inspect the house, then rhapsodized about several projects he planned to undertake as soon as we took possession. Marjorie Wolcott called to tell me how happy she was that Dylan and I had bought the house.

And suddenly I was too excited to get anything done. I was getting married, and soon I would be living in my new home! My life was changing quickly, and I was eager to take the next step.

Trish arrived and I told her about the house we were buying.

Her eyes lit up with delight. "Your children will be going to the same elementary school my kids attend."

"Really? I didn't realize."

"Yes. It's the best elementary school in the district."

Trish went on to tell me more than I needed to know about the excellent teaching staff and advanced methodology at my future children's school. I was too wired to sit still, and I needed to burn some energy, so I left to check on the programs in progress.

Now that all the rooms in the new wing were being used, half an hour had passed by the time I returned to my office. I heard shouting as I opened the door. There stood my easygoing assistant, hands on hips, her face red with emotion as she ordered someone to get out of the office. But the intruder, a scrawny man only inches taller than Trish, refused to budge.

"Can I help you?" I said.

They both turned to me.

Trish opened her mouth to speak, but he got there first. "My name is Garrett Grimm. I have a bone to pick with you."

So this was Garrett Grimm! He wore jeans and a T-shirt that revealed tattoos on both arms, and appeared to be in his late forties to early fifties. His black hair was streaked with gray and pulled back in a ponytail. His pointed nose and beady eyes reminded me of a rat.

"Fine," I said meeting his angry scowl. "I'll talk to you as soon as you calm down."

"Shall I call Max?" Trish said, referring to our head custodian.

"*Are* you going to calm down?" I asked.

"Yeah. Sure." He turned to Trish. "This is personal, so if you don't mind . . ."

"Carrie, would you like me to leave?" Trish asked.

"No need."

Garrett Grimm's laugh was derisive. "She wants you here for protection."

I glared at him. "I don't need protection, and I won't put up with your insults. Perhaps *you* should leave, Mr. Grimm." I sat down at my computer.

"Hey, sorry."

I spun around, startling him. "What exactly do you want to tell me?"

He cleared his throat. "I don't like what you said about me in the *Gazette*."

"That makes two of us because I didn't much appreciate your letter."

The anger was back. "Just because you read Verity Babcock's diary, you think you know what happened all those years ago."

"And you do?" I said.

"I've read several accounts of what was going on at the time. Many people died. They were sick people who depended on Babcock to make them well."

"And this has nothing to do with the fact that John Whitcomb is your ancestor?"

"Of course it does!" he sputtered. "That Babcock woman poisoned him! She was getting revenge because a few of the Whitcomb cattle happened to graze on her land. Get all your facts, Ms. Singleton!"

"That dispute was settled in Verity's favor. As for John Whitcomb, his wife, Hester, came to Verity begging for her help after he'd been sick for days. Verity told her the herbs might not save his life. She wrote that in her diary."

I gave a start as Garrett Grimm stepped closer to me. "Yeah, well, I want to see that diary for myself."

"I'm afraid that's not possible right now. We're waiting for a forensic specialist to advise us on how best to make a copy of the diary so patrons can read its contents themselves."

He scowled at me, then shook his head in disgust. "You're pathetic, and this pardon business is pathetic. Mark my words, Verity Babcock will never be exonerated." He stormed out the door.

Trish and I stared at each another. "That's one angry man," I said.

"I don't get it. Why does Garrett care about something that happened hundreds of years ago?" Trish said.

"Verity's neighbor, who died after taking her herbal medicine, was his ancestor."

"I heard that, but Garrett Grimm doesn't care about family trees. He's a grifter who never worked a day in his life." Trish laughed. "Both his wives divorced him. He's no more than a petty thief."

I shook my head. "I don't understand why he insists that Verity's a murderer. I hope this is the last we've heard from him on the subject."

* * *

After lunch, I stopped by Sally's office. She listened with pursed lips as I told her about Garrett Grimm's unpleasant visit.

"He had no business haranguing you. If he comes back, call me immediately. If you can't reach me, call Max."

We both knew it wasn't in Max's job description to handle unruly or difficult patrons, though he took it upon himself to do so on the rare occasions it was necessary.

"Interesting that he wants to see the diary," Sally said.

"So does Winnie Thompson. In fact, she thinks the diary should belong to her since she's Verity's closest ancestor."

"Don't I know it. Have you seen today's issue of the *Gazette*?"

"No."

Sally typed in the newspaper's URL on her computer. A minute later she turned the screen to face me so I could read the letter Winifred Thompson had written in the Letters to the Editor section.

"It is only right and proper that the diary be returned to Verity Babcock's family, namely, me, as I am her closest living descendent," I read aloud.

"That's not going to happen," Sally said grimly. "The diary belongs to the library."

"I wonder if, given its age and historical importance, the diary is worth a lot of money," I said, "and that's why Winnie wants it."

"Could be. We'll find out what it's worth when the forensic expert examines it. Meanwhile, no one handles the diary. It remains in the display case, under lock and key."

I sighed. "With so many people interested in the diary, I wish the security system were already in place."

Sally sat back in her chair. "Carrie, don't worry so much. By next week, our security system will be extended to include the Historical Room. Surely nothing will happen till then."

I returned to my office, shaken by the attention Verity's diary was stirring up. Garrett Grimm probably wanted to read it in hopes of finding proof that Verity had actually murdered his ancestor, whereas Winnie wanted the diary as a family heirloom. We wanted it kept here in the library so everyone could see it as part of our local history. For sure, an ugly side of our history, but a side no one could ignore. I believed strongly that presenting our history, warts and all, was the only way we could move forward and hopefully never repeat the damaging actions and events of the past.

Reading Winnie's letter in the *Gazette* made me wonder if joining the Wise Women's Circle was right for me. While I agreed with its mission statement and appreciated that its membership included many women I liked and admired, Winnie Thompson's high-handed attitude regarding Verity's diary bothered me. What good would the diary be hidden away in her home, when so many more people could see it here in the library? I couldn't wait for a copy to be made so patrons could read it for themselves, and we could perhaps offer another copy to Winnie.

As Angela and I walked over to the Cozy Corner Café, I told her about Garrett Grimm's unpleasant visit and Winifred Thompson's letter in the *Gazette*.

"Interesting how they're both hung up on their ancestors, people they never even knew," Angela said.

I thought a minute. "I suppose that's one way of looking at it. Grimm insists on regarding his relative as a homicide victim, while Winnie wants to exonerate her ancestor, which is what I want for Verity too."

"Except Winnie Thompson lays claim to the diary, which doesn't belong to her," Angela said.

"No, it doesn't. I'm wondering how far she'll go to try to force the library to hand it over."

Chapter Twelve

A chat with my best friend over a delicious baby greens salad had its usual soothing effect, and I was in better spirits when we walked back to the library. Smoky Joe was waiting for me outside my office. I fed him and gave him some attention; then he scampered off to socialize with his many admirers.

I turned to my computer to see what new email had come in. I forwarded the run-of-the-mill requests to Trish and asked her to answer them. The last post had my heart racing:

Dear Ms. Singleton,

I am writing to you because you are a good detective and you have solved some murders in Clover Ridge. I have information that might help you solve the two recent homicides. Write back and let me know if you can meet me at six p.m. this evening to talk. If you promise to come alone, I'll tell you where to meet me. Don't waste your time trying to figure out who I am. Please keep this between us.

A Friend

I stared at the email and read it again. Who had sent me this? Was it from Tino, the third friend who had taken part in the bank robbery? Should I show it to John?

No. Whoever had written this was frightened and didn't want to contact the police. I started typing.

Dear Friend,

From your email, I understand that you don't want to go to the police for some reason. I will be happy to talk to you. Where shall we meet?

Carrie Singleton

The reply came immediately: *"The parking lot of the Elm Street Elementary school. Six p.m. Come alone."*

I answered: *"I will. How will I know you?"*

"I'll be standing by the door that leads to the gym. It's right on the other side of the fence from the parking lot."

"The door to the gym near the parking lot. Got it." I exhaled loudly as I shot off my email to my mysterious correspondent. The sound caught Trish's attention.

"Everything okay?" she asked.

"Just a crank email," I fibbed.

"Yeah, we get too many of those," she said.

Maybe it is a crank email. How quick I am to assume it came from someone who actually has information about the murders.

With all the attention Verity's diary had been receiving lately, I suddenly felt the need to make sure it was safely inside its case. Smoky Joe joined me, tail held high, as I headed over to the Historical Room.

Since the newspaper article was inspiring more patrons to stop by to get a glimpse of the diary, Norman had spent the last few days putting the room in order. He'd asked Max and Pete to bring whatever items still needed sorting down to a storage room in the basement, along with the many old papers and mementoes that patrons were dropping off by the droves. It seemed that the diary was inspiring residents to go through their family heirlooms and donate whatever they considered of historical importance.

I paused in the doorway of the Historical Room, impressed by the display before me. Objects were set out on the new shelves that Max and Pete had built, and a large glass case was filled with small farming tools from colonial times. In a far corner, Norman had arranged a display of centuries-old kitchen utensils. I chuckled. Before we knew it, we were going to have to feature exhibits while other items remained in storage.

The display case showcasing Verity's diary stood in the center of the room. While three women slowly circled the room, studying everything on display, an elderly couple had planted themselves in front of the diary, where they conversed in animated whispers. Words like *witch* and *hung* occasionally rose above their low tones.

The man standing behind the display case caught my attention. He was close to my age and stocky, no more than five feet eight inches tall. His dark hair was gelled, his facial hair a grubby stubble. He was dressed in jeans and a T-shirt. His upper arm muscles were extremely pronounced, as if he'd put in hours of working out to make them this way. The way men in prison built up their muscles—at least the way they did in movies.

His intense gaze wasn't on the diary but focused on the back of the case as his eyes moved from one corner of the sliding door to the other. When he realized I was watching him, he gave a start and strode out of the Historical Room.

Uh-oh! I thought as I stared at his receding figure. He turned to glare at me, but I caught a flicker of fear in his eyes before he disappeared from sight. I had no time to give him further thought because the elderly couple had spotted me and started plying me with questions about the diary, which I was happy to answer.

Later that afternoon, Dylan called to say the engineer had called back and would be inspecting the house the following week.

"That's good," I said.

"I want to have that done ASAP to make sure we're not running into any huge unexpected problems. We can deal with the closing when we're back from our honeymoon."

"Okay."

"We never discussed when we want to move in," Dylan said.

Anxiety swooshed through me. "No, we haven't. Deciding to buy the house came about so unexpectedly. Our wedding's coming up, and then we'll be away for weeks."

"We needn't move in as soon as we get back from our honeymoon." Dylan said. "I figured there will be plenty of small decorating jobs and minor repairs requiring our attention, as well as a paint job. They'll be easier to deal with while the house remains empty."

"Our lives are suddenly filled with so many new changes, and they're all coming at the same time."

"I know. We might consider the cottage our summer home and not think about moving until the fall."

I exhaled loudly, releasing a load of anxiety. "I like that idea."

Dylan chuckled. "I kinda thought you would."

"Dylan," I began, about to fill him in on the tumultuous events of my day, when he broke in.

"Sorry, babe, I have to go. Talk to you later. Love you."

"Me too," I said and disconnected.

I was relieved when Evelyn made an appearance.

"I thought you might want to have a little chat," she said by way of a greeting.

"I do!" I said. "How did you know?"

Evelyn shrugged. She moved to the corner of Trish's desk, then said, "It's been a day full of surprises. I figured you might want a sounding board."

"I do," I said, forgoing the impulse to ask if she'd been observing me. "Someone contacted me, claiming to know about the murders." I read the emails aloud. "I've agreed to meet with him or her at a local elementary school at six this evening."

"And?" Evelyn prodded.

"And I'm beginning to worry that I've made a mistake. Maybe I'm dealing with a dangerous killer."

"There will be plenty of other people around you. Kids play in schoolyards until dark."

"Unless the email writer is a sniper," I said, "and wants to kill me."

Evelyn nodded. "Farfetched, but a possibility, of course. What does your intuition tell you?"

"That the writer means what he or she has written and is desperate for help," I said without thinking.

"Mine tells me the same. I believe the writer is very frightened."

I nodded, glad that Evelyn and I were on the same page.

"You'll only find out if you go to meet this person," Evelyn said gently. When I made no comment, she went on, "Anything else bothering you?"

"Aside from Garrett Grimm and Winifred Thompson, you mean?"

"There's not much you can do about them right now."

I told her about the young man I had seen in the Historical Room, how he bolted when he noticed me watching him.

"Again, I trust your instincts."

"He was studying the back of the glass case holding the diary. I got the definite sense he was checking it out because he was planning to steal the diary." I shook my head. "Or am I being paranoid?"

"I don't think so, Carrie. The diary might be worth a lot of money."

"It might."

"Why not tell Sally? After all, she's the director."

I nodded. "Good idea. And I'll mention it to Max. I'll feel more secure when the alarm is finally installed in that room."

I walked over to Sally's office. She was out, so I left her a note informing her about the suspicious character I'd seen in the Historical Room. That done, I returned to my office and settled down to some much-needed paper work.

At four thirty I called Dylan to tell him about my upcoming meeting with my mysterious contact. Though I felt more comfortable about the meet after talking to Evelyn, I knew I'd feel even better after telling Dylan. Rosalind, Dylan's amazing office manager, told me he was in a meeting. On impulse, I filled her in on the meeting I'd agreed to.

"Be careful, Carrie," was Rosalind's advice. "Someone with information about two homicides either knows the victims or the killer or both."

"And is afraid to go to the police," I added.

"Could be he or she wants you to hand over the information he's about to give you."

"Like the name of the killer," I said, feeling curiosity building up. "Maybe someone he or she is related to?"

"That's a possibility. I'll tell Dylan. Where is this rendezvous?

I told her the address. "Please tell Dylan I should be home no later than seven."

Not five minutes had passed when Dylan called me. "You're sure you want to do this?" he asked.

"I do. It's the only way to get a break in the case."

My beloved released a huge gush of air. "I can leave in time to shadow you."

"Dylan—"

He laughed. "I may not have trained as a detective, but I've nabbed my share of thieves. Are you questioning my surveillance skills?"

"Of course not." I stopped to think. "In fact, I'd feel so much better knowing you were on the scene."

"Then it's settled. I'll leave now and meet you where?"

"At the library."

"Be there as soon as I can."

I disconnected, thankful that Dylan would be close by when I followed up on this mysterious meeting. My fear that I was in danger was abating. Still, there were too many unknowns for me to be completely relaxed. It was comforting to know that Dylan would have my back, as the saying went.

He arrived at the library at five fifteen. We decided to have coffee and a bite to eat in the library coffee shop, then have a light dinner at home after I'd met with my mysterious letter writer.

I hunted down Smoky Joe and found him curled up on a patron's lap in the reading room. He meowed his displeasure as I lifted him up and disturbed his nap, but he quickly settled against my shoulder as I carried him to my office.

"Do you realize this is our third caper together?" Dylan said as I put Smoky Joe in his carrier.

"Right! Last fall we proved that Victor wasn't a murderer."

"And there was the time we traveled by ferry to Long Island so you could interview a woman who was the key to several murders,"

Dylan reminisced as he took the carrier from me and we exited the library.

I wrapped my arm around his free arm. "I do like solving mysteries with you."

"Like Mr. and Mrs. North," he quipped.

I chuckled. "I loved reading those books! We *must* watch some of the movies of Nick and Nora solving crimes in old New York."

* * *

At a quarter to six Dylan and I got into our respective cars and drove to the elementary school a mile away. I pulled into the parking lot on the side of the school while Dylan parked in the circular driveway in front of the building. His plan was to walk around to the playing field that stretched out behind the school. If a game was in session, he would pretend to watch it, then slowly make his way to the side near the parking lot.

We were approaching the middle of June, and the sun was bright above us. Which meant I shouldn't have been surprised at how much activity was going on. The parking lot was two-thirds full of cars because, I soon realized, a girls' softball game was in progress. There were spectators in the bleachers, and the playground was filled with younger siblings playing on the monkey bars and swings in the adjacent playground. Did my mysterious friend realize the school grounds would be this active, or was he or she counting on the crowd in hopes of not being noticed?

At five to six I left my car and walked past the playground and along the playing field. I passed Dylan, who appeared to be watching the game.

"Any sign of your friend?" he asked.

"Not yet."

I walked back and slowly circled the parking lot. No one was standing near the door to the gym. I returned to my car and watched for someone to appear. No one did. At five after six I walked back to the field. Dylan ambled over to join me.

"Not there?"

"Not yet," I answered.

Time moved slowly when you were waiting for someone to show up, I thought as I returned to my car.

At twenty past six, Dylan came to stand outside my car. "I don't think your friend is coming."

I sighed. "Me neither."

Dylan rubbed my cheek. "He or she got spooked."

I nodded. "I'll see you at home."

"I'll stop for pizza on the way," Dylan said.

I leaned over to kiss him. "I'm glad I'm marrying you."

* * *

At home, I fed Smoky Joe, then set the table for dinner. Tears filled my eyes. I couldn't help it; I was so bummed out that the person never showed. Was it just a case of bad nerves, or had he or she been shadowing me at the library and seen Dylan leave and follow me to the school? Regardless of the reason, I was feeling pretty low. I hadn't realized how much I'd been counting on having this person tell me who had killed Billy Carpenter and Luke Rizzo.

Dylan arrived a few minutes later with pizza and a large salad. As I doled out slices, he opened a bottle of red wine. He knew I was upset but didn't say anything until I'd finished one slice and was reaching for a second.

"I can't tell you how many times I've been disappointed by what looked like a promising lead only to have it turn cold."

I frowned. "I know I shouldn't be getting so upset, but after thinking the email was phony, then being afraid I was being targeted, I finally decided the writer meant what he said and we'd find out who killed those two men."

"It could have been someone pulling your leg. Or the writer got scared. It happens."

I scoffed. "You're just trying to make me feel better."

"That too, but I mean it. Don't be surprised if you hear from your friend again."

Chapter Thirteen

Tuesday morning I stopped to buy a copy of the *Gazette* on my way to work. I turned the pages as I walked back to my car, curious to see if there were any letters in the Letters to the Editor section regarding Verity's diary.

A woman had written in, saying she believed the library should keep the diary because that way more people had the opportunity to see it. "Besides, who but another relative of Verity Babcock could have donated it to the library since the library has owned it all these years? Perhaps Mrs. Thompson is eager to get her hands on the diary so she can sell it and profit from her ancestor's misfortune."

"Right on!" I thrust my fist in the air.

I sat behind the wheel and read the other letters on the subject. Two writers were outraged that Verity still hadn't been pardoned for the ludicrous charge of witchcraft.

The last was a letter from Garrett Grimm. "It is unfortunate that since the discovery of Verity Babcock's diary, Winifred Thompson is seeking exoneration for her ancestor who was hung as a witch in the 1600s. Her secret society of like-minded women supports her in this foolish enterprise. Foolish because whether or not she was a witch,

Verity Babcock murdered her neighbor, John Whitcomb, who happens to be *my* ancestor. She got what she deserved."

My mouth fell open as I read further. "Mrs. Thompson's coven of troublemakers meets regularly to create havoc and disaster. I, for one, would not be surprised if the recent murders of two young men are not evidence of their handiwork."

Coven? Handiwork? Grimm had referred openly to the Wise Women when everyone knew they preferred anonymity, and he had all but labeled them witches and implied they were responsible for the two unsolved homicides. And once again he had besmirched Verity's reputation by calling her a murderer. I drove to the library, seething with anger as I mentally composed my response to Grimm's infuriating letter.

I pulled into the parking lot and was surprised to see a police car parked near the entrance. I peered through the glass as I drove past but didn't see anyone. A chill ran up my spine. Why was someone from the police department here before the library had even opened?

I entered the building cautiously. The lights were on. Nothing seemed amiss. Smoky Joe let out a yowl, reminding me I was still holding his carrier.

"All right, all right." I placed the carrier on the floor and set Smoky Joe free, then slowly followed him as he dashed across the reading room and made a beeline for the circulation desk where, despite my strict orders, Angela fed him treats.

"Carrie!"

Sally was beckoning to me from the doorway of her office. I went inside and found Danny Brower sitting in one of the visitors' chairs, munching on what looked like a large piece of cake.

"What's up?" I asked.

"We've had some excitement," Sally said as she took her seat behind her desk. "Max started work at seven this morning because he was leaving early to watch his granddaughter's ball game this afternoon. He noticed an unfamiliar car parked near the back door of the new addition and called the police.

"John told him to wait outside the library, but Max couldn't resist checking the door, which he knew he'd locked last night. When he found it unlocked and the security system shut off, he walked quietly down the hall and saw a man about to enter the Historical Room. The would-be thief spotted Max and tried to make a run for it. Max tackled him just as John arrived."

"Oh no!" I sank into the other visitors' chair. "Is Max okay? Was the thief after the diary?"

"Max is fine, and so is the diary," Sally said.

Danny swallowed the last of his cake and said, "Don't worry, Carrie. Max acted so quickly, the perp never got the chance to pry open the case. The loo arrived in time to haul him off to the precinct."

I nodded as I tried to absorb what had happened. "Who broke in, Danny? Do you know?"

"This is the burglar." Danny held out his cell phone to show me a photo of a young man struggling to free himself of Max's hold.

"That's him!" I said. "That's the guy who was checking out the back of the display case in the Historical Room yesterday."

"The lieutenant said to tell you his name is Fred Rawlins."

"Fred Rawlins," I repeated. "I've heard that name. Who is he?"

"Rawlins was Billy Carpenter's cellmate in prison," Danny said.

"That's right. Isn't he a suspect in Billy's homicide?"

"Kind of. The lieutenant interviewed him a few times, but since we didn't find any evidence tying him to the murder, the loo couldn't hold him."

"He's not from Clover Ridge, but he stuck around anyway. I wonder why."

"Good question," Danny said.

I shook my head. "What on earth could he want with Verity Babcock's diary? Sell it, I suppose."

"That's what we'd like to know," Danny said. He gestured to Sally. "Mrs. Prescott told the lieutenant that you'd seen someone suspicious sniffing around the diary yesterday. He wondered if you'd be kind enough to come down to the precinct later today."

"I'd be happy to, but there's not much I can tell him."

"Great. He'll call to let you know the time. It probably won't be till later in the day."

Danny crumpled up the paper plate and napkin he'd been holding and dropped them in the wastebasket along with the plastic fork. "Looks like everything's in order, so I'll be heading back to the precinct. I checked the lock on the case that holds the diary. It's secure, but you'll feel a lot more comfortable once it's hooked up to the security system. And get them to figure out how Rawlins managed to bypass the alarm to get inside the library. Thanks for the snack, Mrs. Prescott."

Sally and I said goodbye to Danny. I remained seated when he left, still too shaken to move.

"I'm sorry, Carrie," Sally said.

"For what?"

"For asking you to write an article about the diary for the *Gazette*. All the publicity led to angry letters in the paper, and now someone actually tried to steal the diary."

I released a gush of air. "What kind of security system did we install that Rawlins managed to bypass it so easily?"

Sally grimaced. "John said Rawlins is a crackerjack at breaking in and disabling alarms. I'm going to insist that the security company send over its top engineer to look over our system to make sure it doesn't happen again. After all, we hold art shows here, and some of the artwork is very valuable. Not to mention Verity's diary."

"I'll feel a lot better when the Historical Room is armed and the diary is safe," I said. "At least John hauled Rawlins off to jail, so we don't have to worry about him anymore."

"The diary has become our top priority. In fact, I'm going to speak to the board about having the security system extended to all the windows."

"A good idea," I said. "I wish it weren't necessary, but it is." I thought a minute. "By the way, where did you get that piece of cake Danny was scarfing down? The coffee shop's closed."

Sally turned away but not before I caught her guilty expression. "He said he missed breakfast because John told him to get to the library ASAP. What could I do but find him something to eat? Danny's a growing boy. Katie won't mind."

No, kindhearted Katie Rollins who managed the coffee shop and made many of the items she sold wouldn't mind at all that Sally had raided her pantry. The image of Danny Brower stuffing his face came to mind, and I started to laugh. Sally joined in. We were still laughing when Marion entered Sally's office.

"I just heard what happened! Why are you laughing?"

Sally and I exchanged glances and burst out laughing again.

"Nervous energy, I suppose," I said feeling considerably better as I headed for my own office, to start the day.

I sat down at my computer and read through my emails, then went to check on the programs in progress. Evelyn appeared at my side as I was returning to my office. I told her that Billy Carpenter's cellmate had tried to steal Verity's diary early that morning.

"That diary has become very popular" was her comment. "What did you find out from the person who emailed you?"

"He never showed," I said as I unlocked my office door.

"That's too bad. This murder investigation is going nowhere. It's in desperate need of a witness."

"And you think the person who contacted me witnessed the murders?"

"One of them—and perhaps both, which is why he or she is terrified and was too frightened to meet you yesterday."

"I guess." I slumped down in my chair.

"But this person wants to do the right thing. I think you'll be hearing from him or her soon."

Evelyn left me as suddenly as she'd arrived. I never knew if her proclamations of future events were based on knowledge she had access to or were simply the results of her intuition. Regardless, they rarely disappointed me, so I was feeling positive as I focused on my library duties.

I decided not to write a letter to the editor in response to Garrett Grimm's diatribe. There was no point in stirring things up further. The man was spiteful and malicious. He was angry at Winnie for wanting to exonerate Verity, and so he besmirched the Wise Women, going so far as to call them murderers. Retaliating in print would get me nowhere and only turn his bile against the library and me.

An hour later, Sally called me, sounding excited. "I called the security system company and told them about our break-in—how the intruder had bypassed the new back entrance they'd installed a few months ago. They agreed to arm all the windows and provide CCTV for a very low fee. But they can't get to it until next week, when they come to arm the Historical Room."

"That's great," I agreed. "After all, who would dare to steal the diary so soon after Rawlins tried and failed?"

* * *

It wasn't until four thirty that John called to ask me to stop by the police station. I told Sally I was leaving early and went in search of Smoky Joe. I found him in the coffee shop, being fussed over by two girls who couldn't have been more than fifteen. From their nervous giggles and the crumbs on Smoky Joe's whiskers, I knew they'd been feeding him.

"We're off to the police station," I told him as I helped him into his carrier.

Five minutes later I was parking in the precinct's lot. Since I had no idea how long I would be, I brought Smoky Joe inside with me.

Gracie Venditto greeted me from her seat behind the glass barrier. "Hi there, Carrie. And hello, Smoky Joe! We don't get to see you here very often." Gracie was a cat lover with three of her own.

Smoky Joe must have sensed it because he rubbed his cheek against the door of his carrier and began to purr.

"Care to park your furry friend with me while you talk to John?"

"If you don't mind."

"Mind? I'd love it after the morning we've had. Go right on in. He's expecting you."

I walked down the narrow hall to John's office. He was on the phone, sounding harried with the person on the other end. He hung up a minute later. I waited while he drank deeply from his coffee cup.

"Ah, Carrie. Thanks for stopping by."

"Of course." I sat down in one of the two visitors' chairs.

"Sally told me yesterday you noticed a guy checking out the back of the display case containing the diary. He took off when he saw you."

"That's right. Danny said the guy you arrested is Fred Rawlins. He showed me his photo. It was the same guy I saw yesterday."

"So Danny told me," John said.

"Good thing Max happened to come to work early and noticed the car and the unlocked door. Max and Pete would never leave a door unlocked when they left for the night. How did Rawlins disarm the security system?"

"I've no idea." John grimaced. "He swears he found the door unlocked—not that I believe him—and wandered inside, not realizing how early it was."

I laughed. "As though a library would be open at seven in the morning. Did he damage the door?"

"Not at all, but then, according to his record, breaking into homes and businesses is his specialty."

"Do you think he's involved in the two homicides?"

"It's possible. Billy may have told him about the money he stashed away. Now Billy's dead and the money's nowhere to be found." John sighed. "I can't rule Rawlins out, but I can't hold him—not for the homicide or for his latest misadventure."

I stared at him. "You let Rawlins go? How can that be? You caught him in the Historical Room, about to steal Verity Babcock's diary."

"Actually, he never touched the diary. Max got to him before he broke into the display case. Before he even set foot in the room."

"But it's so obvious what he was after!"

"I had to let him go, Carrie. I could only charge him with trespassing, and believe me, I did. And I plan to talk to his parole officer. But I'm still trying to figure out why he went after the diary."

"It's centuries old and has historical value, but until we have it evaluated, we have no idea if it's worth a lot of money. Besides, he'd need a special buyer. And how would he find one?"

"Which means he might have gone after the diary on someone's behalf. I got the definite sense that he was hiding something. You're familiar with the history of the diary, Carrie. Who has shown a special interest in it?"

I scoffed. "That's easy enough. Winifred Thompson, Verity's descendent, tops my list. She thinks the diary should be hers. Check out her letters in the *Gazette*."

"Anyone else?"

"Garrett Grimm. He wants to read the diary. In fact, he stopped by the library yesterday to give me a piece of his mind."

"Did he?"

John's expression grew dark as I told him about Grimm's hostile visit. "The guy's a sleazeball and a trouble maker. I'm sorry he bothered you. I'll talk to him if you like."

"Thanks, John, but he's turned his focus on Winnie. He's against Verity Babcock getting pardoned. He claims she murdered his ancestor all those years ago. In fact, he's been writing letters to the editor in the *Gazette*."

I hesitated. Of course John knew about the Wise Women Circle, but what I told him now was sure to anger him.

"Go on," he urged.

"In today's paper he all but accused Winifred of leading a witch's coven that could be responsible for the two homicides."

"Did he?" John thundered.

I shuddered even though his fury wasn't directed at me.

"Sorry, Carrie. I didn't mean to kill the messenger. I see I need to start my mornings by reading the *Gazette*."

He stood and stretched his arms overhead. "I think that about covers what I wanted to run by you. I'll talk to Fred Rawlins again, see how he reacts to the two names you've given me."

To my surprise, he stood and, after I retrieved Smoky Joe, escorted me to the main entrance of the precinct. "Feeling nervous?" he asked.

"About what?"

John roared with laughter. "Did you forget you're getting married in a week?"

I found myself laughing too. "With so much happening around me, I haven't had time to be nervous."

Chapter Fourteen

J ohn's comment about my upcoming wedding reminded me that I wanted to stop by Victor's house to check on the deck lighting and a few other things. I doubted Victor would be home this early, but I knew he wouldn't mind my stopping by, as he'd told Dylan and me to do so anytime. Still, it was only courteous to call and let him know I was on my way.

"Hi, Carrie. Nice to hear from you. How are all your plans going?"

"Fine, as far as I know. I'm on my way to your house to check on outdoor lighting."

Victor laughed. "I'm in Manhattan and don't expect to be home until seven or eight, but be my guest."

I smiled, glad to hear him sounding happy. "Thanks, Victor. Talk soon."

I disconnected and ran through my wedding to-do list as I drove. Everything had been rented, arranged, and ordered, and I could only hope that everything would arrive exactly as we'd planned. For the first time I wondered if we hadn't taken on too much. But then I thought about Victor's beautiful house, and I smiled as I imagined how wonderful it was going to be to have the ceremony in his living room, the cocktail hour on the deck, and the party in the tent on the lawn. The weather report called for clear skies and a temperature in the high sixties the evening of the wedding. Thank goodness, no rain was expected.

My thoughts returned to that morning's break-in and my conversation with John. How frustrating that although he could arrest Fred Rawlins on a lesser charge, it wasn't worth the bother because he'd be released soon after. And so he'd only been slapped with a fine.

John's theory that someone had probably offered Rawlins money to steal the diary made sense. Even if the diary proved to be worth a lot of money, it was a specialized item, and only a fence that dealt with antiquities would be willing to take it off his hands. Or had a private collector hired him to steal it for his collection?

Unfortunately, I had the feeling that Fred Rawlins wouldn't be leaving town any time soon. He was probably hanging around Clover Ridge in hopes of finding the money from the bank robbery. Maybe he figured that Luke Rizzo had murdered Billy and gotten his hands on the money. Then Luke had been murdered, and now *his* killer had the money. Once Rawlins worked out who the second murderer was, he'd go after him for the loot.

I realized I was only a few blocks from Winnie Thompson's street. I slowed down as I approached the left turn that would take me past her house. I wondered if she'd hired Fred Rawlins to steal the diary, and if she'd go so far as to hire another thief to steal what she considered rightfully hers.

I drove as slowly as I could until I reached the edge of Winnie's property, which proved to be a good thing. A gray Sentra with a noticeable dent in the right rear door sprawled across the double driveway, as if its driver had pulled up in a hurry. Winnie and a rough-looking character stood confronting each other on the step outside her front door. It was Fred Rawlins, the same guy who had broken into the library.

I opened the passenger window to hear what they were squabbling about.

"It's not my fault the custodian showed up," Fred said. "I did what we agreed."

"You're lucky you get to keep what I already paid you. And for what? You screwed up."

"That's not how this works. You owe me money. I want it now."

Winnie shook her head. "You didn't get what *I want*, so you don't get paid. What about that don't you understand?"

Someone inside the house pulled aside the drape covering a bay window on the ground floor. It was Winnie's son, but neither Winnie nor Rawlins had any idea that Leslie was watching them.

Rawlins lunged forward until his face was inches from Winnie's. She drew back.

"I got in and was about to carry out my job when I got nabbed for my efforts. You swore up and down that the coast would be clear. Only it wasn't, was it? You should be grateful I didn't tell the cops who put me up to it."

Winnie looked affronted. "I don't pay for *efforts*. I pay for results."

"Yeah? Well, here are some results."

I gasped as Fred Rawlins shoved Winnie to the ground. He grabbed her pocketbook and strode off, cursing as he headed for his car.

I sat there, too shocked to move. By the time I had the presence of mind to see if Winnie was all right, she'd disappeared inside her house. I considered following her, then realized that was a bad idea. I didn't want her knowing I'd overheard her conversation with Fred Rawlins. And judging by how fast she'd gotten to her feet, she hadn't been seriously injured.

Rawlins was backing out of the driveway when Leslie Thompson raced out of the house and pounded on the car's roof to get Rawlins's attention. Was he about to demand that Fred Rawlins return his mother's pocketbook?

Rawlins braked and opened the passenger's window. "Yeah?" he growled.

He didn't appear to know Winnie's son. Or maybe his anger at Winnie had spread to the rest of her family. Leslie Thompson didn't seem put off by the unfriendly greeting. He stuck his head inside the car and began a conversation. Curious to hear what they were talking about, I lowered the passenger window as far as it would go, but I still couldn't make out one word. To my surprise, Leslie opened the passenger door, got in, and Rawlins took off.

My first thought was to let John know what I'd witnessed ASAP. I called his cell phone, which never left his side, even when he was in the office.

"I see," he said when I'd finished. "Interesting how you happened to be outside Winnie's house just as Rawlins was demanding the rest of his payoff."

My ears grew warm. "I was on my way to Victor's to check out a couple of things, and took a detour."

"Hmm. Did you notice the direction Rawlins was heading when he drove off?"

"Sorry, no. But isn't it weird how Winnie's son went off with him? I saw Leslie when I was at the Wise Women's meeting the other evening, and thought he looked kinda out of it."

"If you ask me, Leslie's a lost soul who would do himself a favor by getting out from under his mother's thumb. He's Winnie's youngest and never left home—not that they get along. He works in the local deli. Far from a high achiever like his two sisters."

"Has he ever been arrested?"

"We've pulled him in for a few DUIs. Joyriding when he was younger."

"Was he friendly with Billy Carpenter and his pals?" I asked.

"Couldn't say, though they're all around the same age."

"What could he possibly want with Fred Rawlins?" I mused.

"Hey, are you suddenly on the payroll of the Clover Ridge Police Department?"

"John, I just want—"

"Sorry to be abrupt, but I need some information right now, and I don't have the time to chat about Leslie Thompson. What kind of car was Rawlins driving? Did you catch his license plate number?"

"It's an old gray Sentra with a dent on the rear right door. But I was too far away to see the license plate." *Though I should have made a point of seeing it. Something to remember next time.*

"Thanks, Carrie. Tell me you're not on his tail as we speak."

"Of course not." *He's too far gone by now.* "I called to let you know what I'd seen."

"Smart move. We'll talk later," John said and disconnected.

I made a U-turn and headed back to the main road and on to Victor's house. Coming upon Rawlins and Winnie arguing about his failed attempt at stealing the diary proved that my suspicions were right. Winnie wanted the diary badly enough to hire someone to steal it, and Rawlins had taken the job to earn himself some money. I chuckled as it occurred to me that I hadn't even considered chasing after him. That was something for the police to take care of. No doubt, John would talk to Winnie and maybe even arrest her for hiring someone to steal the diary.

But Rawlins hadn't succeeded in stealing it, and Winnie would probably deny the entire transaction. Except she'd paid him half the agreed-upon amount. And if the sum had been large enough, she'd needed to withdraw the money from a bank account, something the police could check. I shook my head, refusing to speculate further. I'd only driven by Winnie Thompson's house because I was certain she'd been involved in that morning's attempt to steal the diary. I had been proven right and was only too happy to pass along what I'd seen to John and have him take it for there. After all, he was the law.

I called Dylan to fill him in on my afternoon.

"I'm glad you didn't go chasing after Fred Rawlins," he said when I was done.

"So is John. Those days are over, my love."

"I should be getting home by seven."

"I'm on my way to Victor's. I want to check out a few things."

"Sounds good. Let's have something light for dinner. I ate a big lunch."

"That's easy enough. See you later."

I pulled into Victor's circular driveway and unlocked the front door. The house was cool. I was surprised when Rasputin, Victor's beautiful Borzoi pranced over to me and nuzzled my hand.

"Raspi, how did you get here?" I asked. Because Victor worked long hours, he brought Rasputin to a doggie day care, where he was adored and pampered.

"Hey, Carrie. I'm in the kitchen," Babette called.

I followed the whir of the blender and found Babette at the counter, adding olive oil to the ingredients in the glass jar before starting the blender up again.

"I decided to make gazpacho for our dinner tonight, so I picked up a few ingredients and brought Raspie home. I'm making it now so it will be nicely chilled by the time Victor comes home. Would you like some?"

"No thanks. I only stopped by to check out a few other things."

"Yes, Victor told me." Babette blended the ingredients another minute, then poured the gazpacho into a large bowl that she covered and placed in the fridge. "Anything I can help you with?"

"I'm wondering if we should rent lighting for the deck, and I need to decide on the best location for the outdoor bathrooms." I smiled at Babette. "I'd appreciate having your artist's eye on this."

We stepped out onto the deck, where we were having the cocktail hour before dining and dancing under the tent. Raspie followed and stayed close to us. Babette turned on all the lights and suggested that a string of lights hanging from one end of the deck to the other would be a nice touch.

Next, I went to stand on the lawn where the opening of the tent would be. "We're renting three portable toilets. They need to be visible without being too obvious," I said. "Where's a good spot for them?"

Babette pointed to the right. "Against the trees over there. Your guests will notice the bathrooms as they file into the tent and hopefully remember their location when they need to use one. At the same time they're far enough away. I recommend renting six pole lamps to light the way."

"I'll get on that tomorrow, along with the string of lights for the deck. And of course we'll make an announcement that guests are to use the portable toilets and not the bathrooms in the house," I said.

"It sounds like you have everything under control."

"I hope so, now that you've mentioned the pole lamps. I'm so afraid we're going to forget something important." I sighed. "I'm thrilled that Victor is letting us hold our wedding here, but if I'd realized how much planning and arranging it required, we might have gone with a hall after all."

"Are you kidding? This way your wedding is going to be exactly how you and Dylan want it to be. And your guests will have the chance to wander outside and look up at the stars."

I smiled at Babette. "You're right. Besides, I really didn't like any of those places."

"Victor and I will make sure that everything goes just as you planned it, Carrie."

I hugged her. "Thanks, Babette. I know you will." I paused then added, "I'm glad we're friends."

"Me too," she said as we headed back toward the house.

I started to walk around the side of the house to my car, when Babette stopped me. "Come into the kitchen."

"Okay."

Inside, she opened the refrigerator and handed me the bowl of gazpacho. "Here—you and Dylan have this for your dinner."

"No, I can't—"

"Yes, you can. I bought too many ingredients. I'll mix up another batch for Victor and me."

Babette's expression told me I had no choice but to take the bowl. "Thank you. Dylan and I both love gazpacho."

She was already bisecting a tomato on the cutting board. "Talk to you soon."

*   *   *

Dylan loved the gazpacho. When he'd finished his second helping, he said, "I could eat this every night through the summer. Make sure you get Babette's recipe."

"I will."

I filled two dessert dishes with ice cream. "Let's have this out on the patio."

"Good idea."

We walked through the den and onto the brick patio. Jack Norris, the handyman for the Avery property, had brought out and arranged the summer furniture weeks ago, but until tonight, life had been too hectic to even consider spending time out here.

We sat down on two cushioned chairs at the wrought iron table. Dylan started eating his ice cream while I gazed beyond the lawn, to the river that ran along this part of the property.

"I'm going to miss this," I said.

Dylan laughed. "When was the last time we sat out here?" He cocked his head. "Did we ever sit out here?"

"Maybe not, but I love the cottage. I'm going to miss it."

"Are you sorry we'll be moving to the house on Old Willows Road?"

I shook my head. "No, but this is where I was living when we fell in love."

"We can always keep it, you know."

I took Dylan's hand in both of mine. "Maybe for a while."

We'd just finished our ice cream when I heard the jingle of my cell phone. I hurried into the house to find out who was calling. It was John.

"I just spoke to Winifred Thompson," he said.

"And?" I asked, excited to hear what Winnie had to say for herself.

"She came into the precinct to complain that some young thug stole her pocketbook."

"That's interesting. And where did she say this theft took place?"

"In the parking lot behind the shops that face the Green."

"Really?"

"Oddly enough, someone had already found it and brought it in to the precinct. Winnie claimed the only thing missing were the few hundred dollars that were in her wallet."

"I'm sure you asked her if she knew Fred Rawlins."

John scoffed. "Of course. She categorically denied knowing him, much less that she'd hired him to steal her ancestor's diary. She put on the grande dame act and asked where I had gotten such strange ideas. Of course I didn't tell her."

"How disappointing," I said. "Had she made any sudden bank withdrawals?"

"She withdrew five hundred dollars in cash last week, but that proves nothing. I don't have one shred of evidence to link her to Rawlins."

"I wonder how she even hooked up with him," I mused. "After all, he's a stranger in town."

"Good question, Carrie. For all we know, she caught him shoplifting small items in a store and figured he was desperate for money and would do what she wanted on the cheap. And I can't for the life of me figure out what her son, Leslie, wants with the likes of Fred Rawlins." He sounded discouraged. "I plan to question Leslie when I locate him. He's not answering his cell."

"I'm sorry nothing's panned out."

John released a deep exhalation. "Well, that's the news for tonight."

"Good night, John. Thanks for letting me know."

I disconnected and joined Dylan in the living room, where he'd gone after bringing in our dessert dishes and stacking them in the dishwasher. I cuddled up next to him on the sofa as Smoky Joe sauntered over and plopped down between us.

"Poor guy hasn't caught a break in the two homicides, and he has no way of disputing Winnie's lies," Dylan said.

I sighed. "If only I'd thought to snap a photo of Winnie and Rawlins arguing. Then she'd have to admit that she knew him and would have to explain what the dispute was about."

Dylan rolled his eyes. "I, for one, am very glad you didn't get involved. John's a good detective. The attempt to steal the diary may be a dead end, but he's not finished investigating the murders."

I stretched out my legs and rested my feet on the coffee table. "I feel guilty not telling him about the emails I received from that person claiming to have information about the two murders."

"To what purpose?" Dylan asked. "We've learned nothing so there's nothing to share. If you hear from your mysterious friend again, then you'll decide what to do with the information he or she provides."

I exhaled loudly. "I've had enough thinking about crime and sleuthing for one day. I simply want to relax with the man I love."

Dylan shot me a mischievous grin as he pulled me closer. "In that case, I've a suggestion we'll both enjoy."

Chapter Fifteen

S ally was waiting for me when I arrived at the library the next morning. My heart was pounding as I placed Smoky Joe's carrier on the floor and set him free. Had I done something wrong? It wasn't like Sally to waylay members of her staff when she wanted to tell us something. Her usual style was to send word, asking us to stop by her office.

"What's wrong?" I asked.

"Can we talk in your office?" she asked.

"Of course."

I'd been so absorbed by my own reaction to the situation, but now I was first noticing that Sally was nervous. Her eyes darted from side to side as we walked the short distance to my office. I unlocked the door, flipped on the lights, and set Smoky Joe's carrier in its usual corner.

I sat down in my chair and gestured to the chair behind Trish's desk. "Have a seat."

But Sally remained standing. "There's nothing wrong, at least not where the library's concerned, but I need to speak to you. About something else."

"Oh. The Wise Women's Circle."

She nodded. "I—that is, *we*—were wondering if you've come to a decision about joining us."

"I admire the members of the circle and the work that you do, but I haven't had any time to consider joining since I attended the meeting."

"I get it," Sally said quickly. "You're overwhelmed with personal stuff. You're about to get married. You just bought a house. These are biggies. Still, the Wise Women's Circle is a vital asset to our residents. If you join now, you needn't get involved in any projects just yet. Only when you're ready."

I looked at Sally. She seemed so vulnerable. Was my joining that important to the group? I had no idea why that would be the case, but I felt compelled to give her an honest answer.

"I can't commit to joining the Wise Women right now. Not while Winnie Thompson is heading the group."

Sally sighed. "I think I will sit down," she said as she sank into the chair behind Trish's desk.

I waited while she gathered her thoughts. "As you know, Winnie is determined to see that Verity Babcock is exonerated. Some of us aren't at all pleased with the way she's going about it, sparring with that awful Garrett Grimm in the newspaper. Did you see today's paper?"

"No, I haven't."

"She wrote a long letter in response to his. She said calling her ancestor a murderer and alluding to her own friends as witches in the local newspaper are offensive out-and-out lies. She's threatening to sue him for libel."

"Oh."

Sally sighed. "The Wise Women don't need that kind of attention. Neither does the library."

"Have you been getting flack since Fred Rawlins tried to steal the diary?"

"Oh yes. A few patrons asked if we plan to employ guards. I had to reassure them that it was still safe for them to visit the library. Others weighed in on both sides of Winnie's claim that Verity's diary should belong to her. As if *we* stole it when someone in her very own family must have gifted it to us."

Sally lowered her voice, though no one could possibly hear us. "Liane Walters called me, very upset about this 'unwanted, ugly publicity that detracts from the lofty purpose of the Clover Ridge Library'—her exact words."

"Maybe if our board president hadn't insisted that I write that article about the diary for the *Gazette*, we wouldn't be dealing with this problem."

"There's no point in rehashing something that's over and done with," Sally said coldly, rightfully assuming that I was including her in the list of people responsible for making me write the article about Verity's diary. "I told Liane the matter would blow over, and there was no way we were handing over the diary to Winifred Thompson or anyone else who claimed it."

I debated whether or not to share what I'd seen at Winnie's house yesterday, then decided that Sally deserved to know.

Sally's mouth fell open as I proceeded to tell her exactly what I'd witnessed. I finished by saying, "This proves she's behind the attempted theft. When John questioned her, she denied even knowing Fred Rawlins."

Sally blinked as she absorbed everything. "How did she even meet someone like Fred Rawlins? He's not from Clover Ridge."

I laughed. "John said she might have seen him shoplifting and decided he'd be up for the job. He just got out of prison and must be hard up for money. I found it very odd that Winnie's son rushed out to talk to Rawlins, especially after seeing how Rawlins treated his mother. Then the two of them drove off together."

Sally shook her head. "Leslie is a troubled young man who's made plenty of bad decisions. Growing up, he gave Winnie and her husband plenty of grief. But I thought he was doing better since he'd started working at Moe's deli."

"The fact that he took off with an ex-con can only mean he's up to no good," I said.

"I have sympathy for Winnie when it comes to her son, but her obsession to gain possession of Verity's diary has driven her to act in dangerous ways, ways that reflect poorly on our circle. I feel obliged to inform the Wise Women that she's behind the attempted theft." Sally hesitated. "Do you mind if I tell them what you observed yesterday?"

"As long as you leave my name out of it. Fred Rawlins is a felon and may be a suspect in the two recent homicides. I don't want him finding out that I saw him arguing with Winnie."

"I understand. I'll report that a reliable witness saw them arguing. As if Winnie's letters to the editor aren't worrisome enough." Sally released a deep sigh as she stood. "I'm almost sorry you found that diary, Carrie. It's caused so much discord and distress."

"Nothing compared to what Verity suffered," I said. "Her pardon is long overdue. When I return from my honeymoon, I'll do my utmost to see that she gets one."

Sally smiled for the first time. "If you say so, Carrie Singleton, I know it will happen."

* * *

The photos arrived as attachments to an email an hour and a half later. There were two. One showed a man entering an apartment building. He wore jeans, work boots, and a hoodie that hid his face. The second photo showed the same person exiting. This time the camera caught his face. There was no question the man in both photos was Fred Rawlins. I gave a start as I read the message in caps: *THE KILLER*.

132

"What's wrong?" Trish asked from her seat at her desk.

"Nothing. I just . . ." My first instinct was to call Dylan. "I'll be right back," I said.

"Sure." Trish rolled her eyes at my strange behavior but returned to the task she'd been working on without another word.

I strode over to the conference room, which was empty, as I figured it would be, and called Dylan. When Rosalind told me he was on a call, I said I'd wait to speak to him because it was very important. I breathed a sigh of relief when he came to the phone two minutes later.

"My secret informer just sent me two photos of Fred Rawlins and wrote *killer* on the email."

"Where were they taken?"

"One is of Rawlins entering an apartment house. The other is of him exiting the building. It's the building where Luke Rizzo lived."

"You need to give this to John."

"I will, but I wanted to tell you first."

"Call him now."

"And prepare to be yelled at," I said ruefully.

"Ignore it. Is the email on your cell phone?"

"No, my computer. Trish is in the office, so I'm calling you from another room."

"Call John and return to your office ASAP."

I called John's cell phone. He picked up immediately. I drew a deep breath. "I need to show you something connected to the two homicides."

"What exactly?"

I told him.

"I'll be right over. Don't let anyone see those photos. I mean *anyone*."

I returned to my office, feeling more jittery than when I'd left to call Dylan. Trish was gone. She returned a few minutes later with a sandwich and a paper cup of coffee. "I have to eat something. I missed breakfast."

"John Mathers will be here in a few minutes. We need to talk."

"So you're investigating the attempted theft of the diary. Or is it the two homicides?"

When I didn't answer, Trish grinned. "I get it. Top secret." She swept out of the room.

John came in five minutes later, red-faced and out of breath. "Show me the photos."

I opened the email and the two attachments. He moved closer and clicked on the necessary keys to send them to his phone. Then he studied them carefully. Finally, he said, "Rawlins."

"Yes."

"Who sent these to you?"

"I don't know. I received the first email yesterday." I proceeded to tell John about the email exchange, then showed him the emails. When he finished reading them, he asked, "Did you go meet this person?"

"We—Dylan and I went to the school, but he never showed."

John's face turned redder. He breathing grew more labored. "Now you're dragging your fiancé into your escapades? And you never thought to call me?"

"Please sit down, John. I'm afraid—"

"You're afraid I'm going to tell you what I think of your behavior? Of your obstruction in my homicide case?"

"Please sit and try to calm down."

"Calm down? How can I be calm when you withhold evidence?" He sank into Trish's chair.

I released the gush of air I'd inhaled, still worried I might have caused him to have a coronary or a stroke.

"Please understand, John. This person is terrified and afraid to go to the police. Even too terrified to meet me."

John nodded. "Could you get me a glass of water."

I hurried to the coffee shop for a small bottle of water. I returned and handed it to John, then watched as he drank the entire bottle.

"The heat got to me today," he said by way of an explanation. I was relieved that he definitely seemed much calmer now.

"I called you as soon as these photos arrived. As for notifying you about the emails, I had nothing to report."

John nodded, and I was relieved that he no longer seemed to think I was holding out on him.

"Whoever sent these photos was watching Luke Rizzo's apartment house and assumes Fred Rawlins murdered Rizzo for the money from the bank heist."

"Only Rawlins didn't find the money," I said. "Which is why he's been hanging around Clover Ridge."

"It looks that way, doesn't it? But not finding the money doesn't mean he didn't kill Luke Rizzo."

I laughed. "You sure love a double negative."

John smiled. "Sometimes it's the only thing that works."

"But getting back to the identity of my mystery pen pal: Who sent me the emails and photos, and why is he or she so afraid to go directly to you?"

"Good questions." John got a faraway look in his eyes as he thought. "The one person I can think of who might have been watching Luke's place is Tino Valdez. Most likely, he took part in the robbery and maybe even in killing Billy Carpenter."

"But why would he be afraid to send you these photos?"

"Another good question, and one I intend to ask Tino soon as I get him down to the station."

"Have you had a chance to talk to Winnie's son, Leslie?" I asked.

"This morning I stopped by the deli where he works to ask him a few questions," John said.

From his grim expression, I gathered their talk wasn't very productive. "And?"

"And nothing. At first he denied ever speaking to Fred Rawlins. When I told him he had been seen in his car, he laughed and said he wanted to ask him about life in a federal prison. When I asked if he knew where Rawlins was staying, he said he had no idea. Said he hardly knew the guy. Just ran into him in a bar. Which one, he couldn't remember. The kid's learned to stall and deflect. I wasn't getting anywhere, and his boss kept giving me the eye. Since I didn't want to be the reason Moe fired Leslie, I left."

"I have a feeling Leslie Thompson is up to something," I said.

"So do I," John agreed. "I'll put Danny on his tail. The kid's a loose cannon."

Chapter Sixteen

As soon as John left, I called Angela. "I have an urge for a roast beef sandwich on rye. Would you mind if we bought lunch at Moe's Deli instead of going to the café?"

Angela laughed. "Why? What's the big draw? Are we going sleuthing?"

"Yes, we are. I'll fill you in on the way."

Fifteen minutes later we were in my car, en route to Moe's Deli, which was located in a strip mall a half mile drive from the library. "And so," I said as I finished my spiel, "though John couldn't get anything out of Leslie Thompson, I thought it would be helpful to see him at work."

"How strange that he took off with Fred Rawlins after Rawlins pushed his mother down and grabbed her pocketbook," Angela said.

"Right. You would think that a son would rush to his mother's defense."

"Can we assume he hates his mother?" Angela said.

"Could be. Or maybe Leslie's not capable of caring for anyone." I turned into the strip mall where the deli was located between a Dollar Store and a card shop.

"I wonder if he knew that his mother hired Rawlins to steal the diary, and the reason why Rawlins got so angry at Winnie," Angela said.

"That's what I'd love to know," I said. "Along with why Leslie decided to hook up with Rawlins and why Rawlins was willing to spend time with him. I think it's pretty obvious that Leslie has serious emotional problems." I pulled into a spot and turned to Angela. "Not that I expect to have any of our questions answered here. Still, I'm curious to have another look at Leslie Thompson."

The deli was mobbed, as I figured it would be at lunchtime. It was a popular place, especially for people who worked in the area. The line for orders started just inside the door. There were three people behind the counter—an older man who was probably Moe, a young woman, and Leslie Thompson.

Angela studied the blackboard above the wall behind the counter. "I think I'll get a shrimp salad sandwich on a roll." She turned to the refrigerated section set against the far wall. "Want anything to drink? I'm getting a lemonade."

"A small bottle of water, thanks."

The line moved faster than I'd thought it would. It was my turn to order as soon as the young woman handed the customer in front of us his sandwich. "Yes?" she said to me.

"I'm still deciding. Angela, why don't you order?"

Angela ordered and her server went to make her sandwich. The older man—Moe—was now on the phone, jotting down a large order. My heart began to pound as Leslie Thompson came to stand opposite me. I wondered if he remembered me from my visit to his home when I'd attended the Wise Women's meeting, and was relieved when I saw no sign of recognition.

"What can I get you?" he asked.

"A roast beef sandwich on rye with Russian dressing." I set the small bottle of water on the counter. "And this."

"Lettuce? Tomato?"

"No, thanks."

He turned to prepare my order. I watched him take two slices of rye bread from a bag and place them on the cutting board. Someone's cell phone rang. Curious, I looked around to see whose it was, then realized the sound was coming from the other side of the counter. Leslie glanced at the older man still speaking on the phone several feet from him. Noting that he was facing the window, Leslie pulled his phone from his pocket.

He was too far away for me to hear any of his conversation, but there was no missing the excitement in his eyes when he slid the phone back in his pocket and returned to his task of making my sandwich.

Angela nudged me. "I wonder if he was talking to Fred Rawlins," she whispered.

"My thought exactly."

A minute later, Leslie was grinning as he placed my sandwich, halved and bagged, on the counter. "Sorry for the delay, but it was a call I've been waiting for."

I merely nodded as I handed him my credit card.

"Have a wonderful day!" he sang out when he returned it to me.

I stepped back, ready to leave, when I noticed that Leslie's smile had changed to a scowl. Curious to know the reason, I followed his gaze. Winifred Thompson had joined the line of customers waiting to place their orders.

"What are you doing here?" Leslie demanded.

All eyes were on him, but he was oblivious to the attention.

"Leslie, dear, why are you getting upset?" Winnie's laugh was forced. "You know I always shop here. I've come to buy some turkey and ham. And perhaps a container of potato salad. You love Moe's potato salad."

"You came to spy on me!"

"That's ridiculous."

Leslie's face contorted with rage. "I don't want you here while I'm working."

Moe walked over to Leslie and put his hand on his shoulder. He turned Leslie away from the staring eyes and spoke softly.

"Yeah, but I told her—" Leslie began.

Moe cut him off and spoke again, his voice gentle but firm. Whatever he said managed to calm him down. Leslie, his face still red with emotion, stepped up to help the next customer, a workman for one of the utility companies, and took his order.

I looked to see how Winnie was reacting to her son's outburst, but she was nowhere to be seen. She must have left the deli.

"That was weird," Angela said as we climbed into my car.

"We sure got a bird's-eye view of their relationship," I said. "Winnie came to check on Leslie at work, probably to see if he's doing what he's supposed to be doing, and he didn't like it nohow." I started driving back to the library.

"He sure didn't," Angela said. "And Winnie knew it, judging by that fake laugh. So why did she come, knowing it would annoy and upset her son?"

"I suppose if she's a helicopter mom, she can't help herself. Especially since Leslie clearly has emotional problems."

Angela pressed her lips together as she thought. "Maybe Moe told Winnie that Leslie's not doing his job, and she's afraid Moe will fire him."

"A possibility, but you saw for yourself that Moe knows how to deal with Leslie. Which leads me to think he's well aware that Leslie would never want his mother showing up at the deli at the busiest time of the day."

"So Winnie came, knowing it would rile Leslie?"

I shook my head. "I couldn't say, but it's obvious she doesn't know how to help her son."

"Leslie sounded like he hated her," Angela said.

"He did."

We rode along in silence, pondering their relationship. As I pulled into the library's parking lot, I asked, "Do you still think it was Fred Rawlins who called Leslie when we were in the deli?"

"I don't know." Angela shrugged. "Could be we were too quick to come to that conclusion. The caller could have been a friend—if Leslie has friends."

I thought about that. "Though the call sure got him excited."

"If it was Rawlins, he might be planning a robbery. After all, he is a criminal. Maybe Leslie got excited because Rawlins is letting him in on it."

"And Rawlins would include someone like Leslie because?"

"Because Leslie Thompson knows Clover Ridge, and Rawlins doesn't. Besides, Leslie's the same age as Billy Carpenter, Rawlins's cellmate," Angela said. "Could be Leslie was part of the crew that robbed the bank all those years ago."

"His name was never mentioned in connection to Billy Carpenter, Luke Rizzo, and Tino Valdez. So I'd say tying him to the bank heist is nothing but conjecture," I replied.

Angela laughed. "You sound like a lawyer."

"Ange, I agree there's a possibility it was Rawlins who called Leslie. Even that he called Leslie about a crime they'll be committing. But we have no proof."

"John could always check Leslie's phone."

"Not with the little I'd be giving him. Besides, Rawlins could be using a burner phone that can't be traced."

"Still," Angela said, "considering how Leslie reacted to the call, it's the most logical conclusion."

"Trust me, John wouldn't thank me for telling him what we're assuming. All conjecture. And he'll be pissed because we went to Leslie's workplace, where we had no business going. I don't want to rile him up—again."

Angela rolled her eyes. "Fine. You know John better than I do."

* * *

Back at the library, I found it difficult to settle down. Like Angela, I couldn't help feeling that Fred Rawlins and Leslie Thompson were about to do something illegal, but it was impossible to figure out where, what, and when. Of course, Rawlins would be doing the planning since he was the seasoned criminal. Not a very good one, since he'd been caught and arrested for whatever crime had landed him in prison. And he hadn't succeeded in stealing the diary.

The diary! That had to be it! Fred Rawlins must have assumed that the diary was worth a lot of money if Winnie wanted it so badly, and now he was determined to get it any way he could. Maybe Leslie had discovered that his mother hired Rawlins to steal it, and decided to help Rawlins actually succeed this time. What better way to get the diary for himself and thumb his nose at his mother?

If only the diary were protected by our security system! But though Sally had tried to move up the date, the company wasn't able to work on our security system until next week. Nervous now because of the possibility of another burglary attempt in the near future, I speed walked over to the History Room to make sure the diary was still there.

Yes, there it was, safe in its showcase, under lock and key, but visible to whoever wanted to see it. A few patrons stood staring at the diary as one of them read aloud what I'd written about Verity Babcock. One of the group, a woman in her forties, spotted me.

"Here's Carrie! She discovered the diary tucked away among papers and pamphlets. Carrie, could you please take out the diary and show it to us?"

"I'm sorry, but I don't have the key. But I'm happy to tell you more about Verity and what she wrote in the diary. In a few weeks, we hope to have a copy of the diary available to patrons, so you'll be able to read it on your own."

I told them what I knew about Verity's life—that she could read and write, which was unusual for a woman in the mid-1600s; about the death of her husband; her knowledge of plants and herbs; her disputes with neighbors; and the accusations and trial. More patrons joined us as I spoke.

"How awful!" several commented when I finished speaking.

"It is awful," I said. "There's a movement to have Verity Babcock and others who were hung as witches exonerated."

"Is there a petition we can sign?" asked the woman who had called me over and asked me to take out the diary.

"No, but why don't we draw one up right now?" I suggested.

The same woman whipped out a notebook and began writing on a page. "Please sign this if you want to see Verity Babcock exonerated," she said. "Be sure to include your address and phone number."

I signed the petition and left the group busily filling out the page. If we left forms for patrons to sign and encouraged other libraries in the state to do the same, maybe we'd get enough signatures to convince the state government that it was time they pardoned Verity and the others who had died under the charge of witchcraft. Feeling more optimistic, I headed back to my office, prepared to do some work.

"Carrie, dear, you must be so excited."

I stopped near the reference desk and smiled at Milly Carrigan, who had just celebrated her ninetieth birthday, and was beaming up at me.

"Excited?" For a moment, I had no idea what she was talking about.

"Your *wedding*, dear. It's this weekend, isn't it?"

"Yes, it is! And of course I'm excited!"

"Oh. For a moment I thought I had it wrong." She shook her head. "These days I sometimes get things a bit mixed up."

I felt a stab of guilt as I watched Milly head for the circulation desk to check out the two audio books she was holding. My wedding *was* coming up and I hadn't given it much thought lately. Dylan and I had everything planned and under control, but that was no excuse. I'd allowed myself to get wrapped up in murder and mayhem when I should have been focusing on my upcoming nuptials.

Both my parents and their spouses would be arriving in a few days. Thank goodness my father and my aunt and uncle were taking care of the rehearsal dinner on Friday night. And Dylan had been speaking to the caterer. Since I'd put in a call regarding the outdoor lights, there wasn't anything else I needed to do. But still, I should be focusing on our big event. It certainly deserved my full attention.

Chapter Seventeen

The engineer whom Dylan had hired to look over the house we were buying told Dylan, who had accompanied him, that everything looked good, though he'd discovered a few minor issues that required attention. He was putting them in his report, which we'd be receiving in the next day or two.

It dawned on me that I'd only seen the house we'd be living in, for many years to come, on the afternoon we'd decided to buy it. I was suddenly overcome by the strongest desire to go through the house and examine every nook and cranny. Not to be on the lookout for flaws and problems, but as part of the process of making it our future home.

We had put down a deposit and chosen a date for the closing in late July, when Dylan and I would be back from our honeymoon. I called Marjorie Wolcott, and luckily she was at home. She sounded relieved when I told her why I was calling.

"I'm so glad to hear from you, Carrie. Ted and I were afraid you didn't want the house after all."

"Why would you think that?" I asked. "We have a date for the closing, and our engineer has already checked out the house. We planned to call you as soon as we received his written report."

"I know, dear, but I haven't heard from you since the day you visited the house. And you haven't been back."

"I've been terribly busy, but that's why I called. I'd love to take another look at the house after work. Can I stop by your house for the key, say about five fifteen?"

"Certainly! Even better, I'm coming into town to do some shopping this afternoon. I can drop by the library and give you the key. Save you some time."

"That would be wonderful. Thank you, Marjorie."

"You're welcome. I'm so delighted that you and Dylan are going to be living in the house where my family spent many happy years."

I was tempted to tell her we'd met the girl ghosts, but decided that could wait till after we moved in. "See you soon."

"I should be dropping by in the next half hour."

True to her word, Marjorie Wolcott knocked on my office door twenty minutes later. I must have met her when I was very young, but I didn't recognize the slender, gray-haired seventy-something woman. Without missing a beat, she hugged me, then held me at arms' length and scrutinized me from head to toe.

"Carrie Singleton! You've grown into a beautiful young woman, just as your Aunt Harriet said."

"Thank you."

"And I've been hearing what a wonderful job you're doing on the town board and here at the library. I'm surprised our paths haven't crossed since you've been back in Clover Ridge, but then again Ted and I have been traveling quite a bit these past few years." She sounded sad when she added, "There's nothing here to keep us at home anymore."

I put my hand on her arm. "I was sorry to hear about your daughter."

"Thank you, my dear." Marjorie sniffed, then pulled back her shoulders. "And here are the keys, front door and back. Keep them. As far as I'm concerned, the house is now yours."

Impulsively, I hugged her. "Would you and Ted like to come to our wedding this weekend? We're having it at a dear friend's home on the Sound."

"We'd love to."

"I'll text you the time and address."

Marjorie grinned. "I bet Abigail and Lucy can't wait for you and Dylan to move in."

"Such sweet little girls," I said.

"They were our delightful house guests. Our daughter's best friends when she was growing up."

"But why did you put the house on the market, knowing most people would be frightened by the little girls' antics?"

"What else could we do? Ted and I knew it would take a while for the right people to buy the house, though we had no doubt it would happen. And we're doubly glad that you and Dylan will be living there."

I cocked my head, suddenly curious. "Do my aunt and uncle know about the two little occupants?"

Marjorie laughed. "I couldn't say since the subject never came up in conversation. Though Ted and I were a bit surprised when we ran into Harriet and Bosco in town—how excited they both got when we told them we were having trouble selling the house." She fixed her gaze on me. "It's almost as though they both knew you and Dylan were the perfect fit."

As soon as Marjorie left, I called Dylan to tell him about our conversation.

"I'm glad you invited them to our wedding," he said when I was done. "They can sit with Harriet and Bosco."

"Yes. That's what I was thinking. I wish you were coming to the house with me."

Dylan laughed. "Now's your chance to walk around, get familiar with our new home. Get a sense of how you want to furnish and decorate the place. Bring a pad and pen so you can jot down your ideas."

"What about your decorating ideas?"

"I made a few notes as I went over the house with the engineer. We'll compare what we've come up with and make the house ours."

I sat back in my chair and thought about my conversation with Marjorie. How interesting that she and her family had enjoyed having Abigail and Lucy as part of their household, while the potential buyers who had looked at the house before us had been frightened by the little girls' chatter.

And how curious that Harriet and Bosco were determined that Dylan and I look at the house. Had they seen the girl ghosts during one of their visits when Marjorie and Ted were living there? Had they somehow found out about my relationship with Evelyn? Or was it simply intuition on their part that Dylan and I would fall in love with the house and want to live there? I sighed. Whichever it was, I wasn't about to ask, so I supposed I'd never find out.

I turned my attention to library business and made a few calls regarding upcoming programs. At four o'clock I decided to look in on the programs in progress. They were all doing fine. Since I found myself in the new wing, I couldn't help checking on the diary once again. The Historical Room was empty. I hurried over to the glass case that held the diary. It was still there! Only a few more days before the case would be armed and protected by the security system.

I started down the hall, intending to return to my office, when I became aware of a slender man in jeans and a polo shirt walking toward me. As the distance between us diminished, I realized it was Leslie Thompson.

He recognized me immediately. "Oh, hello. Didn't I wait on you in Moe's Deli earlier today?"

"Yes, you did." My voice came out an octave higher than usual, like I was embarrassed at being caught out stalking him when I was doing nothing of the kind—at least not at the moment.

"What a coincidence, running into you like this," Leslie said.

"Not really," I said. "I work here."

"Oh, okay. See ya." He continued walking past me. Straight toward the diary.

"What brings you to the library?" I called after him.

He stopped and turned around. His eyes flicked from side to side. "I thought I'd take out some movies."

"The movie collection's in the other direction, in the old section of the library."

"Thanks. I'll go there after I check out what's to see in the new part." He moved on and turned into the Historical Room. I stayed in the corridor, wondering what I should do. Follow him? Call Max? Call John? I decided to wait and see.

Leslie exited the Historical Room a few minutes later. He didn't seem to find it odd that I was standing only a few feet farther down the hall from where I'd been when we first chatted.

"You sure have lots of old stuff in the Historical Room," he said.

"We do. Did you see anything real interesting there?"

Leslie shrugged. "Where are the movies? I wouldn't mind watching a few good action films tonight."

"They're near the reading room in the older part of the library," I said. "Follow me and I'll show you where the movie section is."

I left Leslie poring over the new movies section, feeling uneasy as I returned to my office. Should I call John and tell him that Leslie was in the library and had gone into the Historical Room? If I did, I'd have to risk inciting his wrath when I mentioned the phone call he had received when Angela and I were in the deli where he worked.

"You look perturbed, Carrie. Is something bothering you?"

I jumped at the sound of Evelyn's voice.

"Yes. I'm upset and worried that there's another plan to steal Verity's diary." I told Evelyn about Leslie's phone call, his reaction when he saw his mother in the deli, and his appearance in the new section of the library just now.

Evelyn thought as she perched on the corner of Trish's desk. "I can see why you're concerned."

"You can?"

"Of course, dear. Why are you so dismissive of what's obvious when you usually trust your instincts, and rightfully so?"

"I don't know. I suppose because I can't believe that Fred Rawlins would go after the diary again so soon after his failed attempt to steal it." I laughed. "And I hate to think that Leslie Thompson is involved in his plan."

"You feel sorry for him."

"I do, and I'm not quite sure why."

"Perhaps it's because you're not too fond of his mother right now, and you think she might be responsible for some of his problems."

"Am I right to think that she's responsible for some of his problems?"

Evelyn let out a deep sigh. "I've always admired Winifred, and I think she's a good part of the reason why her two daughters are so successful in their careers and their personal lives. But Leslie was a troublesome child. And while she arranged for tutors and a therapist, she never took the trouble to give him the attention he needed from her, and so he began to act out."

"What about Winnie's husband—Leslie's father?"

"Roger was often away on business and not very involved in the lives of any of his children, though he took to bragging about his daughters once they were out in the work world."

"Are they divorced? Did he die? I never hear anyone talk about Roger Thompson."

Evelyn laughed. "None of the above. As far as I know, he and Winnie simply moved apart. Roger lives in Manhattan and comes back to celebrate holidays with his family."

"I'm not sure what to do about this latest problem. If I should tell John . . ."

"Which obviously you don't want to do."

"I don't."

"I don't see what John can do. Didn't he just question Leslie?"

I nodded.

"It's not like John can have someone stand guard and prevent the diary from being stolen."

"That's true." I felt relieved that Evelyn considered my coward's way out to be the best decision after all.

"Why not tell Max? Explain the situation to him and ask him to keep an eye on the diary."

"Good idea," I said. "And I'll mention it to Sally—but not about my visit to the deli, since I already told her about Leslie driving off with Rawlins yesterday after his encounter with Winnie."

"Good! Put Sally on the alert." Evelyn smiled and winked at me. "It's not your job to safeguard the diary, Carrie, dear. You have other things on your mind."

* * *

A few minutes past five, I placed Smoky Joe's carrier in the passenger seat of my car, slid behind the wheel, and set out for the house on Old Willows Road. I thought about Marjorie and Ted living there with their daughter; about the two little ghost girls whom I hoped to help send where they belonged. I looked forward to decorating each room with Dylan and making our house a loving home for our own children and pets in the coming years.

As I pulled into the driveway, I decided to bring Smoky Joe inside with me. After all, this was going to be his home too. He stood in the hall and looked around. Then he moved into the living room and cautiously began to sniff along the wall.

I left him to get acclimated at his own pace and wandered into the kitchen. The sun was streaming in through the windows. I glanced down at the hardwood floor, the shining updated appliances, the cabinets and counters. Nothing here needed attention except the addition of a round table and four chairs in the eating area, and dishes, utensils, and cookware in the cabinets.

I wandered from room to room, more to get a sense of each space than to imagine it filled with furniture, window treatments, and pictures. I'd rather do that with Dylan, I decided. I gazed out of every window, taking in views of the backyard, of the neighboring houses across the road. My new home seemed to welcome me, bestowing warmth that filled me with a definite sense of belonging.

There was no sign of the little girls. I wondered if they were staying away in order to give me privacy as I entered every room and marked it as ours, Dylan's and mine. I was upstairs in the smallest bedroom when Smoky Joe came scampering into the room. I picked him up and held him tight.

"Welcome to your new home, Smoky Joe."

Downstairs, I put him in his carrier and walked around the perimeter of the backyard. Bushes and trees formed a natural barrier along the three sides, giving us total privacy. I gazed down at the running water in the brook, at the weeping willow in its full glory. A few rose bushes in bloom grew along one side of the property.

The lawn was covered with crabgrass and would no doubt require a good deal of money and attention to get it into shape. I wasn't a natural gardener, but I intended to learn how to cultivate a small vegetable garden. I'd grow tomatoes and cucumbers and zucchini for starters. But that was something to think about next summer.

Smoky Joe was meowing mournfully from his carrier as I carried him back into the house. "Sorry, boy. Soon as I lock up here, we're going home."

I double-locked the front door, then placed the cat carrier inside my car. As I walked around to the driver's seat, I noticed a gray car passing by on the road below. The damage to the rear passenger door caught my eye. It was Fred Rawlins's car! Seconds later I was heading in the same direction.

"I'm not doing anything I shouldn't be doing," I told Smoky Joe.

He didn't bother to answer, but curled up in his carrier and went to sleep.

I had no idea where Fred Rawlins was headed, but I decided to follow him. It wasn't taking me out of my way since we were traveling in the direction of home. There was a car between us, so Rawlins couldn't have any idea that I was on his tail. Not that I had reason to worry. The only time we had crossed paths was when I'd watched him confront Winnie Thompson from a safe distance, and he'd been much too angry that afternoon to have noticed me.

The car between us turned into a driveway. I hesitated, then closed the gap between Rawlins and me. The light was red when we reached the main road, so I had to pull up right behind him. He turned left into a development of homes, and I did too. Soon he made another left and then a right, finally stopping in front of a ranch-style corner house with lovely pink and purple flowers, set in black mulch that bordered the house.

I drove across the next intersection and continued on a few hundred feet, my eyes never leaving my rearview mirror as I watched Fred Rawlins. Instead of knocking on the front door, he ambled around to the side of the house, unlatched a gate, and entered the backyard. I made a U-turn, circled back, and parked across the street from the gate.

Questions swarmed around in my brain. Who lived here? What was Rawlins doing here? Was he planning to rob the place? From the way he'd avoided the front door and instead walked around to the side of the house that led to the backyard, I had the definite impression that he knew no one was home.

I cut the motor. "Be right back," I whispered to Smoky Joe, though there was no need to lower my voice. I waited while two boys about twelve years old whizzed by on their bicycles, talking loudly to each other; then I exited the car and crossed the street.

The side of the backyard facing me was bordered by evergreen trees. I glanced from side to side before setting foot in the backyard. There was no sign of Rawlins. A wooden deck a few steps up jutted out from the house. I climbed onto the deck and peered in a window. I could make out the living room and part of the dining room. There were no lights on inside the house, which appeared to be unoccupied.

A covered barbecue was the only item on the deck. There was no outdoor furniture to be seen, which was odd since we were in the middle of June, and the weather had been warm for weeks. The lawn was green with new grass that needed mowing. A white shed occupied the far corner of the yard. Its door stood ajar.

Chapter Eighteen

I paused, aware that I was in a potentially dangerous situation. Because I suddenly knew what Fred Rawlins was after. At least I was pretty sure I was on the right track. There was a good chance that Luke Rizzo had murdered Billy Carpenter and absconded with the loot. He in turn had been murdered by Tino Valdez or Fred Rawlins, as my pen pal wanted me to believe.

But what if Luke Rizzo never told his killer where he'd hidden the money? What if no one knew where it was right now? I felt a rush of adrenaline. That *had* to be the reason why Fred Rawlins was still hanging around. And he had good reason to think that Luke Rizzo might have hidden the loot in the white shed.

A frisson of terror quickly replaced my sense of excitement. There was no telling what Fred Rawlins would do if he found me here. He was a felon and possibly a killer, dead set on claiming the stolen money. His first instinct would be to get rid of the witness and the spy.

Despite my trepidations, I found myself creeping closer to the shed. I felt the sun's rays on my bare arms. Children's voices carried from a nearby backyard. Other sounds of normal activities echoed around me. Of people nearby enjoying the lovely June weather. Surely nothing evil could happen in broad daylight!

I crossed the lawn to the shed, steering clear of the partly open door, and paused in front of a small window. The glass was grimy and looked as though it hadn't been washed in years, if ever. I peered inside. Rawlins had switched on a naked light bulb that hung from the shed's ceiling. I watched as he pushed gardening tools aside and knocked items from shelves, laying bare every inch of the shed.

There could be no doubt he was searching for the money from the bank heist. Suddenly, knowing I'd been right about his intent was all I needed at the moment. I had no idea if he'd find it hidden in the shed, or whom the shed belonged to. It was time to make a hasty retreat before Rawlins realized I'd been on his tail. But before I could turn around, my head exploded with the most awful pain. Another blow followed. I crumpled to the ground and blacked out.

* * *

I sat up, holding my hand to my aching head, wondering what I was doing sitting on the lawn in some stranger's backyard next to a shed. Slowly, my memory returned. I'd been watching Fred Rawlins search for something inside the shed. The bank money. I blinked, suddenly frightened that he would find me sitting here in broad daylight. But the shed's door was wide open, which meant that he was gone.

I breathed a sigh of relief that Rawlins hadn't murdered me when he found me lying outside the shed he'd been ransacking. Then I gingerly touched the two lumps on my head. One of them felt sticky. Blood. Oh no! I was getting married in a few days! How could I have my hair done, wear my veil with these awful, painful bumps?

Thoughts of my wedding impelled me to move slowly to my knees. I managed to stand but felt dizzy, so I leaned against the shed until the swaying went away. *Almost* went away. I felt for my car fob in my skirt pocket. Thank God it was still there!

I walked slowly out of the yard and crossed the street to my car. I slid into the driver's seat, panting with exhaustion. Smoky Joe opened his eyes and looked at me. "Hi there," I said.

He yawned and started to groom himself.

I glanced at my watch. Only ten or twelve minutes had passed since I'd parked and gone to see what Fred Rawlins was after. But Rawlins hadn't struck me. Someone else must have. Someone who had followed him or me and didn't want me anywhere near that shed.

I made a U-turn and drove past the front of the house. As I'd expected, Fred Rawlins's car was no longer there. I jotted down the address and called John.

* * *

Dylan was waiting for me at home. I was almost sorry I'd asked John to call him for me because I'd never seen him so upset. "What were you thinking?" he murmured as he held me close.

"I had no idea someone was following him. Or me."

"A tail is something every self-respecting investigator keeps an eye out for. Here." He handed me an ice pack.

I held it to my head and walked into the living room.

"Don't get too comfortable. We're going to the ER so a doctor can examine your head."

"Meow," Smoky Joe complained because I'd neglected to release him from his carrier. I moved to set him free, but Dylan stopped me and bent down to open the door.

"Not the ER," I said. "We'll be at the hospital for hours."

"John called South Conn. They know we're coming," Dylan called from the kitchen, where he was getting Smoky Joe's food from the fridge.

Five minutes later we were in Dylan's car, heading for the hospital. I leaned back in my seat and sighed.

"Are you okay?" Dylan asked.

I smiled at him. "As okay as can be expected. I'm so glad I have you to look after me."

Dylan made a sound I couldn't quite interpret. I closed my eyes and drifted off.

A handsome young doctor with a charming accent examined me almost as soon as we arrived at the hospital. He thought I wasn't concussed, but he wanted me to have a CT scan, and for that we had to wait. Meanwhile, I had to answer several questions. Had I lost consciousness when I was struck? Yes. Was I dizzy? No, though I was dizzy right after I came to. Did my head hurt now? Yes. How bad was it, on a scale from one to ten? Eight.

Officer Danny Brower showed up and asked me questions too, but his were about my activity prior to being assaulted.

"Where's John?" I asked after I'd answered Danny's third question.

"Looking for your assailant."

"But we don't know who that is."

"The loo has a pretty good idea who attacked you," Danny said grimly.

"Tino Valdez."

"Who else?"

I hesitated, then said, "Of course there's the slight chance it might have been Leslie Thompson. I saw him at the library earlier today, though I'd never seen him there before." *And I saw him at the deli where he works.* "Yesterday he drove off with Fred Rawlins after Rawlins came to his house demanding that Winnie pay him the money he felt she owed him."

Danny scratched his neck. "Yeah, the loo told me about that. But why would Leslie follow you when you left the library? Did he catch you watching him yesterday at his house?"

"I'm pretty sure he didn't."

"Still, he probably knows you're our local Nancy Drew, and might have been curious to see where you were going, especially if he's planning something with Rawlins, who he has to know is a murder suspect and therefore on your radar."

I shook my head, which I quickly regretted. "Leslie strikes me as flaky and not one for making connections. He'd met me at his mother's house once, but didn't seem to recognize me when he waited on me at the deli where he works."

"And Fred Rawlins doesn't know you," Danny said.

"We've never met."

"We'll continue to look for Rawlins, and I'll swing by the Thompson house to talk to Leslie."

"I'm glad you're covering all bases," Dylan said.

Danny left and I was called in to have my CT scan. Finally, we were free to go. "You're not concussed," the cute doctor said with a smile.

"Thank God," Dylan said. No smile.

We stopped for something to eat on the way home. I had scrambled eggs. Everything seemed surreal, as if Dylan and I were part of a dream. I was certain it was very late, like four in the morning, and was surprised to learn it was only a bit past nine thirty when we returned home. I was suddenly exhausted. I changed into my pajamas and got into bed.

* * *

Dylan was asleep when I awoke the next morning a little past six o'clock. My head ached but I was thinking clearly and, if not exactly energetic, at least feeling more like myself. I was getting married in two days, and today was my last day of work before our wedding.

Dylan must have set his brain to react to any movement I made, because he was instantly awake. "Where are you going?" he asked as I sat up.

"Where do you think? To take a shower and get dressed for work."

"Carrie, I called Sally last night and told her what happened. She said you don't have to go to work today."

"But I want to. I'm feeling better."

"John wants to talk to you. I invited him over for breakfast at eight fifteen." He glanced at the clock. "That gives us a few more hours of sleep."

"Not if we have a guest for breakfast," I grumbled. As fond as I was of John, I wasn't up for company, much less in the mood for one of his "interviews" that consisted of going over the same questions again and again.

"John's bringing bagels and croissants. I'm making coffee," Dylan mumbled as he turned over and went back to sleep.

Smoky Joe chose that moment to leap on the bed. "Come, boy. I'll feed you your breakfast."

My furry feline trotted after me. I felt fine but a bit wobbly after bending down to place his food and water dish on the floor. I decided that going back to bed wasn't a bad idea and slept until Dylan woke me at seven thirty.

John showed up at eight fifteen with fresh bagels and croissants. He was kind enough to ask how I was feeling and not give me a lecture on how I had no business chasing after a known criminal. Dylan served the coffee he'd made. He'd already put the butter, jams, and cheeses on the kitchen table, so there was nothing for me to do but sit down and enjoy my repast.

When the three of us had eaten our fill and were on our second cup of coffee, John pushed his chair away from the table and stretched out his legs. Dylan took an ice pack from the freezer and handed it to me.

"Carrie, you were in the backyard of the home belonging to Gloria and Ralph Rizzo when your assailant struck you," John said.

"Luke's parents?" I asked as I applied the ice pack to my head.

"That's right. They're away visiting their married daughter."

"So Fred Rawlins assumed that Luke Rizzo hid the money in his parents' shed," I said.

"We don't know that for sure, but it's a pretty good bet he was working on that premise."

"Have you caught Fred Rawlins or the person who struck me?"

"We'll talk about that later. And if you don't mind, I'll ask the questions."

"Of course."

John cleared his throat. "I know you told Danny what happened to you yesterday, but I'd like to hear it for myself. So when did you happen to see Fred Rawlins and decide to follow him?"

"I was leaving the house that we're buying on Old Willows Road when I recognized Rawlins's car as he drove by. There's a noticeable dent on the rear door. Since I was going in the same direction, I thought I'd stay on his tail and see where he was heading."

"Was anyone following him?"

I thought a minute. "There was a car behind him when I backed out of the driveway. After a few miles, it pulled into a driveway."

"Did you notice what it looked like? The style? The make?"

I shook my head and immediately regretted it. "Not really. As I told Danny, it was a dark color and really beat up, like it was ready for the junkyard or wherever old cars go when they're done for."

John's eyes lit up for a second, then he recovered his solemn demeanor.

I stared at him. "How stupid of me! The driver in the car *was* following Rawlins. I never made the connection till now."

"It's only a possibility," John said. *He's being kind,* I thought. "Do you remember seeing that car again? Did the driver follow you to the Rizzos' home?"

"Not that I noticed, but whoever attacked me must have followed me there. I was too busy making sure that Fred Rawlins didn't know I was spying on him. I didn't hear the person sneak up on me."

"You told Danny that you didn't see your assailant. Did you get a sense of his height? Notice a fragrance?"

"I sensed he was taller than me—not sure why. Was it Tino Valdez? Have you brought him in for questioning?"

"I did. Right now Valdez is cooling his heels down at the station. He denies being anywhere near you at the time you were attacked. The car you saw following Rawlins fits the description of the car we found at his house when we picked him up. But since you can't ID him, I'll be releasing him as soon as I run through his statement again, because I doubt he'll change one word," John said grimly. "And Rawlins is in the wind."

"What about Leslie Thompson?"

"His mother said he never came home last night. But she said he often stays overnight with friends."

"Really? I find that very suspicious," I said.

"Don't worry, Carrie. I plan to follow through on Leslie Thompson's whereabouts yesterday, though honestly I don't see him as your assailant."

"So that's that," I said flatly." "Tino Valdez gets off scot-free because I never got to see my attacker, and the bank job money remains hidden away."

"Looks that way. We don't think Rawlins managed to find it in the short time between your attack and the time he took off—no doubt frightened when he heard sounds outside the shed. Danny and another officer searched the shed, but they came up with zilch."

"Maybe the money was never there," I said.

"A possibility." John stood. "That's it for now, Carrie. Take it easy. You want to be well rested for your big day."

Chapter Nineteen

After John left, I straightened up the kitchen and gave myself the luxury of watching one of my favorite TV shows that I'd recorded. And so it was eleven fifteen when I arrived at work. I sensed something was wrong the moment I stepped inside the building. A smog of anxiety permeated the air. Smoky Joe noticed it as well. Instead of running off as usual when I opened the door of his carrier, he rubbed my leg and meowed before sedately starting his round of social visits.

Evelyn appeared as soon as I entered my office. "Carrie, my dear, prepare yourself for a piece of bad news. The diary's been stolen."

"What!"

"Shh," she admonished me.

"No one called to tell me."

"Sally and the others figured the news would hold until you came to work." Evelyn eyed me carefully. "I heard about your unfortunate misadventure yesterday afternoon. Are you sure you're well enough to work today?"

"My head hurts, but I can manage to do some paperwork. Did you see what happened? Who stole the diary?"

Evelyn shook her head. "Sadly, I wasn't here when it happened."

My office door opened and Trish appeared.

"I thought I heard voices," she said.

"I was on the phone with a patron," I fibbed.

"I'm so sorry, Carrie," Trish said. "I know how important Verity's diary is to you."

"And to the library. Do you know if Sally's in her office?"

"I've no idea, but she might be. We all hurried to the Historical Room when Max told us what had happened. Sally stayed there till John and Danny showed up. They left only a few minutes ago."

I walked over to Sally's office and found her on the phone. She ended the call and shook her head in disgust. "After that last attempt, I should have insisted that the alarm company arm the Historical Room that very same day. They've agreed to send someone here tomorrow—now that there's nothing to protect."

"We'll get the diary back," I said more forcefully than I felt. "At least we know who's responsible."

"You think Winnie hired someone else to steal it?"

"My money's on her son."

"Leslie? The boy has problems, but he's never stolen anything, as far as I know."

Boy? "Then tell me, why was Leslie in the library yesterday, when I'd never seen him here before, and in the new section, no less? I know he went into the Historical Room, though he didn't stay long."

"Carrie, you ran into Leslie before you went home at five," Sally said.

"Yes, I did. Did anyone see him leave the library?"

"Not that I know of. It's not something we keep track of."

When I didn't answer, a light went on in her head. "Are you saying he stayed here after the library was closed for the night?"

"Why not?" I asked. "Did Max or anyone see him leave?"

"No," Sally admitted, "but after you told me that Leslie was in the library, I had both Max and Pete look for him in every nook and cranny of the building, including the attic and the basement. They found no trace of Leslie. Pete worked late last night. He said he looked in at the Historical Room before he set the alarm and went home. The diary was safely locked in its case."

"The theft happened after hours, when the library was locked and the alarm was armed," I said.

"If that's the case, how did Leslie exit the library without setting off the alarm?"

"That's easy," I scoffed. "Fred Rawlins knew how to bypass the alarm when he broke into the library. He must have told Leslie how to get out without setting it off. Further proof that they're in on it together."

Sally looked sad. "Unfortunately, everything you've said makes sense. I wonder what Leslie and Rawlins plan to do with the diary."

"Sell it. Certainly not give it to Winnie."

"I wouldn't be surprised. Mother and son never got on."

"What did John have to say about the theft?"

"The usual—he'll question the suspects: Leslie, Rawlins, and Winnie."

"I think he's going to have a hard time finding the first two."

"My thought exactly," Sally agreed. "But how are you, Carrie? I'm so sorry you were assaulted while you were following Fred Rawlins. What on earth made you take such a risk so close to your wedding?"

I laughed. "Good question. I recognized Rawlins's car and decided to follow him. I didn't think I was in any danger, but obviously I wasn't the only one tailing him. I suppose it was Tino Valdez, or even Leslie Thompson."

"I can't see Leslie striking you like that. He was such a sweet child. Shy and always a bit strange, but sweet," Sally said. "As a child he would cling to his mother, which exasperated Winnie. She never was patient with him."

"Leslie's the same age as Billy Carpenter, Luke Rizzo, and Tino Valdez. Was Leslie friendly with them in high school?"

Sally shrugged. "I don't know, but I wouldn't think so. Those three used to get into trouble. I don't remember Leslie's name ever being linked with theirs." She gave a start. "You don't think Leslie was involved in that bank robbery. Or do you?"

"Not necessarily. But we know Leslie's gotten involved with Fred Rawlins. Could be he lied and told Rawlins that he and Billy were good friends in high school. Or even that he did take part in the bank heist."

"So that's why Rawlins drove off with him after his spat with Winnie," Sally mused.

"A good possibility."

*　*　*

I returned to my own office and had no sooner started wading through my emails when the door flung open and Angela rushed in. Trish must have texted her the moment I'd returned from Sally's office.

"Poor baby, how are you feeling? Does your head hurt?" Angela asked as she gently rubbed my back.

"It does, but I'm okay."

She looked at me carefully. "You know about the diary."

"Yes."

Marion joined us, a mug of tea in her hand. "Have some chamomile tea. It soothes and it heals."

"Thank you." I took a sip and set down the mug. I hated chamomile tea and only drank Earl Grey when I was sick.

Marion's assistant Gayle poked her head in my office. "I just wanted to say hi and see how you're feeling."

I looked at the faces of my dear friends. They cared that I'd been injured and knew that the theft of the diary was both a personal affront and a deep loss.

"Thank you," I said. "I love you all and appreciate that you care. I promise to have a quiet day and not do anything rash. You can all go back to work—except for Trish who belongs here."

They proceeded to leave, but not until each had gently hugged me, murmuring how glad she was that I was all right. It was touching and a bit irritating. I didn't like being treated like an impetuous child. At the same time, I felt guilty for having scared them. I'd been reckless trailing after a known felon, and I now had two painful bumps on my head as a result. Trish said nothing, though her knowing expression spoke volumes.

I immersed myself in library work until John called half an hour later. "I figured I'd give you some time to recover from one assault before talking to you about the burgled diary."

"What is there to say? It's gone. I think Leslie Thompson stole it. He stayed in the library after hours, removed the diary, and got out safely because someone told him how to open the glass case and bypass the security system."

John exhaled loudly. "I'd say there's a good chance that's what happened."

"Have you spoken to Leslie?"

"Nowhere to be found. Neither is Fred Rawlins."

"What did Winnie Thompson have to say?" I asked.

"She had no idea where her son was. She said he never came home last night." John laughed. "She asked me plenty of questions about the theft and got real snippy when I couldn't provide answers for her."

"She must have been angry that someone—very probably her own son—beat her to it."

"Danny and a few others are out there looking for Rawlins and Leslie Thompson. Meanwhile, I have Tino Valdez in one of our cells. He finally all but admitted to attacking you yesterday. I'm charging him with your assault."

* * *

I didn't feel up to going out for lunch. Angela and I ordered sandwiches from the Cozy Corner Café, and we ate them in the new staff room. The room was spacious and comfortable, with a table by the window, large enough to accommodate eight people.

"Just think, when you come back to work next month you'll be Mrs. Dylan Avery," Angela said.

"Yes, but I'll still be known professionally as Carrie Singleton."

Angela thought a minute. "Don't tell me you're going to make your kids have a hyphenated last name with six syllables."

"I wasn't *planning* to, but then I've never given the subject much thought."

"We really have to consider how a first name goes with our last name. I think Angela Prisco sounds okay. Steve Prisco sounds great. I suppose most boys' names go well with Prisco. We'll have to be more careful with a girl's name. Though she'll probably marry and change her last name. Or"—Angela got a dreamy look in her eyes—"she can use a nickname that she likes."

My mouth fell open. "Ange, are you trying to tell me something?"

Joy lit up her face. "I am!"

I rushed over to her and hugged her tight. "You're going to be a mother!"

"And you're going to be an aunt."

* * *

169

Back at my office, I discovered I couldn't stop grinning. Good thing Trish was staffing the hospitality desk, since I didn't know if I could keep from telling her Angela's secret, at least for the next month. My best friend was going to be a mommy! She and Steve were going to be wonderful, loving parents. Their wedding had only been a year ago, and now their family was starting to grow!

I texted Dylan to tell him Angela was pregnant. *Wonderful news!* he texted back. *How's your head?*

Hurts a bit, but I'm okay.

I'll be home early, he replied.

The door flew open, and a boy about eighteen ran into my office. He was tall and gangly and out of breath.

"Can I help you?"

"Are you Carrie Singleton?"

"I am."

"My name is Albi. Alberto Valdez. I need your help."

His dark brown eyes shimmered with fear, concern, and determination.

I grimaced. "You're related to Tino Valdez."

"I'm his brother." Albi's ears turned red as he looked down at the floor. "He didn't mean to hurt you."

"Is that so?"

"He gets confused, and when he's confused he sometimes does things he shouldn't."

Like striking women? Killing his friends?

"I apologize for Tino," he said softly.

"Did you send me those emails?" I asked.

Albi Valdez nodded, still not meeting my gaze.

I gestured to Trish's empty chair behind her desk. "Why don't you sit down and tell me what you want me to know."

He hesitated a minute, then did as I'd asked.

"Tino's in jail," he said.

"I know. How do you know he attacked me?"

"He called me last night and told me what happened."

"*Happened?* Nothing *happened.* Your brother assaulted me."

Albi cringed. "Tino was tailing Rawlins, and you were kinda . . . in the way," he finished lamely.

"Your brother was hoping Fred Rawlins would lead him to the money that Tino stole with his two dead friends."

Albi's glance moved from me to the floor. He wanted both to tell me something and to simultaneously fly out of my office. "Kinda. It's complicated."

As much as he wanted my help, the kid was still on the fence. A compelling nudge on my part was called for.

"Complicated, eh? Did your brother kill his pals?"

"No! I swear he didn't! You saw the photos I sent you, of Rawlins going into Luke's apartment and then leaving. He must have killed him, even though he didn't get what he was looking for."

"The money your brother and his two dead friends stole from the bank."

Albi nodded once. "But Tino's no killer. It had to be Rawlins who murdered Luke. Only Rawlins couldn't make Luke tell him where he hid the money, so Tino's been following him. And now he's in jail."

Albi's held his head in his hands. "You have to convince Lieutenant Mathers that Tino didn't kill anyone. He has to get out so he can . . ."

"So he can what?" I asked.

"Nothing!" Albi shouted. "I just want him out of jail."

I looked at him. Something else was going on in his brain. Something I didn't understand. "You do know it's going to come out that your brother was in on the bank robbery. He will go to prison."

"Oh yeah? Is there any evidence he was in on that heist? Any proof whatsoever?" Now Albi was on the offensive.

"I have no idea," I said. "And I don't exactly know what you want from me."

"To help Tino! To prove Fred Rawlins murdered Luke so my brother gets released and can . . ."

"Released to do what?" I asked.

Albi sprang out of the chair. "Coming here was a mistake. Sorry, Ms. Singleton. I wanted you to know my brother's no killer. Again, I'm sorry that he hurt you."

He flew out of the office. Something else was bugging Alberto Valdez that was more troublesome than the charges that would be brought against his brother for assaulting me.

I was still staring at the slammed door when Evelyn appeared. "That's one troubled young man," she commented as she perched on the corner of Trish's desk.

"You think?" I scoffed. "First he sends me anonymous emails; then he sets up a meeting and doesn't show up. Just now he stormed in here like a tornado, wanting me to convince John that his brother is innocent of the two homicides and didn't mean to hurt me, in hopes that John will release him."

"So I heard," Evelyn said, "and I find it as puzzling as you do." She cocked her head. "It's almost as though Tino needs to be free in order to do something."

"Do what?" I pounded my fist on my desk in frustration. "Find the money from the bank robbery? That's what he's been chasing."

"Albi seems to be under a tremendous pressure on his brother's behalf," Evelyn said. "He wants to convince you that Fred Rawlins killed Luke Rizzo."

"But why didn't Albi go directly to the police? And let's not forget that brother Tino was willing to knock me down because I got in between him and Rawlins, whom he assumed was about to find the money."

Evelyn pressed her lips together as she thought. "There's a sense of urgency about it all."

I nodded. "I get that feeling too. Almost as though Tino's driven to locate the money from the bank heist ASAP. But why the sudden pressure?"

Evelyn stood. "That's the million-dollar question. Answer that and you'll know what's troubling Albi."

I expected Evelyn to make a fast getaway, as she always did after delivering her words of wisdom. Instead, she came to stand beside my chair, beaming at me in the most loving way. I tried not to shudder from the chill of her close presence.

"My dear, I wish I could hug you as I offer my heartfelt best wishes on your upcoming nuptials. You and Dylan were so wise to choose each other as lifelong partners. I know you will be a very happy couple. You're well suited and complement each other in every important way."

"Thank you, Evelyn. That means a lot to me. I wish you could attend our wedding."

"Oh, so do I." She sounded so sad, I longed to put my arms around her. "Carrie, you are the daughter Robert and I never had. The daughter I wish we'd had. I'm so proud of you and all you've accomplished in the short time I've known you. You will achieve much more in future years. I'm not talking about amassing a fortune, but doing kind deeds and looking after people who do a poor job of taking care of themselves."

"Like Tino Valdez?" I said, partly to lighten her mood.

"Ah, Tino and Albi. You will help them as best you can, and solve this mystery surrounding them."

On impulse, I lifted my arms and wrapped them around her transparent form. I shivered with cold, but I continued to squeeze tight until I felt a core of warmth that I knew was the essence of Evelyn Havers.

"Ah, Carrie. I love you so much. We'll meet again when you're back from your honeymoon."

I watched her disappear from sight, my heart considerably lighter because I knew how much she cared.

Chapter Twenty

Of course now I was too agitated and pent up with emotion to get any work done. Not that Sally expected me to be productive today, my last workday before my wedding. When Trish returned from her stint at the hospitality desk, we went over everything I wanted her to keep up to date during the two and a half weeks that I'd be away. Finally, she hugged me and said she'd see me on Saturday at my wedding, then left for the day.

I walked over to the circulation desk to tell Angela about my visit from Tino Valdez's brother, as well as about Evelyn's heartfelt good wishes. As I was crossing the reading room, the sound of quarreling emanated from Sally's office. Despite all the excitement I'd had for one day, I slowed down in case Sally needed my assistance. A shout reverberated, loud enough to cause nearby patrons to stare at the office door. It suddenly swung open, and a red-faced Winnie Thompson stormed out.

"And I'll never forgive you for accusing Leslie of stealing my ancestor's diary!"

"All evidence points in that direction," Sally answered.

"You have no proof! Some money-hungry thief managed to steal it because you didn't care enough to keep it safe. When my investigator finds the diary—and he will—I'm taking you to court to gain possession. Verity's diary will be mine, if it's the last thing I do."

"Over my dead body!" Sally retorted, and slammed her door with a bang.

I exchanged glances with Marion Marshall, who had come to stand beside me.

"Winnie Thompson's gone crazy over that diary," Marion murmured. "And we've no idea where it is."

"She hired someone to steal it, but that didn't work. I'm pretty sure it was her son who took it last night."

"I'm not surprised."

I stared at Marion. "Because they're Verity's descendants?"

"Because Winnie is desperate for money. She made some reckless investments and remortgaged her home. I heard she's about to lose it, poor thing."

"And she thinks she'll get a windfall is she sells the diary?" I shook my head. "We have no idea what it's worth, which is why we're having it evaluated."

Marion shot me a puzzled look. "What I don't understand is, if Leslie took it, why has Winnie come here pretending some unknown person stole it? Wouldn't he have stolen it for his mother?"

"That's the one genuine part of her complaint—she's offended that Leslie's considered a suspect. I think Leslie stole it in cahoots with someone else, with the intention of selling it. He has no intention of handing it over to Winnie."

"Interesting. They never did get on." Marion cocked her head "Regarding Smoky Joe—is Saturday morning still a good time for me to pick him up?"

I grimaced. Marion and I had discussed this earlier, but I hated the thought of being apart from my feline companion for almost three weeks. But whoever heard of someone bringing a cat along on her honeymoon?

"Yes. I appreciate your taking care of him while Dylan and I are away. I'll have everything ready for you—his food and toys and kitty litter." *And a list of instructions,* I thought but didn't mention.

"Forget the litter box, litter, and treats. I saved all of that from when I had Mittens," Marion said. "Just in case I adopt another kitty."

"And you'll need his carrier."

"Of course, since I'll be bringing him to work with me."

I nodded, suddenly too choked up to speak. Marion put a hand on my shoulder. "Don't worry, Carrie. Smoky Joe will be fine. He knows me, and he'll be spending his days in the library as usual. And I promise not to give him too many treats."

Marion returned to the children's section, and I decided to check on Sally after her shouting match with Winnie. I found her speaking to someone on the phone.

"Okay . . . I see . . . Well, that's good to know. Thanks . . . Yes, I'll have someone do that."

She sighed as she put down the receiver. "That was Ted Ramisson, the library's lawyer. He was kind enough to alert antiquarians who buy and sell old books, pamphlets, and papers, in a fifty-mile radius, to be on the lookout for Verity's diary."

"That's helpful unless there's a private buyer interested in the diary," I said.

"In which case there's not much we can do. But I don't think either Fred Rawlins or Leslie Thompson would have a lead on that."

"No, but Dylan might," I said.

"Good to know," Sally said. "Ted also reminded me that we are the legitimate owners of Verity Babcock's diary, though we can't stop Winnie from suing us if that's what she decides to do. She might just be talking out of her hat, because suing the town will no doubt cost a good deal of money, money Winnie doesn't have."

"So there's nothing to worry about," I said.

"Ted suggested we search through our papers to try to find out who donated the diary. I'm going to ask Trish to sort through the letters and pamphlets in the Historical Room, though there's a good chance there's nothing there for her to find. People don't necessarily include a note with their donation."

"Besides, we have no idea how long the diary's been in the library," I said.

"True. We don't have to prove that a relative of Verity's gave us the diary, but I thought the suggestion was a good idea to follow up on. Anyway, this is a moot issue until we get the diary back."

If we get the diary back, I thought but didn't say. I was sick at heart that two mercenary thieves had managed to steal it from under our noses.

Sally stood and walked around her desk. "Carrie, I know how much you care about Verity and her diary, but please put them out of your head. You have a wedding ahead of you and out-of-town relatives about to descend on you and Dylan."

I laughed. "You're right. My father and Merry are flying in later today; my mother and Tom will arrive tomorrow. Neither couple is staying with us."

Sally hugged me. "Go home, Carrie, and enjoy a few hours of peace while you can."

"Thanks, Sally. I will."

"We'll see you Saturday night."

* * *

I heard familiar voices as I unlocked the front door to the cottage. My father and Merry were here! I put down Smoky Joe's carrier and set him free. A moment later I was in Jim's arms, holding him close and feeling like a little girl again.

"I'm so glad to see you!" I said. To my amazement, I burst out crying.

"What's wrong, Caro?" My father stroked my head, which made me sob harder.

"Just pre-wedding jitters," Merry said as she joined us.

I nodded. "She's right. I'm just so happy." I took the tissue she offered, wiped my eyes, then hugged her.

"When did you get here?" I asked.

"Fifteen minutes ago," Jim said. "Dylan said to have our driver drop us off at the cottage instead of at the motel."

Dylan handed me a glass of chardonnay. "Take a sip."

I drank more than a sip, then followed them back to the living room, where Dylan had been entertaining my father and Merry. I noticed he'd brought out cheese and crackers.

"I didn't know you'd be coming home early," Dylan said.

"Sally sent me home to relax. It's been a very hectic day: first, learning the diary was stolen, and then Winifred Thompson coming in and squabbling with Sally about it. She's hired an investigator to find it; when it's found she plans to sue us for it." I scoffed. "And she refuses to believe her own son might very well have taken it."

"That woman won't give up," Dylan said.

"Dylan's been telling us about the house you're buying," Jim said. "I don't suppose we could go over and see it now."

"Why not? I have the key."

"Then we can stop by Bosco and Harriet's house and all go out for dinner," my father said. "My treat."

"It's kind of early for dinner. Besides, we don't know what plans they might already have," I said.

Merry burst out laughing. "Your father is starving. We didn't have a proper lunch."

I exchanged glances with Dylan. He shrugged. I decided to go with the flow. "All right. Whatever you say."

"And we'll stop by our motel on the way so we can check in and drop off our suitcases," Jim said.

We took my car since it was roomier, stopped at the motel where Jim and Merry were staying, and then drove to our new house.

"So many memories," my father said as we passed the B&B that was once the Singleton Farm.

I pulled into the driveway and unlocked the front door, wondering if the girl ghosts would make themselves known. But they were nowhere in sight as Jim scrutinized every room, shooting out questions about insulation and the quality of the water supply, subjects I had no idea he knew anything about. But then again, working with Mac in Atlanta and being married to Merry had done a lot to make my father the man I wish he'd been when I was growing up.

"A wonderful house!" my father declared when we'd finished the inside and outside tour. "You two will be happy here."

I called Aunt Harriet and Uncle Bosco to let them know we were on our way to visit them and take them out to dinner. I wasn't too surprised when Aunt Harriet insisted that we eat there since she'd made too much food, as usual. And so, we had her wonderful meatloaf and a few other dishes I'm sure she'd pulled out of the freezer and put in the microwave as soon as she'd hung up the phone.

It warmed my heart to see my father and Uncle Bosco deep in conversation. Uncle Bosco hadn't always had a high opinion of his brother's son, who had spent time in prison. But those days were past, and now they enjoyed a good relationship.

I was telling Aunt Harriet and Merry about Winifred's outburst that afternoon, when my father interrupted his conversation with

Dylan and Bosco to call out, "Caro, when are your mother and her young husband arriving?"

My mother. Though my mother and I were getting along, I still walked on eggshells when she was around.

"They're flying in tomorrow afternoon. You'll probably run into them at the motel. Why do you ask?"

"Just wondering. I want to be on my guard when she shows up."

I drew in a deep breath, then realized he was kidding. Last spring, when my mother and Tom were in Clover Ridge for a filming, my father had flown here to give her some much needed moral support.

We spent the evening reminiscing about the past and talking about the future—probably like any other family getting together two nights before a wedding. Not a word was said about the body found on the lawn of our wedding venue or that the murderer was still on the loose.

* * *

The landline phone rang at eight the following morning. I sprang awake in full pre-wedding mode. Had a catastrophe damaged Victor's house? Had the health department shut down the restaurant where we were having the rehearsal dinner tonight?

Dylan reached over me to lift the receiver. I stared at him as he spoke to the caller.

"Good morning . . . Not a problem . . . Oh, that's too bad . . . Yes, I'll put her on." Dylan frowned as he handed me the phone.

"Carrie, it's John. I'm sorry to bother you so early, and today of all days, but Winifred Thompson was murdered sometime last night. If you came into contact with her at the library yesterday, I need you to tell me exactly what you saw and heard."

Winifred's dead. "I only saw her for a moment as she was leaving Sally's office. I didn't even speak to her."

"Even so. She went to the library to stake her claim to Verity Babcock's diary, an artifact you've been closely involved with."

Fear coursed through my body. Surely John didn't think that I had murdered Winnie because she was about to sue the library to get Verity's diary.

"But the diary's been stolen," I stuttered. "It's a moot point."

"No matter. I'm interested in Winnie's frame of mind when she was in the library. Whom she spoke to, what they said."

"How did you know she was in the library yesterday?"

"Sally told me."

"Oh." Then I realized what he was saying. "You questioned Sally already? You can't think—"

"I don't think anything . . . yet. Carrie, can I stop by the cottage, or would you rather come down to the precinct?"

"Stop by here. Give me forty-five minutes to get ready."

"Will do."

Dylan and I had breakfast, then he left to do some last-minute shopping and work out at the gym while I showered and dressed. John showed up close to ten o'clock. He looked harried, and knowing him, I figured he hadn't stopped for breakfast after a sleepless night.

I led him into the kitchen and brewed a carafe of coffee. "Croissant or bread?" I asked.

"A croissant would be great, thanks."

I let him settle down before I bombarded him with the many questions that had crossed my mind since he'd told me that Winnie Thompson had been murdered. Finally, after he swallowed the last bite of his croissant, I asked, "How did you find out that Winnie had been murdered?"

John moved his chair back and stretched out his long legs. "Lauren, one of her daughters, called me because she couldn't reach Winnie. Lauren had an important meeting in the city and was expecting her mother to be at her house at seven to watch the kids, since both of them were too sick to go to day care. Lauren knew something was wrong because her mother was never late. I went over to Winnie's house. When she didn't respond, I entered and found her lying on her office floor. She'd been stabbed."

"But how did you know she'd been to the library yesterday and that she and Sally had words?"

"Her laptop was open. She'd been writing a letter to the editor, demanding that the library hand over the diary of her ancestor Verity Babcock to her, its rightful owner." John paused. "And we checked her phone calls. She'd been on the phone with Sally that evening."

I stared at him. "You can't imagine that Sally stabbed Winnie. They were both Wise Women. They've known each other for years."

John scoffed. "Since when does being in a long-term relationship stop people from killing each other? Quite the opposite. It's often the reason—long festering resentments and the like."

"But Sally had nothing against Winnie. She was simply annoyed that Winnie was trying to take the diary from the library."

"Is that what you heard yesterday?"

My cheeks grew warm as I recalled Sally's words. "She said Winnie would get the diary over her dead body. I spoke to Sally afterward. She'd called the library's attorney, and he reassured her that we owned the diary. He advised her to search for a note that might have accompanied the diary when it was bequeathed to us, which Sally was planning to do. She didn't seem unduly worried."

"Then why did she call Winnie?" John asked. "Sally's phone records show that she called Winnie at eight thirty. She admitted going to see Winnie a few minutes later."

"I don't know. To make amends of some sort? To explain that what Winnie was doing was having a negative impact on Verity's reputation? On the Wise Women's reputation?"

"What's this about the Wise Women's reputation?" John asked.

I bit my lip. Why had I brought that up? "Sally thought that Winnie was acting irrationally. She was obsessed with getting the diary for herself instead of focusing on getting a pardon for Verity Babcock.

"I mean, look at Winnie's stupid spat with Garrett Grimm in the *Gazette*. Both of them arguing about people who lived four hundred years ago. And Grimm made a nasty crack about the Wise Women. I'm sure it infuriated Winnie."

"I'll have to read it," John said.

"Why don't you question Grimm? Maybe he was angry enough to kill Winnie. Or maybe Fred Rawlins made a return visit to demand his fee."

"Of course I'll question Garrett Grimm. And Rawlins too, just as soon as we can locate him."

"Have you managed to find Leslie to question him?" I asked.

"No, much as I'd like to. I understand he and his mother had an acrimonious relationship."

I released a deep sigh and told him what I'd witnessed when Winnie showed up at the deli while Leslie was working. To give John credit, he didn't berate me for having gone to the deli to spy on Leslie.

"I wouldn't be surprised if Leslie's with Fred Rawlins," I said.

"Me neither," John said, "especially if they were both in on the diary theft."

"And maybe Winnie's murder too," I added softly.

"Is there anything else you remember hearing when Winnie and Sally were arguing?"

"Well, Winnie took offense that Sally had dared to tell her that her own son probably stole the diary."

"Do you think she really was offended or angry? Because if Leslie was the one who stole the diary, he certainly didn't hand it over to her."

"I think she was genuinely pissed at Sally for making such a suggestion."

John grimaced as he stood to leave, looking as discouraged as I'd ever seen him. And who could blame him? He now had three unsolved murders and a robbery to solve. I wished there was something I could do, but I was getting married tomorrow evening and in no position to help him. Although I hoped I had successfully changed his mind about considering Sally Prescott a viable suspect.

"I'm sorry I spoiled your day by questioning you about Winifred Thompson's homicide," he said.

I shrugged. "You have your job to do."

"Still," he said, trying to lighten the tone, "I promise the next time we talk will be at the rehearsal dinner tonight. And it won't be about murder."

I felt unsettled as I walked him to the door. Dylan and I were getting married tomorrow and leaving for Greece on Sunday. I hated going away with unsolved murder cases hanging over Clover Ridge, but there was nothing I could do.

Dylan arrived home at eleven thirty while I was packing for our honeymoon. After he showered and dressed, I told him what John and I had talked about. I finished by griping, "I can't believe he seriously considered Sally a suspect."

"You know as well as I do he has to question everyone who recently argued with Winifred."

"That includes her own son as well as Fred Rawlins and Garrett Grimm. What do you know about Grimm?" I asked."

"Not much," Dylan said, "since he's about fifteen years older than me and we never traveled in the same circles. The word is he's a wheeler-dealer kind of guy. Always looking to make a fast buck on some kind of a scheme, and from what you've told me, kind of obsessed with preventing Verity Babcock from being pardoned as a victim of witchcraft because he believes she murdered his ancestor."

I shuddered. "He's creepy. And he likes to argue with everyone."

"I don't blame you for not liking him, the way he stormed into your office last week." Dylan reached over to rub my cheek. "But let's not talk about this anymore this weekend. We have more important things to do."

"Do we ever."

The doorbell rang. Dylan and I looked at each other. "Did my father say he and Merry would be stopping by today?" I asked.

"Not to me," Dylan said as he went to open the door. "And who might you be?" he asked Albi, whose eyes darted about. He looked frightened and about to run off.

"What are you doing here?" I asked. "How did you find out where I lived?"

Albi cringed. "I went to the library looking for you. They told me you were home because you're getting married tomorrow." He looked from me to Dylan. "I know you must be very busy, but I had to talk to you, Carrie. Miss Singleton. I'm afraid . . ."

"Afraid of what?"

I motioned to Albi to enter the cottage. He hesitated then stepped into the hall.

"This is Albi Valdez," I told Dylan. "Brother of Tino Valdez, who knocked me unconscious."

"Your brother did that, and you expect Carrie to help you?" Dylan said.

Albi reared back. "I'm sorry. Tino's all riled up. He's not usually like that."

His eyes swept from left to right, like he was searching for an escape route, and I knew he was about to take off.

I reached for his arm. "Come on inside and tell us what you're afraid of."

Albi glanced at Dylan, then followed me into the living room, where we all sat down.

"Tino's been released," Albi said breathlessly. "Now he's out searching for the money his pal Luke hid before he was murdered."

"The bank money he, Luke, and Billy Carpenter stole five years ago?" I asked.

Albi nodded.

That confirms one big question, I thought.

"Did your brother murder Luke and Billy?" Dylan asked.

"No! I swear he didn't!" Albi rapped his fingers against his leg.

The kid was jumpy and speaking in riddles. I leaned toward him and gazed into his eyes. "What exactly do you want me to do?"

"Stop him!" Albi drew back, as though his own words had shocked him. "Tino knows Luke killed Billy and hid the money. He figures if it's not in that shed, then Luke stashed it somewhere else."

"Where else?" Dylan asked.

Albi shrugged. "I've got no idea, but Tino said once he finds the money, he'll take off. Leave town."

Dylan and I looked at each other. Why was he telling us this? It made no sense. Albi must have read our expressions because he let out a grunt of frustration.

"You don't get it. My brother's a screwup. He can't take care of himself. I told Tino he has no choice but to find the money and follow the guy's instructions. If he runs, the guy is sure to track him down and kill him . . ." Albi shuddered.

"What instructions? What guy?" Dylan asked.

Albi swallowed. "Tino calls him the Boss. I don't think he knows the guy's real name, or at least he won't tell me who he is." He drew in a deep breath. "Tino says the person disguises his voice on the phone. All I know is the Boss set up the bank job and is furious because the job never paid off. He went bonkers when he found out Billy hid the money and then Luke got hold of it. He thinks Tino killed Luke and stashed the money somewhere. He's giving Tino till five PM tomorrow to hand over the money or he's dead like his friends."

"This guy sounds dangerous," Dylan said. "Are you sure you don't want to go to the police?"

"Don't you think I tried?" Albi said. "Tino says no way. The police will throw him in prison. And for what? Tino says he got nothing from the bank job. So why should he do time when he got nothing out of it?" Albi looked at me then at Dylan. "My brother sees the world from his own skewed perspective. Actually, from Luke's perspective—until he was murdered."

"Was Luke the leader of the trio?" I asked.

"You mean Tino, Luke, and Billy? Yeah, he was. They did whatever Luke said."

"Except Billy ran off with the cash and went to prison for it," Dylan said. "He intended to keep it all."

"It looks that way," Albi said. "I never thought Billy was solid with Luke and Tino, but my brother worshipped Luke. He went along with whatever Luke said."

"Now I have a better understanding of the trio's dynamics," I said. "Albi, what exactly do you want me to do?"

"Talk to Tino. Make him see that running isn't an option. Let's hope he finds the money and settles with the Boss. This way he comes out of it alive. Then we'll make him see that he has no choice but to give himself up. Maybe they'll go easy on him because he didn't benefit from the heist."

Albi shuddered. "And please don't tell the police what I just told you, whatever you decide."

Chapter
Twenty-One

D ylan and I stared at Albi, both of us too dumbstruck to speak. Albi remained silent. He wasn't relaxed, but now that he'd said his piece, he seemed calmer.

Dylan was the first to speak a coherent sentence. "Albi, you know Carrie and I are getting married this weekend. In a few hours we have our wedding rehearsal and then our rehearsal dinner. You can't expect us to get involved in your brother's criminal escapades."

"Tino's not planning anything criminal besides finding that money."

"Either way, absconding with the money or handing it over to the guy who masterminded the heist both sound illegal to me," I said.

Albi nodded. "I know, and I just got an idea that's a win–win solution for Tino—if he finds the money."

"We're listening," Dylan said.

"The cops want to recover the bank money that Luke hid. If Tino finds it and you can convince him to hand it over to the authorities, maybe they won't charge him if he helps set a trap to nab the Boss."

This is one smart kid, I thought.

"That's a great idea," Dylan said. "Lieutenant John Mathers is a good friend of ours. He'll listen to you and Tino."

"No!" Albi shouted. "No police. Not yet. Miss Singleton—Carrie—my brother knows you've helped solve murders. He's terrified of the Boss. I think that's really why he wants to leave town. But he's not smart enough to make it on his own."

He put his head in his hands. "I can't deal with this anymore. I'm supposed to be at my graduation this afternoon and thinking about my future, when all I can think about is stopping my brother from getting killed!"

"Where's Tino now?" I asked.

"Carrie . . ." Dylan said. "What are you thinking?"

"Maybe we should talk to Tino, try to convince him not to do anything stupid."

Albi's fingers were flying on his phone. "I'm texting him right now."

A minute later, he was speaking to Tino. His tone was calm and measured. I got the feeling that Albi had plenty of experience talking his brother down from reckless plans and crazy situations.

"Yes, they've agreed to hear you out," Albi said. "No, they swear they won't rat you out to the police . . .Yeah, you can trust them."

He repeated the same sentences a few times without a trace of impatience. Finally, Tino agreed to meet us.

Dylan and I exchanged glances. I did not want Tino Valdez coming here to our cottage. "Ask Tino to meet us in town in half an hour," I said to Albi. "There's a coffee shop on Walnut Street, a few blocks past the supermarket."

Albi gave his brother the information and nodded to me as he disconnected the call. "Tino knows the place. He'll be there. And he's sorry he hit you, Carrie."

"Do you have a photo of Tino?" I asked.

"Oh, right." Albi got busy on his phone and brought up a photo of the two brothers clowning around, their arms wrapped around each other's shoulders. They both had dark curly hair and narrow faces, and resembled each other, but while Albi's eyes sparkled with life, I saw defeat in Tino's.

I walked Albi to the front door.

"Thanks, Carrie, for helping Tino deal with this problem he got himself into. I know he might end up in prison, but that's better than running away or double-crossing a guy who's threatened to kill him if he doesn't come up with the money."

I watched him drive off in a dark blue sedan at least eight years old. It had been recently washed, and the motor ran smoothly, both evidence of Albi's meticulous care. *Interesting, how two siblings can be so different,* I thought. Tino Valdez was lucky to have a younger brother who loved him so much.

Ten minutes later Dylan and I climbed into his BMW and headed for the coffee shop in town.

"I never expected to be talking down a potential fugitive the day before our wedding," Dylan said.

"Me neither. I wonder who this Boss is who set up the bank robbery," I said. "Tino doesn't even know his name, and yet he's terrified of him."

"Tino must be terrified, period, with John liking him as a suspect for his friends' homicides. I hope he shows up at the diner now and doesn't get cold feet."

"Me too."

My cell phone played it's jingle. "Good morning, Caro! How are you today?"

"Hi, Dad. Were the accommodations all right?"

"The motel is great. We slept well and had a lovely breakfast. Merry and I were wondering if you were up to having company."

"Er, we're not home right now, so we'll see you at the rehearsal. You have the directions to Victor's house, right?"

"Yes, I remembered to bring them—that is, Merry remembered."

"That's great, Dad. See you there at five."

"Are you okay? You sound rushed. Where are you off to?"

"Just to take care of a few things."

"I was wondering—"

"See you later." I disconnected and shook my head. "Right now I wish I could concentrate on our wedding plans and nothing else."

Dylan smiled at me. "We'll hear Tino out, give him our advice, then it's up to him to decide what to do."

I reached over to grasp Dylan's hand. "Should we be telling John what Albi told us?"

"So far it's hearsay, so John can't do anything with the information. And we told the kid we'd hold off, so let's do that until after we speak to Tino."

Though the diner was filling up with the lunch crowd, we managed to snag a booth in the far corner. We were ten minutes early, so I didn't expect Tino to have beaten us there. A waitress in her forties asked if we were ready to order. We said not yet but asked her to bring us coffee.

When the ten minutes had passed, I began to fidget.

"Let's order something," Dylan said.

"Good idea."

I ordered a tuna fish sandwich. Dylan ordered an egg salad sandwich. "And a burger and a coke," he said.

As our waitress returned with our order, I caught sight of Tino Valdez standing in the doorway of the diner. I recognized him from his photo. I knew he was twenty-five or twenty-six, but his scrawny frame made him look both less mature and wizened at the same time—like an apple that had never matured and was drying up.

Tino looked around furtively, as if he had no business being there. When he noticed me waving, he drew in a deep breath before heading to our table.

As Tino approached, Dylan moved from his side of the booth, to sit next to me. Now that he was so close, I could see he was thin almost to the point of emaciation. He looked terrified as he slid into the seat across from us.

"Tino, I'm Carrie Singleton, and this is my fiancé, Dylan Avery. Your brother thinks I—we can help you."

Tino licked his lips. "I sure hope so. Things have gotten real sticky lately, with Luke and Billy murdered and . . . stuff," he finished lamely.

"We're here to listen to you and come up with what we consider the best solution to your situation," Dylan said.

"Yeah." Tino stared at the burger in front of him.

"Why don't we eat first and talk after?" Dylan said. "Tino, the burger's yours. We ordered it for you."

"Really? Thanks."

We ate in silence. Tino wolfed down his food and was the first to finish. If his behavior and appearance were anything to go by, he hadn't been eating regularly. I brushed the observation aside because I didn't want to feel sorry for Tino's no-win situation, which he'd managed to get into all by himself. I was helping him for Albi's sake and hopefully to keep him from doing something stupid. All the while, I didn't for one moment forget that he'd knocked me unconscious.

Tino's thoughts must have been running along the same lines, because he said, "Carrie, I'm really sorry I hit you."

"So am I," I said.

Dylan cleared his throat. "Tino, why don't you tell us what's going on, starting with the bank robbery."

"You know about that," Tino said.

"Not as much as we'd like," I said.

"Okay. About five and a half years ago, this guy approached Luke and laid out plans for him and a few guys to rob a bank in Hartford. He said the two guards were useless, and it would be an easy heist. Luke talked it over with me, and we decided to bring Billy in."

"Just a minute," I said. "Who is this guy that arranged the plans for the heist with Luke? Albi said you don't even know his name?"

"Luke never said, though I know he did a few one-man jobs for him over the years." Tino sighed. "Luke and me were really tight, but this was one thing he always held back—who the guy was. He called him the Boss, so that's what I called him when he contacted me."

Tino gulped down the rest of his water. "Do you think I could have another soda?"

"Sure." Dylan called over our waitress. "Another Coke, please. Carrie?"

"Coffee, please."

"Make that two coffees."

"Thanks," Tino said. "Over the years I asked Luke what the Boss made of Billy taking off with the bank money. Luke told me not to worry, that the Boss could be patient when he needed to be."

"In other words, he was waiting for Billy to get out of prison," I said. "Do you think he killed Billy?"

Tino looked like he was about to cry. "I don't know. I don't know if he did it, if Luke did, or Billy's cellmate. I only know I had nothing to do with his murder."

"What about Luke?" Dylan asked. "He must have been furious at Billy."

"Yeah. He was angry, all right. Luke couldn't believe Billy would double-cross us." He laughed. "Actually, he was kinda shocked that he was smart enough to pull off a stunt like that. Luke said we'd get the money as soon as Billy got out of prison."

"Someone managed to get it," I said.

"Wasn't me. I figured it was Luke or Fred Rawlins who killed Billy, so I took to following them whenever I could."

The waitress brought our drinks. We waited while Tino downed his soda.

"Then Luke was out of the picture, courtesy of Rawlins I suppose, so I followed Rawlins, careful to make sure he didn't make me and off me too. He led me to Luke's parents' home." He looked apologetically at me. "Sorry again."

"How did you know Fred Rawlins didn't get the bank money when he killed your friend Luke?" I asked.

"I know Luke. At least, I used to. He was sneaky that way. He'd never keep all that money in his apartment. Somehow Rawlins figured out that shed behind Luke's parents' house was a possible place where Luke might have hidden the money."

"When did the Boss contact you?" Dylan asked.

"The day after Luke was killed. He called me and said I needed to hand over the money from the bank job on Saturday afternoon or I'd be joining my two friends. I told him I had no idea where the money was. He said maybe that was true, which was why he was giving me a few days to find it. He had no intention of waiting any longer than that. When I asked about my cut, he said he'd let me know after I delivered the money."

"I can't believe this guy, supposedly the brains behind the heist, wants to meet you after all this time he's kept his identity a secret," Dylan said.

"Oh, he doesn't want to meet me. The guy calls me every morning to find out if I've made any progress. When I tell him I've found the money, he'll say where to drop it off."

"Careful, isn't he?" I commented.

"He doesn't like to get his hands dirty," Dylan said. "No offense, Tino, but he picked the wrong thieves for the job."

"And now he's gonna kill me if I don't come up with the dough."
Tino began to sniffle, and I hoped he wasn't about to break down
and sob. "Maybe kill me even if I do. That's why I figure my only
chance is to find the money and leave town. Albi says I won't be able
to make it on my own." He covered his face with his hands.

Dylan and I looked at each other.

"You're sure you don't want to tell all this to the police?" I asked.

"No! I wouldn't have come today if I thought you'd say something stupid like that." Now his face was flushed with anger.

"Easy there," Dylan said calmly. "We're just looking at all the
alternatives."

"Well, going to the cops isn't one of them," Tino growled.

"Is there any other place where Luke might have hidden the
money?" I asked.

"Yeah, there is. But I'm not saying till I go there and see for
myself." He smiled. It wasn't a pleasant sight. "And I'm going there
right now, while the police are questioning Fred Rawlins and he can't
beat me to it."

"How do you know he's being questioned?" I asked.

"I saw him being brought in as I was leaving the precinct."

"I'm glad they caught up with him since he's a suspect in Luke
Rizzo's murder," Dylan said.

Tino let loose a neighing laugh. "And maybe another murder
too."

My pulse began to race. "What are you talking about, Tino?"

"I'm pretty good at tailing people, if I do say so myself. Since I
knew where Fred Rawlins was holing up, I stayed on his tail. And
guess where he led me to last night? Turns out he parked and got out
of his car half a block from where that old lady was murdered."

Chapter Twenty-Two

"We have to tell John that Rawlins was seen near Winnie's house last night," I said as soon as we left the diner.

Dylan laughed. "Tell John something he probably already knows?"

"How could he know what Tino just told us?

"Could be he brought Fred Rawlins in to question him regarding Winnie's murder because someone else saw him there last night."

"Really?" I scoffed. "This must have been after Sally had been to see Winnie."

"Carrie, people walk their dogs late into the night. Other people go running at all hours. Someone might have seen Rawlins. Or seen Tino skulking about. Besides, we don't know if Tino is lying about seeing Rawlins near Winifred's house. He has a particular grievance against Fred Rawlins, who he thinks murdered his friend Luke.

"At the same time, Tino's probably pissed at Luke for not sharing the money from the heist with him after he killed Billy and grabbed the loot. For all we know, Tino himself killed Luke before he could get his friend to tell him where he'd hidden the bank money."

"And what about Leslie Thompson?" I said. "Tino didn't mention seeing someone with Fred Rawlins."

"No, he didn't, though Leslie could have stayed in the car when Rawlins went inside to talk to Winnie. Or not. Maybe Leslie had nothing to do with what happened to his mother."

I sighed. "Too many possibilities."

"Which is why I think it's best to wait until Tino calls us once he's checked out that last hiding place," Dylan said.

"I suppose. This way we'll be honoring Tino's request not to bring in the police, and giving him a chance to find the money. It will look better if he shows up at the police station with the stolen money," I said. "Also, he'll have protection against the Boss, whoever he is."

"Yes." Dylan pulled me close. "I only wish this wasn't going down the weekend of our wedding."

We drove back to the cottage, both of us deep in thought. I ran through our conversation with Tino and was left with the definite feeling that, although he was convinced he was telling the truth, he was strung out—either from drugs or not eating and/or not sleeping—and driven by fear and anger. Tino had given us the bare facts, but there was more to the story.

The only way we could help him was to let him go ahead as he'd planned and take it from there. We'd explained we had our wedding rehearsal and rehearsal dinner and couldn't speak to him until later that evening, around ten and no later than eleven. Tino said he understood and might even get in touch with us the following morning.

I hoped he wouldn't run into any danger in the meantime, but there wasn't much chance of that. Fred Rawlins was down at the precinct being questioned, and the mysterious Boss always called in the morning for a report. Maybe Tino would be lucky for once and find the heist money. Then we could meet him tomorrow morning at the precinct and put in a good word for him—if he agreed with our plan.

It was a little past two when Dylan and I arrived home, which gave me an hour or so to finish packing before I got dressed for the evening's activities. The wedding rehearsal at Victor's house was scheduled for five o'clock, but Dylan and I planned to get there a half hour earlier. I called Victor to find out if the rental chairs had arrived, and he assured me that everything was going as planned. In fact, the crew that had delivered the chairs was now setting them up to our specifications.

My mother called to let me know that she and Tom were in their rental car and en route from the airport to their motel.

"Are you nervous?" she asked.

"Not really," I said.

"That's good. I was nervous for days before both my weddings. I hardly slept a wink or ate a morsel of food."

Before she could elaborate further, I told her I couldn't talk because I had to take care of a few things before the rehearsal.

"Carrie, please tell me how we get to your friend's house. I seem to have misplaced the directions."

I tamped down my exasperation. "The directions are up on the wedding website. Have Tom check it out if you have a problem. I'll text him the URL."

I disconnected and sighed as I sent Tom the link to our wedding website. My mother was in town.

"I told the maître d' at Due Amici we still needed the three tables for ten that we originally planned for," Dylan said. "He said the boss told him our guests can order whatever they like as a main course for the same price we'd agreed on."

I grinned. "That was kind of him," I said.

I finished packing, showered, then slipped into the silk fit-and-flare midi dress I'd bought to wear to the rehearsal dinner. It had tiny red, yellow, and blue flowers adorning a white background. I stepped into my navy slingbacks and twirled in front of the mirror. It was finally happening! Our wedding weekend was about to begin!

As we were leaving, Smoky Joe sensed something important was brewing and kept weaving around my feet.

"Sorry, boy, you can't come with us." I picked him up and held him close.

He meowed. I started to set him down, but he clung to me.

"I wish I could bring you tomorrow," I told him, "but a wedding is no place for a cat. Besides, I don't think Raspi would be happy to find a cat roaming through his house."

"Rasputin won't be at our wedding either," Dylan said. "He'll be at the house while we rehearse, but not tomorrow. Too much of a commotion for him, even if he were kept in a room upstairs, Victor said. He's boarding him overnight."

I smiled. "Victor has been such a good friend to us, letting us have the wedding at his house. We must find something very special for him while we're in Greece."

"I'm thinking a painting," Dylan said. "We'll search the galleries until we find one that he'll love."

I wrapped my arms around Dylan's neck. "You've come up with the best idea for a gift. One of the many reasons I love you."

His lips met mine, and for a moment I wanted nothing more than to stay in his embrace. But now wasn't the time to dillydally. Hand in hand, we left the cottage to begin the rituals and festivities of our wedding.

* * *

Victor, Babette, and Raspi greeted us at the front door with hugs and a tray bearing four flutes and a bottle of Cristal champagne. Victor led us into the kitchen, where he popped the cork with a flourish, poured, and toasted Dylan and me first in Serbian, then in English. Before we could take another sip, he ushered us into the living room, to survey the room where our wedding rehearsal would soon take place.

"As you can see, the chairs have been arranged so there's an aisle wide enough for everyone's comfort and adequate room for the ceremony in front of the bay window," Victor said.

"The flowers are arriving tomorrow afternoon," Babette said. "I'll make sure they're placed exactly as you want them—in this room and on the tables inside the tent."

A surge of excitement coursed through my body. Tomorrow evening, in less than thirty hours, I was becoming Carrie Singleton Avery. Everything was going to happen exactly as we'd planned because Victor and Babette would make sure that it did.

"Thank you both." I hugged each of them.

"They're coming at nine tomorrow morning to set up the tent," Victor went on. "And the caterers will be arriving no later than five."

"The musicians will arrive half an hour before we all go into the tent for dining and dancing," Babette added.

"It sounds like the two of you have everything under control," Dylan said, his voice trembling with emotion. "I can't tell you how much this means to Carrie and me."

Now it was Dylan's turn to embrace our hosts.

"We're so lucky, aren't we? To have such wonderful friends," I said.

"It's been our pleasure," Victor said.

Babette grinned. "And what fun we're having managing your wedding."

Have you made any plans for your own wedding? I wondered but didn't say aloud. We returned to the kitchen and finished our champagne.

I'd deputized Rosemary, Angela's mom, to send people down the "aisle," so to speak, during the rehearsal, as she'd recently overseen Angela and Steve's wedding a year ago. Babette's friend Danielle, the high school music teacher who also played the organ in her church, was handling the music for our ceremony, playing a tape she had made and used for several weddings.

My mother and Tom, her handsome younger husband, were the first to arrive. Dylan and I had no sooner introduced them to Victor and Babette, when my father and Merry made their appearance. Jim grabbed me in a bear embrace, and I held on to him for what seemed like minutes before greeting Merry. Then I watched as Jim introduced Merry to my mother and Tom while my mother simpered, and Merry, elegant and composed as always, said she was happy to finally meet them.

Great-Aunt Harriet and Great-Uncle Bosco joined us, followed by Angela and Steve and Angela's parents; my cousins Julia, Randy, Tacey, and Mark; and Gary Winton, Dylan's young associate. Dylan embraced Mac and his wife, whom I'd never met; and finally Mayor Al Tripp, who was performing the ceremony, arrived with his lovely wife, Dolores.

But where was Danielle? She came flying in at twenty past five, her hair disheveled as she apologized profusely, babbling about an accident on I-95 and how she should have exited sooner. We assured her there was no need to worry as this was only the rehearsal. Babette spoke to her, and minutes later Danielle had the digital recording going and we were ready to start.

The stirring notes of Pachelbel's Canon sounded, and I felt a surge of emotion as Al made his way down the aisle to the makeshift altar in the bay window. My matrons of honor and Dylan's grooms-men took their places.

"Walk *slowly*," Rosemary instructed, her whisper loud enough for all of us to hear. Though we were walking the length of the living room, the aisle was still considerably shorter than any place where weddings were routinely performed.

Great-Aunt Harriet and Great-Uncle Bosco followed, then my mother and Tom. Mark was solemn as our ring bearer, but Tacey couldn't stifle her excited giggles until her mother left her place to speak to her.

The music changed to Mendelssohn's "Wedding March." My father put my hand in the crook of his elbow and beamed down at me. "Ready?" he asked.

"Oh yes!"

We hugged, knowing what we were really saying. Rosemary prodded me, and slowly Jim and I started down the aisle.

When the rehearsal was over, everyone took turns embracing Dylan and me. We were surrounded by the people we loved and who loved us. Victor served flutes of champagne to the adults, and soda to Mark and Tacey. Then suddenly there was a flurry of activity as we raced from the house and headed to our cars to set out for the rehearsal dinner.

Luigi, Due Amici's maître d', had set up the tables for our party in the far corner of the restaurant, a good distance from the other diners. As soon as we arrived, two waitresses placed a bottle of red wine and a bottle of white wine on each of the three tables. I directed our guests to their seats. In addition to our wedding party, we'd invited Victor and Babette and John and Sylvia to the dinner. My parents and their spouses, Harriet and Bosco, and Mac and his wife were sitting with Dylan and me.

When everyone was seated, my father stood and toasted Dylan and me. Luigi and Dom, the restaurant's owner, joined in drinking a glass of wine to our health and congratulated us while Tacey and Mark sipped soda. Our waitresses brought out baskets of warm rolls and tricolor salads, then went around with large pepper mills.

Spirits were high as we ate and chatted. As the salad plates were being cleared, Dylan and I visited our guests at the other two tables. Victor was holding court at his and Babette's table, where Sylvia Mathers sat beside an empty seat.

"John's on his way," she said before I could ask. "He's busy with the latest case."

"I can imagine," I said. "You must be upset. Poor Winnie."

"Yes. Poor Winnie. She seemed to be going off the rails these past few weeks. Carrying on about that diary as if she deserved to own it because Verity Babcock was her ancient relative."

"She did seem obsessed by it," I agreed.

Sylvia looked around and lowered her voice. Though no one was paying us any attention, I knew what she was about to say had something to do with the Wise Women. "We've decided to go ahead and write to the state legislature again to seek exoneration for Verity. We're also setting up a scholarship to honor Verity and Winnie. After all, Winnie was an important contributor to our group for many years"

"I think that's fitting and will be appreciated by Winnie's friends and family."

Sylvia smiled. "Sally's told me your thoughts about joining us. I know how busy you're going to be these next few years, but I'm hoping you'll change your mind eventually."

"It's a possibility," I agreed.

When Dylan and I returned to our table for our next course, a serving of pasta, we found my parents and their spouses in an active four-way conversation. I'd placed my mother and Tom next to my aunt and uncle, who were excellent conversationalists, if not especially fond of my mother; and Jim and Merry next to Mac and his wife because they knew each other quite well.

My mother reached past Dylan, who was talking to Uncle Bosco, to touch my arm. "Merry was telling me that she and your father are planning a river trip up the Danube. That's just what Tom and I have been thinking of doing."

"That's nice," I said.

To my surprise, she tightened her grip. "Carrie, I can't tell you how thrilled I am that you and Dylan are getting married."

My surprise must have shown on my face because my mother burst out laughing.

"I know I haven't been the mother you must have wanted, and I'm sorry for that. But never doubt for one minute that I love you very much and want you to be happy." She lowered her voice. "As happy as Tom and I are."

I got up and hugged her. "Thanks so much for saying that."

"I mean it, Carrie. From my heart."

John came over to our table while we were eating our main course—Pesce Misto over angel hair for me and Chicken Scarpiello for Dylan. He exchanged greetings with Dylan and my father, and bussed my cheek.

"Sorry to get to your shindig so late but I've been busy interviewing witnesses and persons of interest."

"Regarding Winnie Thompson's homicide?" I asked.

"That and other cases."

Billy Carpenter and Luke Rizzo? I felt a pang of guilt for withholding information, but it was only until tomorrow morning, I reminded myself. Even so, Dylan and I knew nothing concrete about those murders.

I stood and looked around for one of the waitresses. "I'll have someone take your order."

John put a hand on my shoulder. "Please sit down, Carrie. My lovely wife is waving to me. She'll see to everything."

The rest of the evening flew by as I talked to the people dearest to me and dined on delicious food. Soon we were finishing off our meal with crème brûlée and coffee. Julia, Randy, and their kids came over to say good night and tell us they looked forward to our big day tomorrow.

"When you become Mrs. Avery, Cousin Carrie," Tacey added.

I hugged her tight.

"Too bad Miss Evelyn can't come to your wedding," she whispered.

"Too bad is right," I whispered back.

For some reason, we both burst out laughing. I knew that Tacey was going to have fun visiting Dylan and me at our new house, where she could play with the little girl ghosts.

Thinking of Abigail and Lucy gave me an idea. When the last of our guests bid us good night, I turned to Dylan. "How do you feel about stopping by our new house? Remember, I happen to have the key."

Chapter
Twenty-Three

After a flurry of goodbyes that seemed to go on for hours, we drove off. I put my head on Dylan's shoulder as we headed to our new home.

"I thought tonight went very well," Dylan said.

"I did too. Everyone seemed to have a good time. And the food was delicious, as always."

Dylan turned on the radio, and an old love song came on. We rode along without speaking. When the song ended, he said, "Tomorrow at this time we'll be married."

"Husband and wife," I said.

"Part of an age-old tradition."

"I'm kind of surprised we haven't heard from Tino. We told him the dinner would be over by ten o'clock, and it's ten thirty now."

"He might still call tonight. Better yet, in the morning." Dylan rested his hand on mine. "We have enough excitement in our lives without worrying about Tino Valdez. And if we don't hear from him by noon, we'll fill John in on what we know."

"Good plan," I said.

There were streetlamps along Old Willows Road, something I hadn't noticed on previous rides because we'd always driven here in daylight. They shed an inviting glow on the road, which wasn't a busy thoroughfare. Lights from the houses we passed shone as friendly beacons.

"I feel like the neighborhood is welcoming us," I said.

"Funny—I just had the same thought," Dylan said.

I turned to him. "Good thing I'm marrying you. Who else would think that?"

He squeezed my hand. "Who else indeed?"

The heavy foliage on the front lawn gave the house a dark, mysterious air. It cast shadows on the driveway and the path leading to the front door. One of our first projects would be to have the trees pruned and lights installed along the walk, I decided as we parked on the driveway. I unlocked the front door and we stepped inside. As soon as I switched on the light, the house emitted the cozy, warm ambiance I'd felt on my earlier visits.

It seemed natural to wander into the kitchen, which I considered the heart of our new home. The two little ghost girls manifested almost immediately.

"Welcome back, Carrie and Dylan," Abigail, the older sister, said. "We were wondering when you would return."

"Hey, Abigail and Lucy," Dylan said.

"Hello." I smiled at them. "Did you see us yesterday? We brought my father and his wife to show them our new house."

"We don't like to appear when there are too many people," Lucy said.

"I totally get that," Dylan said.

"When are you coming to live here with us?" Lucy asked.

"Not for a while," I said.

"How long is a while?" Abigail asked.

Dylan and I exchanged glances. "Most likely in a few months. Soon after the summer ends," he said.

"That's such a long time to wait." Lucy's face scrunched up as if she was about to cry.

"It's not really that that long," I said quickly. "Did you know Dylan and I are getting married tomorrow night?"

"Really?" Lucy squealed.

"Are you wearing a white gown?" Abigail asked, her eyes large as saucers.

"Of course."

"And then we're going on our honeymoon," Dylan said.

"Where?" Abigail asked.

Dylan and I spent the next half hour telling them about our wedding plans, and promised to bring photos the next time we came.

"And the two of you will take good care of our home until then, right?" I asked.

"Of course we will," Abigail assured us.

Lucy clapped her hands. "I can't wait for you to move in!"

"We're looking forward to that too," Dylan said.

* * *

When we arrived back at the cottage, I realized I was thoroughly exhausted. It had been a long and exciting day. Tomorrow would be even longer and more thrilling. Our wedding was an event we'd been looking forward to for a very long time. I got undressed and put on my nightgown, washed my face, and brushed my teeth.

"I'm going to sleep," I called out to Dylan, who was in the living room.

He looked up from checking messages on his cell phone. "Good idea. I'll be in soon."

"We haven't heard from Tino," I said as I got into bed.

"That's okay. He'll probably call in the morning."

"I wonder if he found the money."

"We'll find out tomorrow."

"It's practically tomorrow already."

I crept under the covers. Smoky Joe jumped into the bed and plopped down beside me. A minute later, I was sound asleep.

* * *

When I woke up, the sun was shining brightly—a perfect June morning, just as the weather forecaster had predicted. A perfect day for a wedding. Our wedding! I gazed down at my soon-to-be husband snoring gently in a deep sleep. Smoky Joe looked up at me from the floor and meowed.

"I'm coming," I said softly as I followed him into the kitchen.

"I hope you're not going to get spooked by the little girl ghosts in our new home," I told him as I dished out his food and put down a bowl of fresh water. "You've gotten less jumpy in the library when Evelyn appears, so hopefully you'll do the same with Abigail and Lucy."

Smoky Joe stopped eating suddenly and looked up at me. Was it possible that he'd understood what I was saying? Time would tell, I decided as he went back to his meal. It was interesting to think that Dylan and I were starting out our married life in our new home with two ghost children and a cat. And more children and pets hopefully to come!

I'd just finished my breakfast of toast and coffee when Dylan came into the kitchen, rubbing his eyes. "Has Tino called?" he asked.

I shook my head. "No, but it's only a quarter to nine."

"I don't like this. He said he'd call last night or early this morning."

"Maybe he went to that place and didn't find the money there," I said.

"He promised to let us know either way. We should bring him to the precinct before the deadline that guy gave him. I want to do it this morning. I'm not letting Tino's problems interfere with our wedding."

"Of course not," I said, managing to sound calmer than I felt. "But we don't have any obligations until four this afternoon, when my hair and makeup people get to work on Angela, Tacey, Julia, and me at Victor's house."

"Right after that we have photos, and then the ceremony at six," Dylan said. "If we're going to help Tino, it has to be soon."

"Of course," I said. "Sit down and I'll make you something to eat."

"Just coffee would be great. I want to finish packing."

I was a bit shaken to see Dylan stressed. He rarely got agitated, and not hearing from Tino wasn't a reason for him to be tense. But maybe it was pre-wedding jitters, I told myself. After all, grooms as well as brides were entitled to feel nervous before their big day.

Angela called to ask how I was doing. We chatted a bit, and I no sooner hung up than my mother called, wanting to know if I'd like her to come over for moral support.

Moral support? "Thanks, Mom. I'm fine."

Jim called a minute later. "How are you feeling, Caro? This is such an exciting day! I'm walking my daughter down the aisle."

"I'm great, Dad." *Why does everyone want to know how I'm feeling?* I glanced at Dylan, who was pacing, something I'd never seen him do before. "Want to speak to the groom?"

"Sure, honey, if you're busy."

"See you later."

"Of course you will."

I handed Dylan my cell phone. A few minutes later he was laughing and shooting the breeze with my father. Relieved, I took my shower and got dressed, prepared to start the day.

"Harriet called," Dylan said on his way to the shower. "She didn't say to call back. I told her you were fine. And that I'm fine."

"Why is everyone checking up on us?" I asked. "Are they afraid we're going to run off and elope? Or worse, cancel the big day?"

"*Our* big day," Dylan called from the bathroom.

Now the landline phone was ringing. It was Victor telling us the tent people had arrived and were setting up the tent. I thanked him and found myself on edge. There was nothing that required my attention. Even our flight to Greece tomorrow evening had been confirmed, along with our hotel reservations.

Smoky Joe came over and butted his head against my leg. I picked him up and kissed his forehead. I had cans of his food and a few of his toys ready for Marion when she came to pick him up later this morning. The thought of being away from my furry feline for such a long time made me sad. Though I knew that Marion would take good care of him, this was the first time we'd be apart since that day, almost two years ago, when he'd wandered onto the cottage lawn from the farm on the other side of the trees, and I'd ended up bringing him to the library with me.

Marion called to say she was on her way, and a few minutes later I put Smoky Joe in his carrier.

"Marion is going to take good care of you," I told him.

"Meow" was his reply.

Marion rang the doorbell five minutes later. I carried Smoky Joe out to her car while she grabbed the bag with his food and toys. She knew how hard this was for me, so she didn't stay to chat.

"He'll be fine," she said.

I nodded. "I know. Thank you for taking him."

"See you later," she called out the window as she drove off.

I watched the car ride down Avery Road until it disappeared from sight.

Now that Smoky Joe was gone, I wished there was something that needed my attention, but the only thing that Dylan and I had planned until later that afternoon was to wait to hear from Tino and escort him to the station. I'd called him twice so far, but both calls had gone straight to voicemail. It was beginning to look like, despite his promise yesterday, he didn't want our help after all.

I wondered if he'd found the money and decided to run off. Or maybe he hadn't found the money but had decided to run off anyway because he was terrified that the Boss—whoever he was—meant what he said and was going to kill him.

I reached for my cell phone to call John. But what would I tell him? That Tino Valdez was searching for the stolen money, but I had no idea where? That someone Tino had never met had threatened to murder him?

I glanced at the clock. It was almost eleven. Tino might still call. As soon as Dylan finished packing, we would decide what to do next.

I was so deep in thought that I jumped when my cell phone rang.

"Hello, Carrie." It was Albi. He sounded agitated.

"Yes, Albi. Where are you? Where's Tino?"

"I'm at a diner. Please listen. Tino's in the bathroom, so I don't have much time."

"Sure. Go on."

"He found the money yesterday, and he's going back there to get it."

"Where is it?"

"I don't know exactly. Luke's family has a cabin on a small lake outside of town. Mr. Rizzo likes to fish on weekends. He sometimes brought Luke and Tino along when they were in high school—not that they were big on fishing. Anyway, Tino figured if Luke didn't hide the money in his parents' shed, it was probably stashed away in the cabin. So he went there yesterday and found the two duffel bags of money. He's going back for them now. Then he's taking off."

"Tino's leaving town? But that's the worst thing he can do."

"I know, and I've been arguing with him all morning, trying to change his mind. He figures his best bet is to grab the money and get as far from Clover Ridge as he can. Start a new life somewhere else. But"—Albi's voice broke—"Tino can't manage on his own. I did my best to convince him to do what you guys arranged, but he's scared that dude plans to kill him, whether he gives him the money or not."

A real possibility, I thought.

"Carrie, you and Dylan gotta stop him."

Of course we do. "Can you keep him at the diner until we get there?"

"I don't know. He's stressed out. When he gets like this, he has to keep moving."

I sighed. This wasn't what we'd signed on for, but we couldn't let Tino carry out his crazy plan. "Are you going to the cabin with him?"

"No, but first he's dropping me off at home and picking up a suitcase and box of stuff he already packed. I'll stall him as long as I can, then hop in my car and follow him. I'll give you directions as we drive. You gotta talk some sense into him."

"Where are you now?"

He named a diner about fifteen minutes away. "Gotta go. Tino's coming back to the table."

"Give me your home address. We'll get there as soon as we can."

"We're at 435 Sycamore."

I disconnected and went to find Dylan. He was on the phone with my father. When he caught my expression, he said a hasty goodbye.

"You heard from Tino?"

"Albi just called. Tino found the money and he's pulling a runner as soon as he goes back there to collect it. But first he's stopping by his home for his things. Albi's going to lead us to the place so we can try to talk some sense into Tino."

"Let's go."

Minutes later, we were in Dylan's BMW, speeding toward Tino and Albi's home. I called Albi. He didn't answer, so I figured he was still in his brother's car, heading for home and not able to talk. He called me back a few minutes later, sounding miserable.

"I'm in my bedroom, waiting for Tino to leave. Mom just came home. She carried on about him not coming to my graduation yesterday, then started crying when she saw him putting his suitcase in his car. Now she's trying to convince him not to leave."

"Why don't we talk to your brother while he's still at the house," Dylan said. "We're only a few minutes away."

"Too late! Tino just stormed out the front door with a box of his possessions. I'll give him a good lead, then follow and let you know where he's heading. The cabin must be north of here."

A few minutes later, Albi called again. "Tino just turned onto Route 77. I'll give him a head start then follow. I don't want him to see my car."

"I hope you don't lose him. What's Tino driving?"

"A gray 2010 Toyota Camry with a dent in the passenger's door." Albi laughed. "Don't worry, Carrie. There's no way I can lose him. When I bought my car a few months ago, we linked up on an app so we can track each other. Tino must have forgotten, but I have him on my GPS."

"If Tino found the money yesterday, why didn't he take off then?" Dylan asked.

"Good question. I thought it was because he'd decided to stay for my graduation yesterday afternoon. Only he never showed. He apologized for missing it and said he had to see a few people before he left. I'm thinking there's a girl he likes, but I don't know her name."

Or maybe he delayed taking off because he's not sure about leaving, I thought. "I hope we can convince Tino to turn himself in, along with the money from the bank robbery."

"It would go a long way to shortening his prison sentence," Dylan said. "Especially if he had no part in killing his two friends."

"He didn't," Albi said.

We drove past a few small towns. The road narrowed as we drove through a rural area with farms and woods on both sides. At one point a huge tractor slowed us down. I began to grow anxious. "We've been driving for twenty minutes," I said to Dylan.

"Call Albi," Dylan said.

He answered immediately. "I think we're getting close. Tino just stopped at a general store. Probably to buy supplies." His voice grew shaky. "He really means to go through with his stupid plan."

"We're stopping," I said as Dylan pulled over to the side of the road.

"Yeah, I did too."

I got out of the car. The sun was strong now, and the air carried the scent of wildflowers growing in the undergrowth of bushes and trees that edged the road. There was very little traffic here, and the vehicles that passed us were old trucks and even older cars.

I called Albi. "Did Tino ever say where he planned to go?"

"He mentioned Canada. When I asked which part, he said he didn't know. Then he said maybe Maine would be far enough away to make his escape. We have cousins who live in Maine, but we haven't seen them in years."

"So he doesn't have a definite plan in mind," I said.

"Are you kidding?" Albi sniffled, and I was pretty sure that he was crying. "It's no surprise. My brother can't make a plan to save himself. He even . . ."

"Yes?"

"He asked me if I'd go with him. I told him I couldn't. I'm starting college in two months. Tino apologized for asking and said he didn't want to ruin my life too." Albi gulped. "Now I feel bad. He's my older brother, but as long as I can remember, I've been looking out for him."

"Try not to feel guilty, Albi," I said. "Tino's right. You have to lead your own life. And right now you're helping him do what's best for him."

"Yeah, so why do I feel so awful?"

Chapter
Twenty-Four

"Tino just left the general store, carrying two bags of groceries." Albi paused. "He's moving on. I'll follow as soon as I'm out of range of his rearview mirror."

"We're right behind you," I said.

A few minutes later, Albi called. "He's turning right."

"Got it," Dylan said.

We drove onto a tarred road in sad need of repair. I caught a glimpse of a lake through the trees.

"I'm slowing down," Albi said. "According to the app, Tino's car has stopped. Oh! I see it. He pulled into a driveway on the right. The car's mostly hidden by some trees. I can make out part of the cabin."

"Stop where you are and wait for us," Dylan said. "We're only a minute or two behind you."

We parked behind Albi's car. I stepped carefully through the undergrowth that grew to the edge of the road, so I could see the log cabin. It wasn't very large, and I imagined there were no more than two rooms inside. Tino's beat-up Camry stood in the driveway. Dylan and Albi came over to join me.

"He's probably inside," Albi said, pointing at the cabin.

I heard a car drive by. It slowed down, and I caught a glimpse of green as it passed our cars, then continued on its way.

"Did you notice the car that just drove by?" I asked Dylan. "I thought I saw it drive by when we stopped near the general store."

He shook his head. "No, but there are more houses and cabins farther down this road."

"Did Tino tell you where the bags of money were hidden?" I asked Albi.

"He found them in the crawl space above the bathroom ceiling. He said they were jammed in tight."

The three of us crept along the driveway to the front door of the cabin.

"Albi, does Tino carry a gun?" Dylan asked.

"Jeez, no! Why would you think that?"

When Dylan made no response, Albi said, a bit embarrassed. "He usually has his John Wick knife with him. That's a—"

"Microtech ultratech?" Dylan asked.

"Not exactly." Albi laughed. "Those cost big bucks. Tino has a cheaper version."

"Good to know," Dylan muttered.

"He keeps it for protection, not to attack anyone. At least I don't think he'll go after you."

"I'll deal with Tino," Dylan said." He focused on me, then on Albi. "I want both of you to remain outside the cabin, understood?"

"All right," I agreed. Dylan had more experience handling guys who might be armed. He wanted to make sure that Tino wouldn't attack me or hold me hostage because I was the weakest link. I felt both grateful for Dylan's presence and guilty for having dragged him into this situation.

We both looked at Albi. "Sure," he muttered.

"Wait here until I come out," Dylan said.

Albi and I watched him turn the knob of the cabin door, pull it open, and enter.

I stared at the cabin, wishing I could see what was happening inside. The exterior was made of smooth slats of wood. The side adjacent to the front door had a large window and a smaller one farther down. I caught Albi's eye and pointed at the large window to let him know I intended to peer in to find out what was happening. I planned to stand to one side so I wouldn't alert Tino and perhaps put Dylan in danger. After all, Tino had a knife, and any sudden noise or the sight of someone spying on him would make him more nervous and exacerbate the situation.

"Get away from that window! Come and stand next to my car!" The voice was low. Menacing. And somehow familiar.

I turned around, into the grinning face of Garrett Grimm. He was holding a gun.

"Jeez! Who are you?" Albi demanded. "Are you . . . the Boss?"

"Indeed I am, and you must be Albi." Grimm pointed the gun at the door. "Is your brother inside?"

"How did you find us?" Albi asked.

"How do you think?" I followed your idiot brother." He looked at me like I was milk that had gone rancid. "And what are you doing here, Miss Nancy Drew. Isn't today supposed to be your wedding day?"

A shiver ran down my spine as I walked past Tino's car and came to stand next to Grimm's even older car. Sally's description of the lime-green jalopy must have come to mind when I saw the car drive past us as soon as we'd stopped at the cabin. But I'd never imagined that the driver was Garrett Grimm. He had doubled back and surprised Albi and me. It was all coming together. Or was it?

Garrett Grimm looked like he'd dressed for a role in a play. He wore a hat like the one Harrison Ford wore in the Indiana Jones movies, along with a suede vest, jeans, and brown boots that appeared to be brand new. From the awkward way he held the gun, I found it hard to consider this writer of disgruntled letters to the *Gazette* as dangerous. Even his death threat to Tino seemed over the top.

"You really set up the bank robbery?" I couldn't help asking.

My incredulity made Grimm scowl. "What? You don't believe I'm capable of it?"

"No, I believe you," I said quickly. "I'm just surprised, that's all."

"Of course you're surprised. I keep a low profile. I prefer to keep it that way." Grimm looked around and returned his attention to me. "I suppose your boyfriend is inside, trying to make Valdez give up the loot like a good little boy."

"Dylan's inside."

"Is he armed?"

I paused. Dylan owned a gun, but he would have told me if he'd brought it along with him today. "No, he isn't."

Grimm turned to Albi. "Does your brother have a gun?"

"No."

"In that case, let's go inside and join the others."

Neither Albi nor I moved.

"What are you going to do?" Albi asked.

"What do you think? Take the money." Grimm let out a weird laugh that sent chills down my back. Suddenly I was terrified of this scrawny man in cowboy duds.

"I mean, are you going to let us go?" Albi persisted. I had to give him points for courage. We were facing possible death, and he was daring to ask about our fate.

Grimm scratched his chin and smiled. Not a pleasant sight. "I haven't decided what to do with all of you."

"Did you kill Billy Carpenter?" I asked.

"I did not."

I breathed a sigh of relief. If Garrett Grimm hadn't killed anyone, maybe he'd balk at killing us.

"Did you kill Luke?" Albi asked.

"Maybe I did. Maybe I didn't." Grimm let loose another burst of demonic laughter.

"So it was you I saw . . .?" Albi began, then shut up when he caught me glaring at him. A witness was all Grimm needed as an excuse to shoot Albi, Dylan, and me.

"You saw me?" Grimm narrowed his eyes as he demanded an answer from Albi.

"I saw someone leaving Luke's apartment the day he was murdered," Albi said. "I was pretty sure it was . . ." He hesitated as though reluctant to give up a name.

"Who?" There was resentment as well as curiosity in the question. Garrett Grimm wanted us to believe he was innocent of murder while getting cred for his dirty deeds, which didn't bode well for Albi and me.

"Billy Carpenter's cellmate," Albi said. "I've seen him driving around town a couple of times. I saw him go into Luke's apartment building."

"Enough of this chitchat," Grimm said. He gestured with the gun that we should move. "We're going inside. Don't try any funny business. I won't hesitate to shoot."

I walked to the front door of the cabin, taking as much time as I could. Albi walked even slower. I cringed when Grimm poked the gun in his back. "Open the door slowly, and don't make a sound."

Albi nodded.

He jabbed me next. "Follow him. Got it?"

"Yes."

"In we go. Quickly. Quietly."

Albi and I did as we were ordered. The cabin was one large room, its wooden floor covered by a faded rag rug that had once been colorful. Small kitchen appliances lined the wall across from the large window. Near it stood a wooden table and three chairs. A worn sofa and two arm chairs occupied the far end.

But my focus was on Dylan, who had his back to the door in a semi-crouched fighter stance. And for good reason. A few feet away, Tino brandished a large knife. Beside him were two long duffel bags. The stolen money.

Dylan glanced around as soon as we entered the cabin. He saw the gun and took in the situation. "Hello, Garrett."

"Dylan Avery, I believe."

"That's me."

Grimm focused his attention on Tino. "Hello, Tino. I see you found the money."

"Yeah." Tino's hand holding the knife was shaking badly.

"And now it's time to put down the knife and hand over the bags."

"No, I won't."

"Of course you will. Or I'll shoot you."

"Tino, do what he says," Albi said.

Tino looked at his brother. His face crumpled. "You shouldn't have followed me, Albi. It wasn't safe."

"Hurry up, Valdez. Get those bags over here."

"Or what? You'll shoot everyone here?"

Grimm wrapped his arm around Albi's neck. "Starting with your brother."

Dylan moved quickly to stand between Albi and me. "Let Albi go," Dylan said. "He has nothing to do with this."

"Don't tell me what to do," Grimm said. "Now, everyone go and stand against the far wall." When we hesitated, he waved the gun. "Go on."

The four of us went over to the wall opposite the door. Garrett Grimm walked over to the two duffel bags. He tried to lift one, but it barely budged.

"All right. Now all of you, toss your cell phones on the floor. Go on. I want to see four phones."

"I left mine in my car," Albi said.

Grimm patted him down while he kept the gun on the rest of us.

"All right. Three phones, then."

Tino, Dylan, and I did as instructed. Grimm swept them up and stuck them in his vest pockets.

"Now, Tino and Little Brother. I want each of you to pick up a bag and carry it out to my car."

Tino and Albi went over to the duffel bags filled with money. Albi struggled to lift one, but he could only raise one end off the floor, or so it seemed.

"They're heavy," Tino said.

"You managed to get them here from wherever they were hidden."

"Not easily."

Garrett Grimm scratched his head with the end of the gun. "I'm curious. Where did Luke hide them?"

Tino pointed up. "There's a space above the bathroom ceiling. I don't know how, but Luke managed to stash them up there without dropping them in the toilet."

Albi laughed. He stopped when Grimm scowled at him.

"He was a tough nut, your friend Luke. Refused to tell me where he hid the money."

"So you killed Luke," Tino said.

"Yeah."

I shivered. Garrett Grimm admitting that he'd killed Luke Rizzo didn't bode well for our future.

"Okay. Here's the plan. There's four of you and two bags of money. First, Tino and Albi will carry a bag of money out to my car. Carrie and Dylan, you'll follow with the second bag when I tell you to." Grimm pointed the pistol at each of us in turn. "Don't try any funny business. I won't hesitate to shoot one of you, and frankly, I don't much care who."

Dylan squeezed my shoulder. It made me feel hopeful. Damn it, today was our wedding day, and I intended to become Mrs. Dylan Avery as planned.

Chapter Twenty-Five

G arrett Grimm propped open the cabin door with a chair. "Okay, Tino and Albi, follow me outside. I'm going to unlock my trunk, and that's where you'll stow the bag. Got it?"

Both Albi and Tino nodded.

Grimm turned his attention on Dylan and me. "Remember, you make a run for it, one of them gets shot." He cocked his head to one side. "Maybe Tino." He cocked his head to the other side. "Maybe Albi." Which set him off on a laughing jag.

I shuddered. Our lives were in the hands of a madman.

As soon as we were alone, I grabbed Dylan's hand. "What are we going to do?"

"We're four people. He has one gun. He can't focus it on all of us all the time. Soon as he's distracted, I'll disarm him."

"Just be careful. I don't want anything to happen to you."

Dylan put his arm around me. "Something will happen to all of us unless I stop him. I've dealt with some bad asses in my time, but Grimm is a loose cannon. I can't predict what his next move will be."

"He's mad, Dylan. Crazy."

Dylan nodded. "He seems unhinged, but it could be an act. Don't worry—I'll be careful. For now, just go along with whatever he says."

I went over to the door and watched Tino and Albi struggle to lift the duffel bag and place it inside the trunk of Garrett Grimm's car. Albi fumbled and lost his grip on the bag. His end dropped to the ground.

"Careful! That's my money your handling!" Grimm snarled.

Dylan's muffled laughter had me spinning around. "What's so funny?" I demanded.

"Albi's one smart kid. These bags aren't as heavy as he and Tino make them out to be. We'll do the same. Take our time, pretend to struggle under the weight of the bag. I think getting it into the trunk will be a good time to make my move."

"All right. Next." Grimm waved his arm to us like he was directing traffic past road work. "Bring out the bag."

"He's left Albi and Tino standing by the passenger's side of the car," Dylan said. "Which tells me he has no idea what to do with them just yet," Dylan said.

The sound of an approaching car gave me hope. I stared at the road not fifty feet away. If only the driver would glance at the driveway and realize something odd was happening. Something very wrong. But the vehicle never slowed down as it drove past.

I heard another car motor. But it must have turned into one of the nearby cottages, because I never saw it pass.

"Stop stalling," Grimm shouted through the open doorway. "Bring the bag outside and stow it in the trunk of my car."

"We're coming," Dylan said. I marveled at how steady and normal his voice sounded. As though he were simply doing a favor for a friend or a neighbor.

"Remember, pretend it's heavy," Dylan said as he lifted one end of the bag. It was only about three feet long, but the bills must have been packed tightly by the dense feel of it.

"It *is* heavy—and unwieldly," I said, finding it difficult to get a good grip on my end of the bag.

"I'll lead," he said. "When I push the bag back toward you, drop your end."

"All right." My heart was thumping madly. Was this how Dylan and I were going to end it all, lugging a bag of stolen money for a crazed murderer?

"Come on! Come on! We don't have all day." Grimm waved the gun at us as we started down the driveway to his car.

Dylan stopped in front of the open trunk. "Do you want us to put the bag on top of the other one?"

I came to stand next to Dylan. I rested my end of the duffel bag on the edge of the car and peered inside the trunk. It was jam-packed with cartons labeled with the names of computer companies. Were they stolen goods? The first duffel bag had been crammed in, though from the looks of it, it probably wouldn't clear the trunk when it was closed.

"This duffel won't fit," I announced, wondering why a man who had planned to hijack bags of money hadn't thought to empty out his trunk. Until I realized that Garrett Grimm was too disorganized to ever plan ahead.

"Sure it will. Push the first bag in farther."

Dylan tried to rearrange the cartons, but they wouldn't budge. "You want me to pull out a few of these boxes?"

"No! Leave them just as they are."

"Okay. You're the boss," Dylan said agreeably.

"Yeah," Grimm muttered, his face red with perspiration and nerves.

Dylan exhaled loudly. "So, what do we do with this bag? Bring it back inside?"

"You're real funny. Stick it on the back seat."

Dylan moved to open the rear passenger door behind the driver's seat, but Grimm stopped him. "That door's stuck. Go to the other side." He waved the gun at us, in case we'd forgotten he still had it.

We walked slowly, carrying the duffel bag around the car to the right passenger door.

"More boxes," I said, peering in the window. They were piled high on the seats and jammed into the floor area.

"Open the door and shove it—hey!" Grimm suddenly realized that while he'd been giving us orders, Albi and Tino had almost made it to the road. He chased after them. "Get back here," he snarled.

The two brothers exchanged glances. Just when it looked like they were going to make a run for it, Tino let out an exaggerated sigh. He and Albi turned and trudged back up the driveway, to stand in front of Grimm's car.

Grimm turned his irritation on Dylan and me. "What are you two waiting for? Stick the bag on top of the cartons. Now! I don't have all day."

When neither Dylan nor I moved to open the door, Grimm let out a growl. "Move out of the way and I'll open the door," he said, like he was doing us a favor.

"I can't lift it that high," I said.

Dylan pushed the bag toward me. I dropped the end I'd been holding. Dylan let go of his end. Holding his hand low, he gestured to me to step back, which I did.

"Hey!" Grimm shouted, sounding aggrieved. "Be careful. You'll be sorry if that bag splits open. I've been waiting a long time for this money. Years."

"Sorry," I muttered. "It's heavy."

Grimm pointed the gun at the two brothers. "You two help Dylan shove the bag in the car. It can't be that difficult."

The three of them told one another what to do as they made a big show of squeezing the second duffel bag onto the back seat. I moved farther away from the car so Dylan would have the space to do whatever he was planning.

But when was that going to be? It had be soon.

I heard footsteps and turned to the road. Two familiar figures were walking up the driveway. One of them was carrying a gun.

"Looks like we're right on time, Les," Fred Rawlins said. He positioned himself in front of Garrett Grimm's car. "They saved us the trouble of hunting for the money. The loot's been found."

"Yeah." Leslie Thompson giggled nervously.

"Drop the gun, Garrett," Fred Rawlins ordered.

Garrett Grimm's mouth fell open as he stared at Fred Rawlins, but he held on to his weapon. "What are you doing here, trying to steal what's mine?" he growled.

"Drop the gun now," Rawlins ordered.

Garrett Grimm didn't move.

A gunshot rang out, deafening me. And I wasn't the only one. Albi and Tino covered their ears. Dylan, I noticed, never took his eyes off Fred Rawlins.

"The next shot might hit your knee. Or your heart," Rawlins said.

Grimm's gun clattered to the ground.

"Leslie," Rawlins said.

Leslie picked up the gun and held it at arm's distance.

"Okay. Time to collect what we came for. Leslie, give me the gun, then grab the bag of money and stash it on the back seat of my car."

Leslie tried to lift the duffel bag, without success. Rawlins scowled. He gestured to Dylan and Tino. "You two, pick it up and set it on his shoulder."

Dylan and Tino did as instructed. We watched Leslie stagger off. Dylan, I noticed, stayed on the driver's side of Grimm's car and managed to edge closer to Fred Rawlins. Rawlins must have sensed his move, because, though he didn't say anything, he stepped back.

"All right. You got what you came for—now leave," Grimm said.

Fred Rawlins nodded and grinned. "You'd like that wouldn't you? But I ain't leaving. I know there's another bag of money. Where is it?"

"There's no more money. And if there was any, it wouldn't be yours, now would it?" Grimm sneered.

Tino let out a loud guffaw.

"What's so funny?" Rawlins demanded.

"The two of you arguing over something that doesn't belong to either of you."

"As if you should have it?" Rawlins demanded.

"Why not? At least I earned it," Tino said.

"Yeah, so did I," Grimm mumbled.

While the others were talking, Dylan had once again inched closer to Rawlins. Would he get close enough to wrest the gun away this time? It took all of my effort not to watch. Watching would draw Rawlins's attention to Dylan, so instead I looked at Albi to see how he was managing the awful situation we were in.

Suddenly Grimm grabbed my upper arm. He slammed the rear passenger door shut and opened the door in front of it. He pushed me inside and over to the driver's seat, got in beside me, and shoved the key into the ignition.

"Carrie, you're gonna drive us out of here," he said as he started up the motor.

"No, I'm not." I reached for the door handle, but the door didn't budge.

"The lock's jammed so it won't open."

"Oh."

I glanced at Rawlins, wondering if he was going to stop us, but he was eyeing Albi and Tino, who must have edged toward the road soon as Grimm opened the car door. It was difficult keeping a gun focused on five people.

"You'll do as I say, Miss Librarian." Grimm reached under the passenger seat where he was sitting and pulled out a wicked-looking knife. The blade was less than five inches long, but sharp and deadly. "Unless you want a taste of this."

I swallowed. "Where are we going?"

"As far from here as possible."

Chapter
Twenty-Six

D riving Garrett Grimm's ancient car was an odd experience. I
felt as though I were sitting in a large upright chair and driving a bus or a van while springs poked at me through the worn seat.
Being a getaway driver for a thief-murderer was nerve-wracking
enough, and I didn't appreciate the commands he screamed at me.

"Faster! Faster!" And "Turn left!" or "Turn right!" whenever we
approached a new road.

The car shimmied from side to side with each turn. Since it didn't
have power steering, I had to exert considerable effort to straighten
out the wheels after every turn, then hug the right side of the road in
case another car came along. How I wished one would, but so far we
were alone on the road.

"Slow down," Grimm said after I'd made the third turn as per
his instructions. "Do you want to get us killed?"

"You told me to drive fast," I complained.

"Yeah, okay. But now we're miles from that thieving felon. No
way is he getting that second bag of money."

My mind was awhirl with all that had happened today, the day
of my wedding. And now I was stuck in a car with a murderer going

God knows where while the man I loved was either taking down a criminal or getting shot in the attempt.

Grimm looked ridiculous as, knife in hand, he kept sticking his scrawny neck out the window to see if anyone was following us. How was it he never seemed to notice that the door to the trunk fluttered up and down with every bump and turn because it had never been closed? I felt every bump as well. The shock absorbers were gone, and the suspension was really awful. It was amazing that the duffel bag of money never fell out, given the jarring ride that had my teeth chattering.

A left turn was coming up, and Grimm told me to take it. We drove past a few cabins and small houses amid the woods and shrubs. A car passed us, then another. On the right side, I spotted a small beach and water through the woods. A lake, most likely.

"Do you know where we are?" I asked.

"As a matter of fact I do," he sneered.

No, he didn't. The man was a loser. He screwed up everything he did. Isn't that what Trish had said about him? He was erratic and he'd murdered Luke. What was he going to do to me?

I heard the familiar jingle of my cell phone. The sound was coming from one of the pockets in Grimm's suede vest, where he'd jammed our three phones. A surge of hope brightened my spirits. *Dylan's safe! He's calling from Rawlins's or Leslie's phone. He's sending the police after Grimm.*

Reality set in and my hopes crashed to the ground. It was my wedding day. Anyone could be calling, most likely my father or Angela. Or Aunt Harriet.

"Don't slow down," Grimm said. He reached for my phone and glanced at it before tossing it to the floor of the car.

"Who called me?" I asked.

"Your mother."

"Oh."

Grimm shot me a spiteful grin. "Were you hoping it was your boyfriend? Do you think he grabbed Rawlins's gun, or did Rawlins catch his play and shoot him?"

So Grimm had noticed what Dylan was planning. Of course he had. That was the moment he'd decided to take me hostage and drive away with at least one bag of the money.

When we came to a county route, Grimm instructed me to take it going north. There was a GPS affixed to the top of his dashboard, but he never glanced at it once.

"Where are we going?" I asked.

"Where no one can find me till it's time to leave. This time tomorrow I'll be far, far away."

So he has a plan, I thought. *I should talk to him. Find out what I can.* But what would Garrett Grimm be willing to talk about? What would set him off?

I cleared my throat. "Did you have any idea that Fred Rawlins followed you to the cabin?"

Grimm pursed his lips. He looked angry. Maybe this was a bad way to start. "No, and I should have been on my guard. I knew who he was. Luke pointed him out to me, told me he was Billy's cellmate. Then suddenly everywhere I went I saw him around town." He let out a guffaw. "It took me a day or two to realize the guy was tailing me."

"So Luke must have told Billy that you'd planned the bank robbery," I said.

When Grimm didn't answer, I took that as a yes, a yes that didn't make Grimm happy.

"Do you think Fred Rawlins killed Billy?" I asked, though I knew Rawlins hadn't.

"Nah. Luke did that." Grimm shook his head. "Luke was a good worker, except he had no patience." Another hoot of laughter. "I told him to wait for Billy to get hold of the loot from wherever he'd stashed it while he was in the slammer, and *then* grab it, but Luke was impatient—not that I blame him after all those years of waiting around. And he was seriously pissed at Billy for hiding it from all of us."

I had the sense not to point out that Grimm hadn't shown any patience when he'd killed his pal Luke. Anyway, Grimm was as eager to change the subject as I was.

"I heard someone broke into the library and snatched the witch's diary." He clucked his tongue in mock concern. He turned to me, his eyes glittering with malice. "Any idea who stole it?"

At this point, I had no reason to hide the truth. "We're pretty sure Leslie Thompson stole it with Fred Rawlins's instructions. But proving it is another story."

"So the kid stole the diary for his mother," Grimm mused. "Who would have thought he'd have the guts to do something so bold?"

Kid? "Leslie didn't steal it for Winifred," I said. "He hates her."

"Interesting. He finally wised up to the kind of person she was. Then I suppose he and Rawlins plan to sell it for big bucks—if Rawlins knows how to find a buyer."

"Actually, we have no idea what the diary is worth. A forensic expert was scheduled to come in next week to tell us its value for insurance purposes."

Grimm had me make a few more turns. From the signs we passed, I realized we were heading back toward Clover Ridge. His cell phone rang. I listened carefully to the conversation, but I couldn't hear what the caller was saying.

"Got it. Not as much as we expected, but enough for now." Grimm said.

Then, after a pause, "I know, I know. I'll be there." He made a face while his caller spoke, probably reminding him of their arrangements. Then he smiled at me as he said, "I took someone else instead of Tino." His burst of laughter sent shivers down my spine. Whomever Grimm was talking to was helping him escape.

The call put Grimm in a real chatty mood. Despite finding Dylan, Albi, and me at the cabin, then losing half the bank haul to Fred Rawlins and Leslie Thompson, he seemed to consider that things were working out just fine.

"What I can't figure out is why Leslie's hanging out with the likes of Fred Rawlins," he said. "Rawlins's a felon, and Leslie's the meekest geek in Clover Ridge. I mean, how did they even meet?"

"I think Leslie's starved for any kind of adventure. He sees Rawlins as some kind of hero."

Grimm shot me a look of disbelief. "You gotta be kidding."

"Somehow Leslie found out that his mother hired Rawlins to steal the diary, only Rawlins got caught in the act. He was furious when she didn't pay him his fee."

"How do you know?"

I shrugged, though my heart was racing. "Things have a way of coming to the surface."

Grimm nodded. "Good! People are finally finding out that Winifred Thompson was a nasty, deceitful bitch. The woman stopped at nothing to get what she wanted. Only this time she picked a bumbler."

He chuckled. "So Rawlins and Leslie grabbed the diary, and Winnie couldn't get her paws on it. I love it." He saw my expression of horror and apologized. "Sorry, Carrie. I know that diary means a lot to you."

"It's part of our town's history and belongs in the library," I said.

Just then my phone's jingle sounded again. Grimm sighed with exasperation as he picked it up.

"Your father," he told me as he tossed it back on the floor of the car.

Maybe Jim will realize something's wrong when I don't answer, I thought.

"What's with all the phone calls?" he asked, suddenly suspicious. Then he remembered. My heart began to pound as a large grin covered his face. "Oh, right. How could I have forgotten? Today is your wedding day."

I blinked back tears that threatened to spill down my cheeks. I would *not* let him see me cry.

"Don't worry." I cringed as Grimm patted my arm. "Maybe you'll get there. And maybe you won't."

To distract myself from worrying, I returned to our conversation. "You really hated Winnie, didn't you?"

"It irked me how she kept trying to make out that her ancestor was a saint. She wasn't, you know. I read a few articles about that period. There were complaints about Verity Babcock. How she refused to help people who couldn't afford to pay for her herbs."

I stared at him. "Was John Whitcomb really your ancestor?"

He shrugged. "Yeah, he was. Not that I cared, except it's kinda prestigious to have an ancestor going back all the way to colonial days. But when I read in your article that he'd died after taking some of Verity Babcock's herbs—Verity, who was Winnie Thompson's ancestor—that took on a whole other meaning."

"So that battle of the letters the two of you played out in the *Gazette* was a cover for something else."

No answer.

"Come on, Garrett. What's the real reason you didn't like Winifred?" I asked.

After a pause, he exhaled loudly and said, "The woman was a snob who looked down on people like me. Despite her fancy house and showy ways, Winnie was desperate for money. She'd heard I'd managed a few deals that weren't quite kosher, and asked if she could get in on one of them. When I told her the risks, she swore she was okay with them." Grimm's face contorted into a mask of hate. "Until she claimed her conscience was bothering her and she pulled out of the deal. Only then it was too late."

"Too late for what?" The words were out of my mouth before I could stop them. Belatedly, I realized it would be dangerous to find out why Winnie had gotten under his skin. After all, Winnie had been murdered, and her killer could very well have been Garrett Grimm.

"Winnie and I go way back," Grimm began, his manner casual. "My father was a gardener. His specialty was exotic plants, and the Thompsons—Winnie's parents—were into exotic plants. They had a large greenhouse filled with them. Anyway, I was eight or nine when I started going to the Thompsons with my father. I loved looking at the koi swimming around in a pond. I could stare at them for hours. The second or third time I was there, Winnie called to me from her window. I went up to her bedroom, which was about the size of our entire downstairs. She asked me if I wanted to help her play a joke on someone.

"I said, 'Sure, why not?' I liked playing jokes, and I was flattered that someone in high school was talking to me. She told me where she wanted me to go—only a few blocks away—and what she wanted me to do. She handed me the bottle of glue and repeated her instructions. Then she called out to my father and told him I'd be running an errand for her close by. Since we were in the posh part of town, my father said okay, and off I went."

"What did she tell you to do?" I asked.

"Pour glue on the car seat of her former best friend's brand new car. I found out later that the girl had gone out on a date with a boy Winnie liked." Grimm laughed. "The following week she had me do something to the guy's favorite tennis racket. Winnie told me that suspicions flew around the high school, but no one could prove anything."

"Lovely," I said. I glanced at my watch. It was two o'clock. My anxiety, which I'd been keeping at bay, was rising. "I need to get home."

Grimm turned to me, his expression dark. "I need you here with me."

"Why?" I asked.

"Because that's the plan."

"Your plan . . . or someone else's?" I asked.

He hesitated, then said, "It was Buddy's idea."

"Who's Buddy?"

"The best pal I've ever had. Get off at the next exit."

I began to panic. Was Dylan safe and able to send the police out to rescue me? Surely Albi would tell the police that Garrett Grimm had abducted me. That is, if they both weren't injured or . . .

"I heard from Winnie occasionally over the years," Grimm went on, as though we were having a friendly chat. "She asked me to do a few more little jobs, as she called them, and I always obliged. Sometimes she gave me money. Other times she gave me gifts, expensive items I could never afford."

He turned to look at me. "Are you listening?"

"When did you meet Buddy?" I asked.

"About a year ago."

And he became your best friend? "Uh-huh."

"We met in a bar in Merrivale and started talking. The more we talked, the more we discovered we have in common. Only Buddy's way cooler than I'll ever be. He's the smoothest guy I know." Grimm chuckled. "He's the older brother I never had."

A chill chased down my spine. This Buddy sounded like a Svengali who had wormed his way into Grimm's confidence and was now calling the shots. Clearly, Grimm had filled his pal in on the bank job, and this Buddy was clever enough to convince Grimm to take drastic steps he'd never come up with on his own to collect the missing money. Like instructing him to get tough with Luke. And when that failed, to give Tino an ultimatum. For some reason, Buddy had told Grimm to take a hostage—probably as insurance if he ran into trouble.

Hostages were dispensable, which meant my life was in danger.

"So your friend Buddy totally gets you," I said. "And he has your back."

"Completely."

"Getting back to Winnie, what kind of plan did she agree to and then pull out of?" I asked.

Grimm chuckled. "That was one of Buddy's brainstorms. When I mentioned to him that a formerly rich woman I knew needed money, he told me about this con he ran a few times over the years. In order for it to work, it requires an inside man—or woman—with wealthy friends."

"Uh-huh."

"Turn here," Grimm instructed.

The new route led to Merrivale, where I imagined Buddy lived. Not a good move, as far as I was concerned, especially since Grimm now seemed more relaxed. He was getting closer to his accomplice, and each mile brought me closer to my demise. I pretended to listen to his story as I plotted an escape route.

"Winnie's part in the scam was to convince some of her well-padded friends to put money into a so-called 'safe investment' that never really existed. She liked how it would get her out of the hole she'd found herself in, until one of her pals called to ask if the deal was really safe, because she was planning to use money she'd been saving for her granddaughter's college education."

"Okay. So Winnie decided to pull out," I said, eyeing the neighborhood I was driving past—private homes with people outside, gardening and chatting with their neighbors. "What was the big deal?"

"Are you kidding?" Grimm's eyes bulged out like frogs' eyes as he gaped at me. "Buddy had brought in guys he's been doing business with for years. They had everything set up and ready to go when I told Buddy that Winnie refused to hold up her end of the scam."

Her end of the scam. I shuddered. This Buddy was pulling the strings. I dreaded to hear what was coming next.

"I explained to Winnie that she had to go through with the plan. Lots of people had invested in it, and they would be royally pissed if it didn't go through as arranged. But she just laughed and said she wasn't about to betray people she'd known since she was a little girl. It had been a mistake to even consider it."

He laughed that awful hyena laugh again. "Her mistake was double-crossing us. So I made sure she'd never make that mistake again."

"You . . .?" I couldn't finish the sentence.

"I sure did."

Grimm's phone rang, and he answered. "Okay . . . Ten, fifteen minutes . . . Okay." He paused and glanced at me. "But you told me—" He took a quick look at me again. "Do you think that's really necessary?" Another pause. "I'm not arguing. I just . . ." Then: "I understand . . . Yes . . . yes, I will."

I clasped my hands together so they would stop shaking. If I had it right, Buddy had just instructed Garrett Grimm to murder me, and Grimm was too far under his sway to disobey.

Chapter
Twenty-Seven

I had to get out of the car and as far from Garrett Grimm as possible if I hoped to make it to my wedding tonight.

"Hey, steady," Grimm chided because the car was veering off course as though a drunkard were driving; only it was my terror that had loosened my control of the wheel.

We had left the section of pretty homes and were now passing more modest houses, many of which were in need of repairs and a paint job. I caught Grimm glancing at me, probably wondering how he was going to carry out the task his BFF had given him.

Well, I had no intention of making it easy for him. I sat firmly in my seat as I gripped the steering wheel and rotated it from side to side. The car swerved to the left, narrowly missing a car coming from the opposite direction. The door to the trunk flipped up and down. The suspension rocked like a bucking bronco.

"Hey! Cut it out!" Grimm shouted. "Do you want to get us killed?" He was nervous now, and I wasn't sure if that was good or bad. Bad, I decided, when he waved the knife at me.

"You're making me nervous," I said.

"Then drive properly."

"Why should I?" I stared into his eyes. The car drifted to the right, barely missing a parked car. "Since your friend wants you to kill me."

"Don't be silly," he said, his rictus grin betraying him.

"Only you won't get the chance," I said. The restraint and caution I'd been holding in check since he'd dragged me into the car were gone. I deliberately drove into the left-hand lane and snapped back into the right lane.

"Cut it out!" He raised the knife.

"Or what? You'll stab me in front of our live audience?"

We peered out at the people on both sides of the street, fear and apprehension in their faces. I turned right at the next block.

"I didn't tell you to turn."

"No, you didn't." I scrutinized the street we were approaching. At the far end of the block, three adults stood chatting in front of a house. I rotated the wheel as hard as I could. The car jumped up on the curb. I spun the wheel in the other direction. The car landed in the street with a shudder.

"Aha!" I said, pleased with my results. "Finally!" I turned to Grimm. "Looks like the bag of money fell out of the trunk."

If looks could kill, I would have died that instant. Grimm's eyes rolled as he considered what to do. Finally, he came to a decision. He yanked the key from the ignition and flew out of the car, but not before he raised the knife. "Don't move!" he ordered, then he ran behind the car to pick up the duffel bag of stolen money that had fallen into the street.

I had a minute at most to exit the car and make my escape. According to Grimm, the driver's door was jammed, which meant he'd be expecting me to leave via the passenger's door.

I glanced at the three men, chatting and laughing. They hadn't even noticed that I'd ridden over the curb. Now they were walking up the path leading to the front door of the house. *No!* I shouted in my mind. *Don't leave!*

I inched away from my seat, prepared to scoot over to the passenger seat and fly out the door. Since my feet were now past the steering wheel, I thought why not kick the jammed door. But first I raised the old-fashioned lever button to unlock the car door, in case that was working.

I rammed the door with both feet. Nothing happened. One more try, then it was out the passenger door and praying I didn't run into Garrett Grimm, who, I noticed, was right this minute struggling to get a good grip on the duffel bag of money. It wasn't really that heavy, but it was dense and awkward for one person to grab hold of, especially when that person refused to let go of his knife.

The third kick did it! The car door shot open. I scooted past the steering wheel and had just stepped on the ground when Grimm let out a shriek. I almost laughed at the expression of indecision on his face. Should he stay with the money or drop the bag and chase after me?

I took off running down the block and was amazed when I heard footsteps behind me. Grimm had chosen to come after me. I glanced back, terrified because the knife never left his hand.

Just then the garage of the house the men had entered began to open mechanically, and a middle-aged woman stepped onto the driveway, a garden hose in hand. I imagined she was planning to water the hydrangea bushes bordering her house.

"Help!" I screamed as I ran. "He's trying to kill me!"

"Don't be ridiculous, Carrie. Come back to the car," Grimm shouted as he chased after me.

The woman, now twenty feet from me, stared at us. I couldn't tell if she thought I was crazy or really in danger. The footsteps grew louder. He was gaining on me.

"He has a knife!" I shouted at the woman. "Help me. Please!"
Grimm held up both hands. "Look. No knife."

I ran as fast as I could, but he was getting closer, panting with every step he took.

And then I heard the most beautiful sound in the world—a police siren.

The sound was coming from the direction I was running toward and growing louder and closer. Yay! Help was coming. I halted in my tracks. So did Grimm. For a moment he froze as what had to be his worst fear was realized. Then he spun round to race back to his car and the duffel bag of money. Which was when the woman with the hose turned it on full force and aimed it straight at Grimm.

Chapter
Twenty-Eight

Three police cars pulled up to where I was standing with the lady with the hose. Seven officers jumped out and came as close to us as they dared while a strong arc of water doused Garrett Grimm.

"We'll take it from here, ma'am," one said to the woman. She turned off the nozzle and set down the hose.

An older officer in civilian clothes, who I assumed was the person in command, approached me. "Are you Carrie Singleton?"

I nodded.

"I'm Captain Chris Donahue of the Prescott Police Department. Are you all right?"

"I think so." Though I was surrounded by police officers, I couldn't stop looking at Grimm, to make sure he couldn't get at me. I released a sigh of relief when two young officers put him in handcuffs and escorted him to one of their cars.

"I've no idea why you're treating me like a criminal," Grimm was saying. "Arrest that woman! She turned her hose on me for no reason. Look at me! I'm soaking wet."

"How did you know where to find me? Did Dylan call you? Is he all right?"

As if in answer to my questions, another car joined the pileup of cop cars. A very familiar car. Dylan got out and ran to me. He enveloped me in his arms.

"Thank God you're okay," he said, as he buried his head in my neck. Were those tears I felt? Tears welled up in my own eyes.

The sound of clapping and cheering broke out. A crowd of about thirty people surrounded us, with grins on their faces, cheering Dylan and me as if we were stars filming a movie.

"Is Albi all right? And Tino?" I asked.

"They're fine. As soon as I disarmed Rawlins, the brothers grabbed Leslie. We used his phone to call the police in that village. They came and arrested Fred Rawlins and Leslie Thompson. I told them Grimm had taken you hostage, and asked them to send out a BOLO ASAP. That done, I gave the officer in charge a statement. He promised to keep me in the loop, which is how I managed to get here so quickly."

"I'm so glad you're here." I sighed. "I was so worried."

Dylan slipped his arm around me. "Looks like we'll make our wedding on time."

I turned to the woman who had set her hose on Grimm. "Thank you for saving me."

"You're welcome. Did you say you're getting married today?"

"Yes. We—"

She turned from me and, putting her hands around her mouth, shouted to her neighbors: "These kids are getting married today! And she just escaped from a criminal I helped catch."

More cheering. Captain Donahue came over to us. He looked harried. "Miss Singleton, we need to take care of some police business before you can leave. First of all, is that Garrett Grimm's vehicle?" He pointed to Grimm's old jalopy.

"It is. Behind the car, you'll find a duffel bag of money that was stolen in a bank job some years ago, along with lots of stolen items in the car."

He nodded. "Wait here." He went over to speak to two of his men. I watched as they walked over to the green car. On the way, one stopped to look at something lying on the ground.

"Grimm had a knife he threatened me with," I said to Captain Donahue as I watched the officer slip on a pair of gloves and pick up the knife.

"I'm afraid you're going to have to come down to the police station and give a statement."

"Now?" I asked, incredulously. "But Dylan and I are getting married in a few hours. I need to go home and shower. Pick up my gown and veil and . . ." I patted my hair, which I imagined looked like a bird's nest, and gaped at Captain Donahue, "I have to leave now! A hairdresser will be at our wedding venue to do my hair in less than an hour!"

Captain Donahue's expression softened. "The station's a short distance from here. I promise I'll be as quick as I can."

"You won't have me answering the same questions again and again?" I asked.

"No, why would I?"

"No reason," I said thinking of John, whose method was to go over the same material several times in hopes of eliciting more information. I stifled a giggle as I realized there was a good chance that John had gotten news of the arrests through the police grapevine and was now shaking his head at the latest escapade Dylan and I had gotten involved in, today of all days.

"In that case, if you're ready to leave and your fiancé will drive you, you can follow me to the precinct."

* * *

Ten minutes later, Dylan and I were seated comfortably across the desk from Captain Donahue. Between us, Dylan and I filled him in on how Albi had approached me and begged us to stop his brother from running off with the bank job money.

Eager as I was to go home, I couldn't help asking, "Is there any way that Tino won't be charged with the robbery and can avoid serving a prison sentence?" I asked.

Captain Donahue exhaled loudly, reminding me of Tom Selleck in *Blue Bloods* when he was faced with a difficult decision. "Impossible to say, but since he helped stop Rawlins from taking the money, and given that Garrett Grimm threatened to murder him if he didn't find and hand over the money, they may go easy on him."

"There's someone else involved in all this," I said. "Someone more dangerous than Grimm. And he's waiting to hear from Grimm."

Dylan and Captain Donahue stared at me.

I told them about Garrett Grimm's friend Buddy, who was orchestrating his actions.

"One of my men is questioning Grimm right now. I'll have him ask about this Buddy."

Dylan and I described the scene at the cabin. How, after we arrived, Garrett Grimm had showed up and pointed a gun at us, ordering us to stow in his car the two duffel bags filled with bank money.

"Then along came Rawlins and Leslie Thompson," Dylan said. "Rawlins had a Glock. He ordered Grimm to throw down his weapon, which he did, and Leslie made off with one of the duffel bags. I was about to make my move to disarm Rawlins, when Grimm shoved Carrie into his car, wielded a knife, and ordered her to drive off."

"With our phones and one bag of money in the trunk," I added. "The trunk door kept swinging up and down, but he didn't seem to notice."

Captain Donahue's head reared back, and he roared with laughter. When he was done, he said, "I apologize for laughing at your situation, Miss Singleton. It had to be terrifying while you were living it, but the escapade sounds like a case of the Keystone Cops, only there were no cops involved."

"I was terrified," I said. "I had no idea what Grimm planned to do with me. It seems Buddy told Grimm to take Tino hostage, but Grimm grabbed me, probably because I was standing closest to him when he made his move to escape Rawlins."

Dylan wrapped his arm around me.

"Who is this Buddy character? Does he have a last name?" Donahue asked.

"I don't know what it is. Grimm never said."

I told Captain Donahue when and where Grimm and Buddy had met. He stopped me to call one of his officers, instructing her to search their online sites for anyone named Buddy who had a record and lived in Merrivale.

"Please continue," he said when he'd hung up the phone.

"Grimm was carrying out Buddy's instructions. From what I could make of their last conversation, Buddy no longer had any use for a hostage. He told Grimm to get rid of me."

Dylan squeezed me tighter. The phone rang and Captain Donahue answered it. I watched him break into a grin. Whoever was on the other line was feeding him valuable information. When he disconnected, he looked at me.

"We think we found the right Buddy. Lives in Merrivale and has a record for getting close to other criminals and coercing them to go way beyond what they would do on their own. This information provides us with a way of making Garrett Grimm talk if he refuses to give up his accomplice."

"Grimm admitted he murdered Luke Rizzo and Winifred Thompson," I said.

Captain Donahue looked at me with admiration. "You got all that while driving around following his crazy directions? Now, if you can tell me everything again in chronological order, and how Grimm's confession came up in your conversation, we can finish up, and I'll text over the report for you to sign."

* * *

I sank back against the leather seat of Dylan's BMW and closed my eyes. Though the agitation caused by my recent abduction had yet to subside, a sense of security was beginning to envelop me. I was with Dylan. I was safe and unharmed. The bad guys had been apprehended, and our wedding was taking place in a few hours.

Our wedding! I bolted upright and stared at the clock on the dashboard. It was almost four o'clock! There was no way I could keep my hair appointment. And the photographer was scheduled to arrive at Victor's house at six o'clock.

I felt panic rising as I wondered how long it would take to get home. I needed to shower and pack up my gown and everything I'd be wearing tonight. Thank goodness Smoky Joe was at Marion's house!

I was suddenly aware that Dylan was conversing with someone in low tones.

"Who are you talking to?" I asked when he ended the conversation.

"Angela. I told her we needed to push the wedding back two hours. She'll contact everyone. I've already called Victor and your father to fill them in on the delay."

I leaned over to kiss his cheek. "I am so lucky to have you."

Dylan blinked quickly. "You have no idea how terrified I was when that weirdo ordered you to drive off in his rickety car. I'll never forgive myself for letting that happen."

"You were busy taking down Rawlins. Who knows what evil plan *he* had for us."

My cell phone rang. It was my mother, sounding hysterical. "Carrie, dear, is everything all right? Your father just called to tell me the wedding has been delayed. He wouldn't say why."

"Yes, I'm fine." Thank goodness Jim hadn't told her why it was being pushed back.

She lowered her voice. "Are things all right between you and Dylan? You know it's normal to have a bout of jitters before one's wedding day. Everyone wonders if he or she is doing the right thing. And we can always have a mother–daughter chat if you'd like."

I cleared my throat to mask the laughter that had bubbled up in my throat. This had to be the most maternal thing my mother had ever said to me. "Mom, I'm fine. Really I am. And Dylan and I are good. It's just that something unexpected came up. I'll tell you about it when I see you later."

"That was very tactful of you," Dylan said when I hung up.

"She means well."

My soon-to-be-husband raised his eyebrows at me as he pulled into the parking area of a casual restaurant.

"Why are we stopping here?" I asked.

"Because we haven't eaten anything since early this morning. You don't want to faint from hunger in the middle of saying 'I do,' do you?"

As soon as Dylan turned off the motor, I threw my arms around him. "I'm so glad I'm marrying you."

"The feeling's mutual."

Chapter
Twenty-Nine

"**D**o you have everything?" I asked Dylan. We'd arrived home forty-five minutes ago. Having showered and dressed, we were now in the process of carrying our wedding finery out to the car.

"I think so—tux, shoes, shirt, cummerbund."

"Socks? Tie?" I asked.

"Those too."

I walked slowly, careful not to trip, and mentally ran through the list of what I was bringing to Victor's home: my makeup kit, my tiny pocketbook that held a lipstick and not much else, and everything I'd be wearing tonight. I checked over everything I'd placed on the back seat of Dylan's car, then went back inside the cottage to find out what was keeping Dylan.

It had felt strange to come home and not have Smoky Joe rushing to greet us, but given today's unexpected events, I was glad that he was safe at Marion's. Considering all the tumult and activity, I knew our wedding was no place for Smoky Joe. Still, part of me wished he would be there. Just as I wished Evelyn could attend. But ghosts, like cats, were not on the guest list.

"I'm ready when you are," I said.

"Okay. Let's go," Dylan said.

I looked around the cottage. When Dylan and I returned later tonight, we'd be a married couple. Though we'd be spending the summer here, this was no longer our home. Come the fall, we'd be moving into our new house—the next step in our new life.

"Carrie?" Dylan turned, wondering why I hadn't moved.

"Coming."

Dylan drove at a leisurely pace to Victor's house. I knew that, like me, he was aware that this fifteen-minute drive was a bridge from our old life to the one ahead of us. It was six o'clock, but since our band, photographer, and caterers had no problem with the two-hour delay, we were doing fine timewise.

I was bubbling with anticipation as I gazed out at the houses we passed, at the trees and flowers and the other cars on the road. An ordinary sight on a late June afternoon, but one I meant to keep as a special memory as we set out for our wedding.

"This was some day we've had," Dylan said.

I laughed. "Yeah! Following Albi as he tailed his brother to the hidden loot. Then Garrett Grimm stealing it, only to lose half the money to Fred Rawlins and Leslie Thompson."

"You know what they say," Dylan joked. "Follow the money."

"I'm glad everything worked out in the end," I said. "All the bad guys are in jail." Captain Donahue had called half an hour ago to inform us that Bruce "Buddy" Colgan had been arrested and was being charged with a variety of crimes.

Dylan took my hand and kissed it. "I'm glad you're here, safe and unharmed."

We were silent for a while.

"Are you nervous?" I asked when we stopped for a red light.

"Not at all." He turned to beam at me. "I can't wait to marry you in front of all the people we love."

"Me too. Tomorrow night we'll be on our flight to Athens."

Dylan laughed. "Don't rush away the next thirty hours. They might prove to be the most memorable time of our lives."

I wrapped my arms around Dylan. "Maybe for a short while, until we start our honeymoon."

I felt a thrill of excitement as we pulled into Victor's semicircular driveway. The florist's van was the only parked vehicle here because Victor had posted a large sign that said, "Parking Only for Our Bride and Groom; Deliveries Can Stop Here Temporarily." Six cars filled the driveway that led to the three-car garage,

Dylan had no sooner cut the engine than Victor, Babette, Angela, and Steve spilled out the front door. They greeted us in a flurry of hugs.

Angela pulled me close. "I'm so glad you're okay. Victor told us what you went through."

"Being Garrett Grimm's kidnapping victim was scary. Especially when the guy manipulating him told him to kill me."

"I can't believe you and Dylan nabbed a bunch of criminals on the day of your wedding."

"Believe me, we didn't plan anything of the kind. It just . . . happened."

Angela laughed. She put her arm around my waist, and we dashed up the steps to the front door, like two school girls. "Now it's time to forget all that, my BFF. You are now in wedding mode."

I halted. "Just a minute. I have to get my gown and stuff and bring them inside. They're in the car."

"Not to worry. Babette and Steve will see to everything." She urged me to walk faster. "Monica Dale is here to do your hair—and mine, Tacey's, and Julia's. Earlier, she was pacing up and down the kitchen, mumbling to herself. If we don't hurry, I'm afraid she's going to take off."

Booked on Murder

"Monica Dale!" I echoed several decibels louder. Monica Dale was an import from a top-echelon Manhattan salon, where she worked for a short stint after catering to the Hollywood stars for many years. She was now the main attraction at my local beauty salon but saw very select clients.

"I had no idea Kathy was sending Monica over to do our hair," I said. "She'd told me she could only spare one of the younger stylists because Saturday was her busiest day."

"Monica happened to catch your latest adventure on TV, along with everyone else in the salon. As soon as Kathy bragged that you were a customer and Monica found out today was your wedding day, she insisted that *she* was doing your hair, and left Kathy to reschedule her appointments."

I laughed. "I suppose notoriety has some advantages. When I tried setting up an appointment with Monica, I was told I'd have a two-month wait."

I gasped when I saw that Victor had placed vases of yellow tea roses, their petals edged in fuchsia, amid white hydrangeas in all the downstairs rooms. They would blend in beautifully with the lilac, white, and fuchsia flowers in gold-colored vases rimmed in teal that Dylan and I had ordered for the wedding ceremony and the dining tables inside the tent.

Tacey came running to me, and I swung her around. "You're getting so big, I won't be able to do this much longer," I told her.

"Cousin Carrie, I heard on TV that you and Dylan caught a lot of criminals!"

"Well, we helped," I said.

"I'm glad the bad guys are going to jail."

"Me too," I agreed.

My little cousin slipped her hand into mine. "Now we have to go have our hair done. Right, Angela?"

"Right, honey."

Julia hugged me. "Monica's waiting for us in the large upstairs bathroom. I suggested she first do Tacey's hair, then Angela's and mine to save time, but she insisted on doing yours first because you're the bride."

"Then let's not keep her waiting. But first I must peek into the living room to make sure everything's set up properly."

"Victor oversaw that, so I'm sure all was arranged to your specifications," Angela said, "but I know you can't resist checking on it yourself."

Everything was just as I'd pictured it—the chairs set in rows with an aisle wide enough to allow two people to walk side by side; and a tall vase of flowers on both ends of the area in front of the bay window, where Al would officiate the ceremony. I had the sudden urge to visit the tent outside, to check on that too, but I would have to do that later. I was keeping Monica waiting.

* * *

"Hmm." Monica stood behind my chair as we both stared at my wet head in the mirror. She was a short, burly woman with fierce dark eyes and long black hair that hung down on both sides of her chest. I tried to tell myself that her hairstyle or lack of one was no indication of how well she could shape other people's hair. I'd seen for myself the results of Monica's haircuts on various library patrons. They were truly works of art.

And now she was clipping up a section of my hair and snipping away on another. I glanced down at the floor, shocked to see two inches of my hair lying there.

"Hold still!"

"Sorry," I murmured.

Angela giggled. Julia smiled.

"You look funny, Cousin Carrie."

"She does now," Monica agreed, her accent pure Brooklynese. "But when I'm done she'll be stunning."

Ten minutes later they were oohing and aahing over my hair. I had to admit that Monica was right. It looked stunning, framing my face while giving the crown the perfect height for the veil.

"Next," Monica said.

"Can I be next?" Tacey asked.

"Of course," Angela, Julia, and I said in unison.

Babette appeared and called me into one of the bedrooms, where she'd set up a table. Spread out was an array of nail polishes, glitter, and decorations as well as all the accoutrements that went along with manicures.

"Surprised, are you?" she said, seeing my astonished expression. "I worked in a nail salon more summers than I can remember. I love doing nails; I especially love decorating them."

I glanced down at my hands. "My nails aren't very long."

Babette grinned. "Tonight they'll be as long as you like."

She showed me a selection of acrylic tips. I chose the set I liked, and then she helped me pick a color. I opted for fuchsia for my mani and pedi. Babette asked what I'd like her to paint on my fingernails.

"Butterflies on one hand; flowers on the other."

"Fun. Soon as your nails are dry, I'll paint them on."

When she was done and her artwork was set, I hugged her tight. "Thank you so much for doing this, Babette."

"My pleasure, Carrie. You and Dylan are our dear friends. Victor and I are thrilled to be a part of your wedding."

Something in her tone made me study her face. She was glowing. "Is there something you're trying to tell me?"

Just then Tacey burst into the room. "Please do my nails, Babette. Please paint them pink!"

Victor entered close behind her. "Carrie, the photographer has arrived. He's setting up his equipment on the back lawn and wants to know how soon you'll be ready."

I felt a moment of panic. "Rienzo is here? But I'm not dressed! I need Angela and Julia to help me put on my gown so I don't muss my hair, and I still have to do my makeup. They need to get dressed, and so does Tacey, and—"

Victor rubbed my back. "Calm yourself, my dear. No need to work yourself into a tizzy. Rienzo can wait." He shot me a wicked grin. "I think he's come ahead of time because he's eager to hear about your adventures earlier today. Frankly, so am I."

"Victor, dear, I think Carrie could use a glass of wine right now," Babette said.

"Coming right up, my love. And I'll bring one for you too."

The smile they shared was brief but electric.

"Can I have some soda?" Tacey asked. "Please."

"Why not?" Victor said, and took off.

Tacey asked for a unicorn on each of her thumbnails, and Babette got to work.

Victor returned with our drinks. I thanked him and took a hefty swallow of my white Bordeaux and immediately felt relaxed.

"What is Dylan doing?" I asked.

"He's dressed and chatting with your dad and Merry. They've just arrived."

Men have so much less to do to prepare for their wedding, I thought.

"Carrie, I placed your makeup bag in the smaller bathroom down the hall. It won't take me as long to do Angela and Julia's nails since I'm simply polishing them. They'll help you into your gown and voilà! You'll be ready to take photographs with Dylan."

"Thank you," I said, wondering when Babette had become such an organized person. Or had she always been organized, and I simply hadn't noticed?

As though reading my mind, she winked at me. "It's really not rocket science. Just a matter of getting you and your attendants dressed and ready for your photos with Dylan. By then your mother, aunt, and uncle, should have arrived, and Rienzo can take several family photos."

* * *

Half an hour later, I was standing on the back lawn in all my finery, with Dylan beside me, while Rienzo, whom I knew from Angela's wedding the previous year, placed us about the lawn and garden and instructed us on how to pose and smile. I followed his directives precisely because his photos were extraordinary. I'd be thrilled if ours came out nearly as well as Angela and Steve's.

Some of our guests had joined us outside to watch Rienzo at work. Victor intercepted my mother just as she was about to interrupt a shot, her arms open to greet me in a melodramatic way. While he and Babette were our hosts, they had also undertaken the role of wedding coordinators, for which I now felt a surge of gratitude.

After he'd shot several photos of Dylan and me amid the rose bushes and other flowers in the garden, Rienzo pointed at the gazebo.

"How about I shoot a few in front of the gazebo with the Sound in the background."

Dylan and I looked at each other. "Up to you," he said.

I hesitated. It was only two weeks ago that we'd come upon Billy Carpenter's body in that very same spot.

"Today we helped find all the links connected to his murder," Dylan murmured.

"Yes, we did." I turned to Rienzo. "Fine. Let's take a few photos there."

"Excellent!" Rienzo agreed, and strode down the lawn to the gazebo.

As we followed Rienzo, I realized our misadventures with Garrett Grimm, Fred Rawlins, and Leslie Thompson would be forever entwined with memories of our wedding day. As Dylan had pointed out, we'd helped solve the case.

I smiled.

"Keep that smile!" Rienzo shouted, focusing the camera on me.

"What were you grinning about?" Dylan asked when Rienzo was done taking a battery of photos.

"I was thinking we make a great team combating felons and killers."

"*Made* a great team—past tense."

"Save the chitchat. Now stand in front of the gazebo with your arms around each other," Rienzo instructed.

When he was done, he called over my parents and their spouses to join us for some family photos. Then we included a few shots with Aunt Harriet and Uncle Bosco, and Julia and Randy and their kids. Then a few of me with Angela, Julia, and Tacey; and of Dylan with his best man, Mac; his groomsmen, Randy and Gary; and Mark, our ring bearer.

Suddenly it was ceremony time. We all made a dash to the house. I clutched Dylan's hand. With the other, I patted my tiny pocketbook that held a lipstick, a tissue, and the printed-out page of my vows."

"I'm nervous," I said.

"Thinking of ditching me and turning into a runaway bride?"

I scowled at him. "If I were planning that, I'd be sailing off in my boat that I'd stashed down in the Sound."

"That would have made a clever getaway. So what's bothering you?"

"My vows," I admitted. "I feel stupid reading them from a piece of paper, but what if I forget some of them?"

"How many are there?" Dylan asked. "Ten? Fifteen?"

"I don't remember the exact number." But I did remember. There were four. "What about you? Did you come up with more than one or two?" I asked.

"Maybe two." He squeezed my fingers. "Later you can write down the vows you forget to mention, so I can hold you to them."

I knew Dylan was trying to make me relax, but my heart lurched as we climbed the steps to the deck. I was growing more nervous by the second. It didn't help that as soon as we entered the kitchen, Mac, Gary, and Randy swept Dylan away while Victor and Babette directed our guests to the living room.

Thank goodness Angela and Julia suddenly appeared. Angela had my makeup bag. They hustled me into the dining room, where they powdered my nose, added lipstick, adjusted my veil, and gave me a once-over. Then they each hugged and air-kissed me and left me on my own.

Before I could feel abandoned, my father came into the dining room, followed by Babette. He wrapped me in his arms. "This is the happiest day of my life, Caro."

When he stood back to look at me, there were tears in his eyes. I felt tears welling up in mine as well.

"Don't cry," he said. "Your mascara will run."

"I won't if you won't."

Babette offered us each a tissue. "You guys are the sweetest. I can tell the two of you have been close from the time Carrie was born."

Jim and I burst out laughing, which puzzled Babette, but now wasn't the time to explain that her assumption was far from the truth. But these days we were very close, and that was what mattered.

The first strains of Mendelssohn's "Wedding March" filled the house. I peered into the hall, where the members of the wedding party were waiting their turn to walk down the short aisle we'd created in the living room. Slowly, the hall emptied out. Babette had my father and me follow her into the hall and wait outside the living room. The music took on a more dramatic flair.

"Your turn," Babette said, urging us forward.

The flutters in my stomach that had just calmed down started up again.

Tucking my hand in the crook of his elbow, my father shot me his cocky smile. "Caro, my love, we're doing this walk in style."

Chapter Thirty

M y father and I stepped into the living room turned wedding chapel and started down the short aisle. I looked around and found myself grinning back at all the familiar faces. We stopped halfway down, and Dylan came to meet us. I was surprised and touched when he and my father embraced, something they hadn't done during the rehearsal yesterday. Dylan took Jim's place and led me to the altar we'd created in front of the large bay window.

The sun was still high in the sky, but not shining into our eyes, thank goodness. Dylan and I came to stand in front of Al Tripp, who was looking both solemn and joyful.

"We have gathered here today to celebrate the marriage of Carrie Singleton and Dylan Thomas Avery," he began, "two very special people we love and cherish who have brought caring friendships into our lives."

Dylan squeezed my hand as Al continued, his words both poignant and filled with gentle humor. He spoke about us as only someone who knew us as a friend and fellow resident of the town we all loved could.

And then it was time for Dylan and me to exchange our vows. My heart seemed to flutter like a leaf in the wind. Was I really nervous about not remembering a few lines, or was it the solemnity of opening my heart and revealing my love for Dylan before everyone dear to us as they witnessed our formal agreement to share our lives from this day forth?

I cleared my throat. "Dylan, I stand before you and our family and friends to say I love you and will continue to love you as long as I live."

A few *aws* sounded from the audience.

"Of course, I'm expecting you to remain lovable so we can share our lives in good times and bad, in sickness and in health."

I heard muffled laughter.

"I will," Dylan adlibbed.

I grinned at him. "I look forward to taking care of you and our future family to the best of my ability, sharing your troubles and your difficulties as I hope you'll share mine."

"I will," Dylan repeated.

"I want us to continue to learn and grow as we grow older together, always eager to talk to each other about any and all topics. I promise to be there for you, supporting you in what you hold dear."

I stepped back to a round of applause.

"You're up, Dylan," Al quipped.

Dylan smiled at me. "Carrie, I love and adore you. I promise to love and adore you as long as I live."

"Thank you," I murmured as a blush warmed my ears.

"I agree with everything you've said, and promise to do the same with you and for you. I look forward to our life together. I know it's going to be a series of adventures, judging by today's events."

Laughter echoed around the room. When it calmed down, Dylan went on. "Carrie, my love, I've watched you develop into a strong, self-confident woman. You are the most amazing person I know. I will support you as you continue to do new and wonderful things. I will care for you and protect you to the best of my ability."

Protect me? I opened my mouth to protest, but Dylan was speaking again.

"I say *protect* because you have a knack of putting yourself in dangerous situations. I can no more tell you to avoid those situations than stop the rain from falling. That said, I want to keep you as safe as I can so we can share a long and happy life together."

Our guests burst out in applause.

Al was about to speak, when I held up a finger.

"Thank you, Dylan. I promise not to rush into danger. You get me, and that's one of the reasons I love you so much."

Dylan grinned. "And I have no problem with you having the last word."

The cheering was even louder this time. We'd *both* managed to have the last word, which was a true reflection of our relationship.

Al went on to the official part of our wedding and declared us married in the State of Connecticut.

I was a married woman! Dylan took me in his arms and kissed me. Our audience roared their approval. And then we were exiting the room and heading for the deck off the kitchen, where we accepted our guests' hugs and good wishes, amid drinks and hors d'oeuvres, as a harpist strummed in a corner, playing light classical music.

An hour later, as the sun was setting on the horizon, Victor and Babette ushered everyone into the tent for an evening of dining and dancing. Dylan and I paused at the entrance to admire the lovely setup. The ten tables decked out in lavender and teal, with tall vases of flowers in the center, were set in a semicircle around the dance floor.

"It's so much prettier than I even imagined," I said.

Dylan chuckled. "It really is."

The tent was surprisingly roomy and well lit. We had chosen one with a transparent top and large "windows" on the sides that brought in the outdoors while maintaining a feeling of shared space.

The four-piece band was playing a lively tune as people found seats at their assigned tables. We'd chosen a small ensemble so that when Tony Milano, our master of ceremonies/male vocalist, wasn't singing, our guests could hear themselves converse.

Tony asked everyone to rise and then introduced Dylan and me as Mr. and Mrs. Dylan and Carrie Avery. Hand in hand, we came to stand in the center of the dance floor, where a small table bearing two flutes and a champagne bottle had been placed. Tony uncorked the champagne and filled our glasses while waiters went around the tables filling our guests' flutes.

Mac and Angela came to face us across the small table, each of them holding a glass.

"As best man and matron of honor, we toast the bride and groom, wishing them every happiness they want for themselves," Mac said.

They sipped and we followed suit.

"Carrie and Dylan," Angela said, "you love each other now, but we know your love will grow with every year you share as a couple and create your family. We all love you and wish you a happy, healthy future together."

We drained our flutes as cheering and shouting filled the tent.

And then the band began to play Harry Styles's "Love of My Life." I slipped into Dylan's arms, and we began to dance. "This is where I've been wanting you all day," he murmured into my ear.

I lifted my face to kiss him and held on to Dylan for a long minute. The music changed, and Tony invited my father to dance with me while Dylan led my mother around the dance floor. Soon most of our guests were dancing. Uncle Bosco cut in. Then Mac. The dance medley ended with me panting after dancing a fast one with Tom, my mother's husband. We sat down to eat our roasted beet salad with walnuts and goat cheese.

I floated through the evening in a dreamlike state, eating and dancing and chatting with dear friends and relatives. Dylan was often at my side, and when he wasn't, I always knew exactly where he was. Dylan, my husband!

Mark and Tacey were the only children at our wedding. They were rarely off the dance floor, often telling our band which songs to play. And why not, since, of all our guests, they knew which songs were most popular? After Tony had arranged a line dance, and the band was striking up a foxtrot, I was surprised and touched when Mark came over to ask me to dance.

"Of course, Mark. It would be my pleasure."

He assumed the correct position, right hand on my waist, his left hand in mine, and proceeded to do the box step.

"You dance very well," I told him.

"My mom taught me. Tacey and me."

We danced a minute or two. When I felt him relax, I asked, "Are you having fun?"

"I sure am! This is the first wedding I've ever been to."

"And you were our ring bearer," I said.

He led me into a walkout step, then had me twirl around him.

"Fancy!" I said.

Mark grinned. Then he asked, "Cousin Carrie, how many kids are you and Dylan going to have?"

"I don't know. I suppose two. Maybe three."

"Three's a good number," he agreed. "That way if you have a son, he has a good chance of having a brother to play video games with."

"Girls play video games too, you know."

"Not Tacey. She'd rather play with her dolls."

"Oh." I said. "After Dylan and I come back from our honeymoon and move into our new home, we're thinking of getting two dogs."

"Two dogs! That's awesome!" Mark got so excited he lost his concentration and stepped on my foot. "Sorry, Cousin Carrie."

"That's all right," I assured him.

"Can I come over and play with the dogs? We can't have any because Dad's allergic."

"Of course you can."

The song ended, and I discovered Tacey at my side.

"Can we dance the next dance together?" she asked.

"Of course."

Mark frowned at his sister. "You're such a copycat."

"Am not!"

"Mark, thank you for dancing with me. I'll always remember it," I told him.

His face lit up. "Me too."

The music started up, a faster beat this time. Tacey began stepping from side to side as she thrust out her arms, one at a time.

"You're pretty good," I told her.

"I love dancing. I'm taking classes in September."

We moved around the dance floor. Tacey *was* good, changing direction easily as well as using arm gestures, and she always kept time to the music.

"I love your wedding, Cousin Carrie. It's the best wedding I've ever been to."

I grinned at her. "I'm so glad you were my flower girl."

"The petals were all gone before I got to you," she said, worried.

"That's okay. Some flower girls forget to throw out the petals."

"Really? That's silly."

We danced a while in silence, then Tacey said, "I wish Miss Evelyn could be here with us. I know she'd want to be at your wedding and see you and Dylan get married."

"Me too. Evelyn is one of my dearest friends. She's your good friend and mine. But we can only see her in the library."

Tacey sighed. "I know." A minute later, she said, "Mommy told me you and Dylan are moving into a new house when you come back from your honeymoon."

"We are!" I hesitated, then said, "Our new house is very special in a way that you will like."

Tacey stopped dancing. "What do you mean?"

I danced toward the edge of the dance floor, where there was an open space. Tacey followed me. I bent down so I could speak softly. "There are two little girls who . . . visit," I said, for want of a better word.

"They're like Miss Evelyn!" Tacey all but shouted.

I put a finger to my lips. "They are."

"Sorry."

"That's all right. No one noticed. But most people can't see these special people like you and I can."

"Why are they there? How old are they?"

"Lucy and Abigail died in a fire in the house many years ago. Lucy's about your age, and her sister's a few years older. I think they'll be very happy to meet you."

Tacey gave me a big smile. "I can't wait to meet them."

While the waitstaff served a delicious amuse-bouche—a tiny glass dish of ceviche—the orchestra took a break, and Rienzo began taking table photos, starting with ours. When he moved on, Dylan and I decided this was a good time for us to make the rounds in reverse order. Our first stop was the table where Victor and Babette, John and Sylvia, Al and Dolores, and Reggie and Marissa Williams were sitting.

John stood as we approached and wrapped me in a bear hug, which surprised me. He and Sylvia had congratulated Dylan and me right after the ceremony, and hugging wasn't his style. My

Allison Brook

astonishment must have showed because John said, "I want you to know I spent most of the day worrying about you," low enough so no one else could hear. He led me to a spot away from the table.

"You knew Garrett Grimm kept me a prisoner in his car?" I asked.

"Dylan called me right after he contacted the Prescott police. Chris Donahue kept me apprised of your situation until Grimm was apprehended." John chuckled. "And then some."

"So Captain Donahue's a friend," I said.

"He sure is. Chris and I went through the Academy together. I'm hoping to have some information for you tomorrow that will put a smile on your face."

I opened my mouth to ask what it might be.

"Not now," he admonished. "No shop talk. This is your wedding, remember?"

"Of course," I agreed, although I longed to raise my fist and shout. No, shop talk indeed! Finally, John had slipped and let me know he considered me an unofficial member of his team.

Chapter
Thirty-One

Dylan and I returned to our seats as the main course was being served. We'd decided to offer our guests a choice of prime rib, salmon, and chicken cordon bleu. Dylan and I shared our entrées of prime ribs and chicken. I was happy to discover that both had been cooked to perfection and were being served piping hot. Our caterers and serving crew, both Victor's recommendations, were proving to be the gems he'd claimed they would be. Once again, I felt a surge of love and appreciation for all that he and Babette had done to make our wedding a wonderful success.

My mother leaned across her handsome husband to cover my hand with hers.

"Carrie, my dear. I can't tell you how happy I am, seeing you and Dylan married. And your wedding is truly a five-star event! When you told me the reception was being held in a tent, I admit I was a bit disappointed, but this is one of the loveliest affairs I've ever attended."

Tom beamed at me. "It's a lovely wedding, Carrie, in every sense. Your mother and I wish you and Dylan a marriage filled with happiness."

"Thanks, Tom, Mom." I felt myself choking up.

"We'd love to have you and Dylan come visit us soon," my mother said. "You both will love Hollywood." She winked. "Who knows? Maybe you'll decide to settle there, and I'll get to see my grandkids every day."

Right, I thought. *We'll pull up roots and move to California.* I couldn't help but remember my mother's reaction two years ago when I'd been at my lowest point and wanted to stay with them, and she told me it wasn't a good time for me to come.

Now I smiled and said, "A visit sounds great, Mom, only it might not be for some time. We'll be on our honeymoon for almost three weeks, and then we'll be busy settling into our new home."

"Of course. Whenever it's convenient. The thing is, I want us to spend time together now that you're entering a new phase of your life."

I almost burst out laughing. For years I'd longed for a close relationship with my mother, and now that I was starting my married life, she wanted more togetherness. Then I reminded myself that she was offering what she was capable of giving. And so, when our server finished clearing our section of the table, I smiled and said, "That will be really nice, Mom. And we can always chat on FaceTime."

My mother gripped my arm. "I'd love that, Carrie."

"Me too," I agreed, and realized that I meant it.

The band began to play some interim music, and I thought the dancing would begin again, not that I was ready to bounce around on a full stomach. Instead, Tony tested the mic and began to speak.

"I know you're all enjoying the good food and company in celebration of Carrie and Dylan's nuptials. A few guests have told me they'd like to say a few words."

My father was the first to walk up and stand in front of the band. Jim took the mic.

"As you all know, I'm Jim Singleton, Carrie's dad. I wasn't always the father of the year when Carrie was growing up. That's my regret and always will be. But I'm a lucky man. Carrie gave me a second chance to have a place in her life, and I jumped to it. What's more she brought me Dylan, whom I love as a son."

Jim raised his glass. "I drink to my wonderful daughter and her wonderful husband. Merry and I wish them every happiness in their married life."

Then Angela got up. I was surprised because my best friend didn't like public speaking, and she'd already made her toast to us privately.

"I liked Carrie from the moment she came into the library dressed in her Goth getup. Then she was hired as head of programs and events, and like everyone else, I got to see just how clever and creative she is. Carrie helps make the library a better place, when she isn't solving mysteries and crimes."

That got a wave a laughter.

"She also ended up being my best friend, steering me through my own wedding a year ago when some unfortunate events took place. Carrie and Dylan are very dear to Steve and me. I'm so happy to have both of them in our lives."

My mouth fell open as Al got up to say how valuable I was to the town board, and Sally spoke about the difference I'd made at the library. Mac talked about Dylan and his best wishes for our future.

Then, hand in hand, Victor and Babette came forward to address our guests. Dylan and I stood to applaud them, and everyone joined in. When it was quiet again, Victor began to speak.

"Welcome to my home. I never expected to have a wedding here, but life is full of surprises. I hope you're as delighted as Babette and I are to have taken part in celebrating the union of Carrie and Dylan."

Applause burst out again.

"Though I haven't known Carrie and Dylan very long, they quickly became two of my closest friends—that is, once they realized I was neither a fraudulent art dealer nor a murderer."

Laughter rippled through the tent.

"I knew that Carrie was having difficulty choosing a venue for their wedding, and I was deeply honored when she and Dylan asked if they could hold the wedding at my home. Hosting their wedding here tonight is the most meaningful event I've taken part in in decades."

The clapping was thunderous.

"All of you present know how special our newlyweds are. I value their friendship, their ethics, and the way they treasure each and every one present. It's an honor to be part of their circle of friends."

When the tumult calmed down, Victor held up the wineglass he'd been holding, and said, "To Carrie and Dylan!"

"To Carrie and Dylan!" Our guests' shouts rang through the tent.

Dylan and I looked at each other. Without exchanging a word, we rose and took Victor and Babette's place in front of our guests. I was too emotional to speak, but my husband was up for it.

"Thank you, Victor. I can't tell you how happy you have made my new bride and me, offering us the use of your home and your backyard. Your generosity has overwhelmed us. We appreciate that you and Babette have seen to every aspect of our wedding ceremony and reception, making sure that everything runs smoothly without a hitch."

I discovered that there was something I wanted to say.

"I agree with all that Dylan has said. Victor, you are a most kind and generous friend. Your gift of allowing us to hold our wedding here is one I will always cherish. I feel so lucky that my life is filled with the most wonderful people, all of whom are with us under this tent. I came to Clover Ridge just over two years ago, feeling root-less and not knowing how I'd be spending the rest of my life. Here I found a home and a purpose, my life's companion, and my chosen family. I thank you all for being in my life!"

* * *

Dylan and I returned to our seats to thunderous applause. The band started up, and dancing resumed while our servers brought out platters of desserts to each table. Our guests oohed and aahed over the selections: red velvet madeleines, mini fruit tarts, tartlets filled with dark chocolate, mini lemon-blueberry cheesecakes, chocolate-covered strawberries, and mini ice-cream sundaes.

A table bearing our three-tier wedding cake was wheeled out, and Tony was charming and funny as he instructed Dylan to cut the first piece and feed it to me. Yummy chocolate mousse was the filling for the top tier. Then I fed Dylan a bite of cake.

We sat down to applause as the cake was wheeled away to be cut up and served.

I floated through the evening, enjoying every moment of our wedding. I was oblivious of time passing as I danced and ate and socialized with our guests. Dylan and I were on the dance floor, swaying to an old Frank Sinatra classic, when Randy and Julia, a sleeping Tacey in her arms and trailed by a sleepy Mark, walked toward us.

"Oh no! They're leaving," I murmured to Dylan.

"It's after midnight. The kids are exhausted," Dylan said.

"But I want our wedding to go on and on. I don't want anyone to leave." I knew I was being childish, but I couldn't help it. Tears welled up in my eyes.

Dylan kissed me, a fleeting kiss that spoke pages of understanding. A husband's kiss to his wife.

Randy wrapped me in his arms. "Cuz, time for us to put the kiddies to bed. I gotta tell you, this was one great wedding. I'm so happy for you and Dylan."

Julia leaned over her daughter to kiss my cheek. "It all went beautifully, Carrie. The kids were thrilled to be in your wedding party."

"Thanks for being my matron of honor," I said.

"It was my pleasure."

"I'm sorry you guys can't come to the brunch tomorrow morning," I said.

"Me too. But we'll get together when you guys are back from your honeymoon."

Mark gave me a hug and shook hands with Dylan.

"I can't wait to meet those little girls," Tacey murmured to me.

I winked at her.

Julia looked at her daughter, then at me. "What little girls?"

I shrugged, feigning ignorance. Julia had no idea that her daughter was looking forward to meeting our two ghost boarders. "Tacey must be dreaming."

"I suppose you're right. She fell asleep at the table, and she's still out."

Like most parties, as soon as the first guests departed, more quickly followed. Aunt Harriet and Uncle Bosco came over to say their goodbyes, followed by Sally and her husband. Then Marion and her significant other came over to bid us good night.

I sighed as I watched them left the tent. Our wedding was winding down.

Chapter
Thirty-Two

I rested my head on Dylan's shoulder as we drove home to the cottage. It was after one o'clock and there wasn't much traffic on the road. We'd left the rental crew packing up dishes and stacking the leftover desserts in Victor's subzero freezer. I'd convinced Angela, her mother, Al's wife, and Rosalind—who were among the last to leave—to take home the beautiful flower arrangements. The large arrangements in the living room were, of course, meant for Victor and Babette.

"They're so beautiful. Won't you be taking one yourself, Carrie?" Rosemary Vecchio asked me.

Angela rolled her eyes. "Mom, they're leaving on their honeymoon tomorrow, remember?"

"Of course. Sorry." Rosemary turned to me. "Why don't you keep them here for tomorrow's breakfast?"

"I've got other flower arrangements for that" I said.

Angela grinned. "Carrie's gone all out for this affair."

"Well, it was lovely," Angela's dad chimed in. "Rosemary and I thoroughly enjoyed ourselves."

Now I sighed contentedly as we drove onto the Avery private road that led to our cottage.

"How are you feeling, Mrs. Avery?" Dylan asked.

"Wonderful. Happily married."

"Enjoy our wedding?"

"It was like living the most marvelous dream, and now I'm awake," I said.

"Do you feel any different?" Dylan asked.

"Yes and no. I'm your wife and you're my husband, but we're still the same two people."

Yet the cottage felt different as I walked up to the front door with Dylan at my side. Though I'd been living here for almost two years, it suddenly seemed more like a temporary home. A vacation home perhaps. And though we'd be staying here when we returned from Greece, I suddenly couldn't wait to move into our new house.

Dylan unlocked the door, and the cottage felt empty without Smoky Joe there to greet us. But I had my husband's full attention.

"Tired, Mrs. Avery?"

I returned his cocky smile. "Not too tired to celebrate."

Dylan took me in his arms and kissed me. "The perfect way to end a perfect evening."

* * *

It was a good thing I'd set the alarm for nine thirty, because both Dylan and I would probably have slept till noon after the very full day we'd had. But our morning-after brunch began at eleven o'clock. This gave us an hour and fifteen minutes to shower and get dressed and do some last-minute packing before we drove back to Victor's home.

Less than half our wedding guests were able to attend our post-wedding brunch. I'd invited Aldi to join us, and he was the first person I saw when Dylan and I got out of the car. He was sprawled out on the front lawn, petting Raspie. That was, until the beautiful borzoi caught sight of Dylan and me and came bounding over to greet us.

"I see you've made friends with Raspie," I said as I petted Victor's dog. "Did you finish eating already?"

Albi shook his head. "I looked in the tent and didn't see anyone my age so I thought I'd wait till you guys showed up."

Dylan threw an arm across his shoulders. "Got it. Who wants to have breakfast with a bunch of strangers?"

"I didn't know I was supposed to wait there."

"Dylan's teasing," I said. "You're welcome to sit with us."

"I'm glad you don't mind if I eat with you," Albi said, some of his natural spunk back in place. "Oh, and congratulations on getting married."

"Thank you," we both said.

Albi looked me up and down. "You seem to be fine, but are you really okay after that guy shoved you in his car and kidnapped you?"

"I'm fine," I told him. "I managed to get away in time before he could carry out his plan."

Albi's eyes widened. "You mean he was about to murder you?"

"Garrett Grimm fell under the sway of a diabolical criminal. He ordered Grimm to get rid of me."

"Do the police know who he is?" Albi asked.

"They do," I told him. "And if he's not in custody now, he will be very soon. Meanwhile, Garrett Grimm is in jail, along with Fred Rawlins and Leslie Thompson."

"I'm really glad Grimm's in jail and you're safe now." Albi shook his head. "I'm so sorry things turned dangerous when you guys were helping me stop Tino from running off."

We walked around the side of the house toward the tent. "Speaking of Tino, where is he?" I asked, though I had a good idea where he was.

"In a cell in the Clover Ridge jail. My mom is there now. She's the worst I've ever seen her. I told her I'd go with her to see Tino, but she insisted I come here this morning. To thank you for keeping Tino from leaving."

"Listen, Albi," Dylan said, "your brother's going to need a criminal lawyer. Have your mom call my office in New Haven tomorrow morning and speak to Mrs. Feratti, my office manager. Mrs. Feratti will give her the name of a good criminal lawyer we know."

Albi's eyes filled with tears. "Thanks, Dylan. I don't know what would have happened to Tino if you and Carrie hadn't stepped in like you did."

"I hope Tino knows how lucky he is that you're his brother," Dylan said.

Albi shrugged.

I rested my hand on his arm. "Albi, Dylan's right. Tino got himself into trouble, and you did everything you could to help him. But you're not responsible for Tino, and you can't control what happens to him. Now it's time for you to focus on your life. On your future." I gripped his arm tight. "Promise me you won't let his problems overshadow your plans and dreams."

Albi nodded. "I get what you're saying, Carrie. My mother told me the same thing."

"Now that we've agreed you're going to listen to Carrie and your mother, let's go inside and eat," Dylan said. "I'm hungry."

The glamorous tent of last night had been transformed into a cozy brunch setting. There was no sign of the dance floor or the brilliant lights. The top now opened to the azure sky. Four tables had been set for the thirty or so guests we expected to show up.

Dylan and I had decided that buffet style would be best, with everyone free to select what he or she wanted to eat. Two tables stood along the far side of the tent. One had an assortment of breads and muffins, coffee cake, butter and jelly, various cheeses, coffee, tea, and orange juice. The other held warm buffet trays filled with scrambled eggs, pancakes, and sausages. Two servers were on hand to dish out portions and refill coffee.

We found my dad and Merry, Al and Dolores, and Victor and Babette inside, chatting away at one table. My father broke away to embrace Dylan and me.

"Here they are, my two children! Sit down and have something to eat."

Babette recognized Albi from school and greeted him as if it were the most natural thing for him to be here with our nearest and dearest. "Hi, Albi. Come and join us."

"I don't know—" he began, noticing there were only two place settings. But Victor was already pulling over a chair from one of the other tables.

Dylan and I introduced Albi to the others. We joined in the chit-chat for a few minutes before Dylan, Albi, and I went up to the buffet. I filled my platter but only managed to eat a few bites because whenever someone new entered the tent, they came over to greet Dylan and me.

My mother and Tom arrived, followed by Angela and Steve, Angela's parents, Aunt Harriet and Uncle Bosco, and Reggie and Marissa. Sally, Trish, Marion, Fran, and their partners showed up, but where were John and Sylvia?

For the past eighteen hours I'd been too caught up in our wedding to think clearly about yesterday's traumatic events. Right now I was fine as I'd told Albi, but I knew PTSD symptoms could set in at any time. I was relieved that Garrett Grimm and Fred Rawlins were now in custody, but I had no idea if Grimm's partner was still at large. And I was curious about John's comment last night. Even later, when we were dancing, he refused to tell me what he hoped to be able to share with me today.

Dylan and I went table-hopping. Mac and his wife came by for a short while before they had to leave for the airport. Albi hugged us goodbye and promised to stay in touch. Where were John and Sylvia?

Finally, as I was being served a second cup of coffee that I was enjoying with a delicious piece of Russian coffee cake, John and Sylvia made an appearance.

"Sorry we're late," he said. "Work." He looked a bit disheveled, but there was a twinkle in his eye.

"Have something to eat," I said after I'd hugged them both.

"We will," John said, then made a mad dash for the food.

"He's been up most of the night," Sylvia said. She winked at me, then followed her husband at a slower pace.

John returned with his tray loaded with eggs and sides, and sat down at an empty table. I went to join him, but instead of joining us, Sylvia went to sit with some of the others. I waited for John to gulp down most of his orange juice and eat some of his eggs and sausages before I asked, "So, what was the outcome of yesterday's arrests?"

John cocked his head and grinned at me. "Quite a lot was resolved, at least from our side of things."

I waited for him to go into detail.

"Captain Donahue booked Garrett Grimm and charged him with kidnapping. Chris is a very competent interrogator. When he was done questioning Grimm, he also charged him with two counts of first-degree murder. Grimm confessed to killing Luke Rizzo and Winifred Thompson as well as masterminding the bank heist. Since more than five years have passed, he can't be charged under federal law, but the state can charge him for his part in the heist. That and his behavior yesterday as a result of the heist will no doubt add to the years he'll spend in prison."

I shuddered. "That's good, but what about Grimm's accomplice? The friend who urged him to kill Luke and told him to get rid of me?"

"We're working on it. We have his name and address, but he's on the run. We've found a slew of his aliases and tracked down two criminals now incarcerated because of what he'd convinced them to do."

"He really is evil," I said.

John put his hand on my shoulder. "Carrie, I promise you needn't worry about this guy coming after you. There's a nationwide BOLO out for him. He'll be caught very soon."

"I'll be happy when he's behind bars. What's going to happen to Tino?"

John stretched out his long legs. "He may be lucky enough to get a suspended sentence after everything he's told us about Garrett Grimm—Grimm's part in the bank robbery and the way he's been threatening Tino." He sighed. "But he's a troubled young man. He needs a support system and a job."

"I know." I thought a bit. "What's happening to Fred Rawlins?"

"He's going back to prison for planning the theft of Verity's diary."

"And Leslie Thompson?"

John shrugged. "I couldn't say. Depends on how good his lawyer is and the judge his case happens to draw." Now he was grinning. "But there's one thing I can tell you, and that is the library will have the diary back very soon."

"How wonderful!"

"Normally a stolen item can spend months stowed away in police lockup. But I've had the diary declared a fragile antique that requires the proper care the library can provide."

"Thank you, John! The security system will be in place next week!" I hugged him tight.

He patted my arm. "I wanted to give you that piece of news before you guys left on your honeymoon."

"That was very kind of you."

John stood. "And now I'm going to get myself a refill of food before this breakfast shindig shuts down."

Barely a minute had passed before Sylvia took his place. She was grinning like the proverbial Cheshire cat.

"What are you up to?" I asked.

Sylvia raised her eyebrows most dramatically. "It just occurred to me that you might want to reconsider joining the Wise Women's Circle."

I blinked. "Why? I haven't given it any thought since I told Sally I wouldn't be joining.

"We thought you might reconsider now that Winnie is no longer with us." Marissa said as she and Sally joined Sylvia and me at the table.

"The truth is, many of us were getting a bit tired of her bossiness and proprietary attitude," Sally said. "We're making big changes—at least in the way we manage projects."

I laughed. "Is it nice to ambush a newly married woman about to leave on her honeymoon?"

"Your honeymoon will give you lots of time to reconsider joining the circle," Sylvia said.

"Why should I?" I asked.

Sally, who knew me so well, gave me a sly smile. "For one thing, we plan to start a movement to exonerate Verity Babcock and the others who were hung as witches. We're asking groups and organizations to join us in approaching the state government. This will be more effective and hopefully finally bring about the desired results."

I couldn't help but nod. It was a solid plan.

"And we're planning to set up an annual scholarship in Verity's name for a young woman who otherwise couldn't afford to attend college." Marissa said.

"As you see," Sylvia said, "we're expanding our outlook, and we thought you might feel more comfortable being part of our new direction."

Everything they said *did* appeal to me. And I had to admit I admired the group's purpose as well as the women who made up the circle. Then I thought of Tino.

"I do like the changes the circle plans to make, and I admit I was put off by Winnie's high-handed desire to keep Verity's diary for herself. But I was wondering, does the scholarship recipient have to be female? Does it have to be for college per se?"

The three Wise Women first stared at me, then exchanged glances. Finally, they burst out laughing.

"What do you have in mind, Mrs. Avery?" Sally asked.

I told them about Tino—his part in the bank robbery, how he sorely needed direction. "He needs a life coach. A mentor. Someone who can show him how to lead a worthwhile life. He also needs job training. Besides, I hate seeing his younger brother feeling responsible for Tino when Albi needs to concentrate on his first year of college."

Sylvia leaned over to hug me. "Carrie, this is precisely why we want you to join us! Your vision has us expanding our horizons even more than we'd imagined."

"More projects mean more responsibility. And we'll need funds to carry them out." Marissa's eyes met mine. "Would you be willing to put in the time?"

"If I find I have a free hour between working and setting up my new home and attending council meetings."

"We're in for it," Sally said darkly. "Carrie's always coming up with new ideas."

I opened my mouth to say something, but it had already been said. Somehow I'd agreed to become a Wise Woman.

Dylan tapped me on the shoulder. "I hate to break up your meeting, but Victor wants to make an announcement, and he'd like you to return to our table."

"Excuse me," I said as I stood.

"Enjoy your honeymoon," Sylvia said. "We'll talk when you're home again."

"What was that all about?" Dylan asked as we walked back to our table.

"They convinced me to join the Wise Women's Circle."

He laughed. "Why am I not surprised?"

As soon as I sat down between Dylan and Victor, Victor stood and clinked a spoon against his glass. "Could I have your attention, please?"

A minute later, our remaining guests were all seated and looking at him expectantly. Victor loved talking to groups, so I imagined he wanted to say a few words about Dylan and me.

"Last night you heard me toast Carrie and Dylan, our newly wedded couple. Today I want to say a few words about myself. I came to this country fifteen years ago from my native war-torn country. While I was fortunate to have been a successful businessman, I wasn't as lucky with my personal life. I lost my second wife shortly after coming to Clover Ridge, and frankly, after that, making friendships wasn't a priority, especially since my business and my art collection occupy so much of my time.

"But friendship and a sense of community are just as important as earning a living and appreciating art. Through events that most of you know about, Carrie and Dylan proved my innocence, and in the process we became very good friends." He looked around. "And I got to know many of you."

Victor smiled down at Babette. "At the same time, Babette and I began to date. We fell in love. And suddenly, I was the luckiest man." He winked at Dylan. "One of the two luckiest men."

Everyone chuckled.

"And so, as Carrie and Dylan's wedding festivities come to a close, I thought it most appropriate to announce that I have asked Babette to marry me, and she said yes!"

The tent roared with cheers and applause. Dylan and I hugged Victor and Babette.

"I'm so happy for you both," I said.

"Me too," Babette said.

"You're crying," I told her.

"So are you."

Everyone came over to congratulate the happy couple.

Dylan wrapped his arm around me and drew me to his side. "Now we're the old married couple," he joked.

"I kind of like it that way."

My husband glanced at his watch. "I've settled everything with the caterers and the rental company. It's time to say our goodbyes."

Tears streamed down my cheeks when we said goodbye to my father and Merry. Jim took me in his arms.

"Caro, honey. What's wrong?"

"I won't be seeing you for a long time."

"It doesn't have to be a long time. You and Dylan will visit us; we'll visit you." His face brightened. "We'll come very often once I'm a grandpa."

"Stop rushing things," I told him.

"I'm just saying."

I kissed Merry. "We'll be in touch," she said.

I nodded, then went into my mother's open arms.

"Carrie, darling. You're always welcome to visit us, you and Dylan."

"We'll come see you and Tom," I said as I hugged Tom goodbye. And we would. I had always wanted to visit Hollywood.

Finally, we were in Dylan's BMW, heading back to the cottage. A hired car was picking us up in an hour and a half.

"So, what do you think of married life, Mrs. Avery?" Dylan asked.

"So far I like it, Mr. Avery."

Author's Note

Verity Babcock's diary never existed because Verity Babcock is a character I created based on what I'd read about people who were accused of being witches when witchcraft was a capital offense in the Colony of Connecticut. Between 1647 and 1663, of the forty-three cases of witchcraft, sixteen resulted in executions, mostly hangings; or at least thirty-four were accused of witchcraft and eleven were hung. Numbers vary somewhat because, in the words of Benjamin Trumbull in his 1818 *History of Connecticut*, "the history of witchcraft in Connecticut is difficult to track, owing primarily to the lack of documentation from the accusations, trials, and executions." This began over forty years before the first case in Salem, Massachusetts, in 1692.

Why were people accused of witchcraft? Many, like Verity, were different in some way from the other residents of their tightly knit communities, which were bound by strict and rigid rules. Women were often victims in this patriarchal society, though a few men were also accused and convicted of being witches. For years the Connecticut Witch Trial Exoneration Project was actively trying to get pardons from the state for those accused and executed as witches. In May 2023, while I was writing this book, both the Connecticut

House of Representatives and Connecticut State Senate voted in overwhelming numbers to exonerate twelve people who were convicted of witchcraft in the seventeenth century. I was delighted that this long overdue wrong had been righted, but for the purpose of my novel, I took literary license and continued to write it as though the victims had yet to be pardoned.

Sources: Wikipedia, and Wetherfield's Historical Society's article "Connecticut's Witch Trials" by Chris Pagliuco: https://www.wethersfieldhistory.org/articles/connecticuts-witch-trials/#:~:text=In%20all%2C%20Connecticut%20heard%2043,their%20neighbors%20and%20their%20times.

Acknowledgments

I am delighted that the eighth and final book of the Haunted Library series is now available to readers. It's also bittersweet bidding adieu to Carrie, Dylan, Evelyn, and the rest of the gang whose lives and adventures have played out in this series. Now Carrie's story arc is complete, and it's time for me to write about other characters in other stories.

I want to thank everyone at Crooked Lane Books who had a hand in making these eight books professionally presented and appealing to cozy readers: my great editor, Faith Black Ross; Claudia Griesbach-Martucci for my wonderful covers; Jill Pellarin for her careful editing; and Rebecca, Dulce, and Thai for answering my many questions. And Mikaela and Mia. It's been wonderful working with you all!